XIAOLONG HUANG

Journey To The Heartland

Second Edition

Second edition

ISBN (paperback): 979-8-218-00614-3
ISBN (hardcover): 979-8-9863563-5-8

Cover art by Andy Bridge
Editing by Vanessa Curtis
Editing by Danielle Anderson
Editing by Donald Weise

This book was professionally typeset on Reedsy.
Find out more at reedsy.com

Dedicated to the everyday people who lived an honest life, struggled, cared for others, and fought for our humanity.

Preface

A story, much like a memory, is rarely finished the first time it is told. It asks to be revealed. This second edition reaches deeper into the father's story — his buried life, the places he lived, and what Hanwei finds when he finally goes looking. It also introduces Rick, a man born into America's promise who finds himself losing ground to addiction and a changing country. Hanwei refuses to let him fall without a fight.

Based on a true story…

The names of some individuals have been changed. The feelings have not. This book was written because the author believed that an honest life, fully lived, is itself a political act — and that those who cannot yet live openly deserve to know that such a life is possible.

Acknowledgments

First and foremost, I would like to give my special thanks to my mother, Yufang, who raised me and supported me in hardship.

I would like to thank my aunts, Hongyi and Yulan, my uncles, Yulin and Mingguang, my cousin, Yuanyuan, and my grandma, Guoyu, for giving my mother and me a helping hand.

I am indebted to Aosong, Priyantha, Kentez, and Raja for the love and life they gave me — and that I carry with me still.

I am deeply grateful to have the love and support from my partner, Ravi, who believed in me and encouraged me in writing this book.

I would like to thank Shuming Fei, Jianfeng Liu, Wei Yu, Xiaowen Lei, Yong Ling, Yvonne, Joshua Lee, Frank Guo, Minjian Liang, Sina Zahedi, Lei Wang, Bernard Jiang, Ethan Lin, Leonce Noel, Bin Huang, Rolf De Vegt, VK Jones, Gopal Ravi, Anu Mandavilli, Ruiqing Ye, Nathaniel Houghton, Linda Johnson, and James Duenas for their friendship and support.

Vanessa Curtis, Danielle Anderson, and Donald Weise gave this manuscript their sharp editorial attention, and the book is better for it.

Andy Bridge created the cover artwork, which gives visual form to the journey at the heart of this book — from darkness toward light.

Arley Concaildi's team worked tirelessly on marketing and

publicity to bring the book to its readers.

And finally, this book owes a debt to the many pioneers who fought for LGBT rights, women's rights, racial justice, and workers' rights. Without their sacrifice, the life this book tells would not have been livable.

Prelude

"Hanwei, you are wandering at the edge of a cliff, seeking suicide. Mom doesn't know how to protect you from the abyss ahead," Rulan said gently and seriously. The lady in her sixties stood in the middle of the living room, looking out the window of her son's home. She held a glass of warm water using both her hands, trying to calm herself from an emotional breakdown she had had moments ago. Her anguish was visible on her tense and reddish face.

"The life you have today didn't come easy. You need to cherish it. Mom couldn't bear to see you go down like your father did, the sufferings and ridicules he went through. Mom wouldn't be able to die in peace thinking your life is hanging in the balance at the edge of society." Rarely expressive, Rulan tried her best to open up her feelings to her son.

Standing to her side, Hanwei answered cautiously and firmly, trying to soothe his mother, knowing the precarious situation they were in. "Mom, I will protect myself and I will protect you. I have friends here. I will be a strong man."

The genesis of their conversation would go back more than twenty years to Luoqi, a factory town by the Yangtze River in Chongqing, China.

Factory Town

During the eighties, with the planned economy in China, people working and living in a big factory town like Luoqi had a sense of security and prestige. The locals sometimes traveled to the city for business or leisure on a nauseating four-hour bus trip through dangerous winding roads along mountain cliffs. After work, families spent time together watching TV shows or gossiping with neighbors in the courtyard. Everyone seemed to know everyone's business in the factory. Work, for most folks in the factory, wasn't difficult, although some had to sweat in the workshop, handling hazardous machinery and chemicals used for producing pharmaceutical compounds.

Factory kids learned to be tough from an early age. They were rarely watched by their parents and could often be found running around basketball courts, playing games and sometimes fighting off opposing gangs. To local villagers, the factory people had it easy: their kids received a decent education, and engineers in the factory's main office building who migrated from the coastal area seemed very knowledgeable.

One day after school, Hanwei was busy drawing on a piece of paper at his desk. Beneath the desk glass top were pictures of scientists accompanied by some of their famous quotes, including Newton and Galileo. On his paper was an almost finished Chinese dragon, full-fledged with scales and mane, limbs and claws extended out in a commanding presence. At eight years old, Hanwei's talent in drawing was already well known among school teachers and family acquaintances.

"Hanwei, Mom is back." Rulan had gotten back from the hospital where she worked as a pharmacist. In her mid-thirties, she was petite and nimble, carrying a friendly smile, gentle and content, especially when her son was around.

"Hi, Mom." Hanwei continued focusing on his drawing.

Rulan walked through the door into the kitchen attached to a small living room and the family bedroom. She sat down on a bench with a bucket and started sorting the vegetables she brought from the farmer's market to prepare the family dinner.

"How was your school today?"

"It was good."

"Are you still working on your homework?" Rulan was rarely worried about her boy's school work, as he was attentive in school without much pushing.

"I already finished it." Hanwei went into the kitchen, holding the globe his dad bought for him, joyfully joining his mom on the bench.

"Mom, if the Earth is round, what about the people in the southern hemisphere? How could they not fall off the Earth?" Hanwei had been bothered by this question ever since he'd heard that the Earth was round. He thought the earthlings might not notice the Earth was round because the Earth is so big that its curvature is subtle. But everyone he saw stood upright because the ground supported them from below. Then what about the people down there? Their world was horrifying to this little boy.

"People there also stand on the Earth just like we do." Rulan continued washing her nicely trimmed vegetables. Still puzzled, the boy pondered what he'd heard, thinking what was "down" as a direction seemed to depend on something more than met the eye. At that age, he did not know about gravity yet.

"Will Dad be home today?"

"Who knows? He is probably hanging out with his buddies."

It would be just Hanwei and Rulan enjoying their dinner and evening together.

"Have you finished the drawing for Grandma? Her birthday is coming this weekend."

"Almost done!" Hanwei answered.

With a smile on her face, Rulan felt a sense of pride that she often had for this little boy.

#

Rulan's mother lived by the Yangtze River bank. End of summer offered nice weather to the town. The water was warm enough for daring young fellows to jump in. Some would challenge others to swim across the river for the title of "The Town's Fittest," although that could be a fatal endeavor with the turbulent water and busy ferries. The more mature fellows enjoyed their walk on the local street in the cool breeze, playing Chinese chess or mahjong with their babies in their arms, enjoying cigarettes and tea around benches in their courtyards, or hanging out in shops, chatting with their friends about what terrible things were going on in the town.

It was a busy day for Wanqing, Rulan's mother, and her big

family. They set up benches and tables in the courtyard. By noon, all her five children's families had already shown up.

Rulan's younger brother was running around in the kitchen, chopping, seasoning, and cooking with the grandma. He was an all-around good family man, funky and macho, worked in the factory's mechanical repair department; he was on the department's basketball team and competed in tournaments against other departments as they were cheered by the town people. He was a role model for the young Hanwei. The locals also said the nephew carried on his uncle's traits.

Rulan threw herself into the busy work, trying to be helpful. The big family wouldn't put her on the chef's spot, though. Not only was the grandma a professional chef in the factory's cafeteria, her other four children were also good cooks and tough critics. And that culinary skill, taste, and critical attitude were among the most exemplifying traits of people in this region of China, which Rulan was a bit lacking in. Rulan's little boy happily immersed himself in that part of local culture. That sometimes made Rulan feel like she was too ordinary as a woman and a mother.

Rulan's elder sister who lived in town, her youngest brother and sister from the city, and their in-laws were all deemed as the adults in the family. Connected and informed of local affairs, sharp tongued, they joyfully led the conversations at the birthday gathering. But those conversations were rarely enjoyable to Hanwei's father, Gaoming, who also came today, sitting in the corner like an outsider.

After his tech institute graduation, Gaoming was dispatched as an engineer under the migration policy of the planned economy to this factory from the coastal Chinese city, Suzhou, a historically famous cultural and economic gem. Working in the factory's main office building, he scouted and read as much as he could to find out about the world. Although the information from outside was limited, in his mind, it gave him a bigger picture, a higher aspiration, and a better understanding of a civilized society. So, listening to the in-laws talking about who won a fight on the factory floor, who maneuvered for a promotion, or who was killed in a factory shop by accidentally stepping and falling into a grinding machine was rather arduous to him. After all, he was the one who put those scientists' pictures underneath Hanwei's desk glass top, taught Hanwei how to use the electronic keyboard, and gave him Transformers and Lego toys.

The kids were raucous. They ran around, skirmishing one another. The oldest two kids already grew feisty, bragging about their mischief, and occasionally laughing at their younger cousins for their inexperience and naivety.

Food and plates were streamed out onto the tables. The sizzling food had everything that locals liked: Chongqing spicy chicken, sour pickled fish, marinated pig ear, twice cooked pork, Sichuan peppercorn eel, dry chilly cooked vegetables, stewed pig feet with beans, and the famous local dish, Luoqi tofu. This was one of the things Hanwei enjoyed most with his extended family.

The feast began.

"You know the amount of cash they hid in the moon cake gift box given to Officer Liu? Three hundred yuan," Rulan's brother-in-law, a factory insider, noted to the family crowd. As factory workers who barely earned two hundred yuan a month, that got their attention. "But you've got to have the connection first. Otherwise, even if you want to bribe, the door does not open; officials wouldn't dare touch it."

"Yep. These days, it's all about commission," Rulan's youngest brother's wife, a trendy lady, added. "Once these kids grow up, they will all have to look for opportunities of getting commissions."

Rulan's pretty younger sister who visited from the city pointed to the kids' table and said, "Well, unless you all study hard and do well in school like Hanwei."

Rulan instinctively felt shy and awkward hearing her son mentioned. Her youngest brother's wife followed not so subtly. "Even for technicians, or those scientists, it will have to come down to getting commission of some sort. That's how people really make money."

Rulan's youngest sister added, "Nowadays, city people have more money than ever. Going out to meet friends or simply walking in the street, you would be judged by your appearance. People say don't judge a person by the looks. But that's how things actually work."

"True. It is the era of open economy and reform. You get more respect when dressed up," Rulan's youngest brother's wife seconded.

Not sitting on the sideline, Rulan's elder sister added her mature take. "People are like that, fake. Other than your own family, you do not know others' agenda. In the office, white-collar people also elbow one another. It's either I float to the top, you sink to the bottom, or the other way around."

"Hmm... This sounds similar to the era of old China," Wanqing laconically commented. To the locals and to Hanwei, Grandma was a nice, warm lady. She grew up in a dismal era of China before 1949, lived through days where she had to go out seeking day labor work to bring food back to her opium addicted father, survived both the Sino-Japanese war and Chinese civil war, and raised her children through the Great Chinese Famine and a decade of cultural revolution. Yet remarkably, she was still here today, and managed to retain a sense of kindness, humbleness, and dignity.

Hearing the talk among the adults, Hanwei looked confused and worried. It was quite different from what he had read in his books.

"The world is colorful, Hanwei, not black and white printed in the textbook." Buzzed with beer, the elder uncle grinned at his nephew, followed by spontaneous laughs from other adults.

Drinks and talks lingered on until it started raining in the afternoon. As stomachs filled and bottles emptied, Wanqing's family rushed to clean up the mess.

Inside the house, everyone was rested. Rulan nudged Hanwei and said, "Do you want to give Grandma your birthday gift now?"

"Yup." Hanwei reached for Rulan's bag, pulled out a scroll, and walked to Grandma.

"Grandma, I drew something as a gift for you."

"Ah? A gift for me?" Wanqing opened the scroll in a delightful smile, while others steered their sights into her direction.

There it was, on that one-meter-long paper, a vivid and commanding Chinese dragon, penciled in black and gray, with its body covered in scales, claws extended from arms, seemingly stepping up and climbing through clouds, with its head rising to the top with a calm yet snarling look, adorned with a fire-like mane and a pair of outstretched horns. On the bottom right corner, there was Hanwei's printed name, which literally meant, "a great Chinese."

Wanqing couldn't hold back her joy. "Hanwei, thank you. Grandma always says Hanwei is the nicest and smartest boy," Wanqing said raising her voice, while turning to the other four grandchildren, "All my grandchildren are good kids. But if all of you listen to your parents and study as hard as Hanwei does, Grandma would be even happier."

Rulan intercepted, trying to spare the feeling of other parents in the room. "Hanwei is just good in books—other things, not so much. Sometimes he is almost tardy."

"Probably it's time to go home," Hanwei's father murmured, seeing that the rain had stopped.

"We also need to get going," Rulan's elder sister seconded.

Streaming out of the house, the family waved goodbyes to one another.

"It looks like it's still drizzling a little bit." Hanwei pointed at the cloud to his mom.

"Don't be a sissy." Gaoming pulled the little boy to the sidewalk, while Rulan followed in a hurry.

Father and Friends

The '80s were a magical era. The entertainment industry in Hong Kong dazzled the Chinese mainlanders, like those in the factory town, with their stars, pop songs, and tempting movie stories. Footage of NBA players, in that distant but shining country, slamming the ball into the net in a way that seemed to defy gravity, captured the hearts and minds of testosterone-filled young men in this newly opened country. Full of life and hope, with ample time at hand, young men in this factory town were eager to explore what was in store for them.

"Rulan, I need to go to the city for business the day after tomorrow. I'll take Hanwei with me." Gaoming sat on one side of the self-made L-shape couch in the living room, jabbing a cigarette, enjoying Alan Tam's classic song playing on his stereo. Hanwei, now eleven years old, was doing his homework in the bedroom.

"Another business trip? You are busy these days. Be careful on the trip, especially with Hanwei," Rulan responded before quickly returning to the kitchen.

The living room was small, barely twelve feet by twelve feet. Gaoming built all the bookshelves onto the wall to save space. A small square dining table was placed in front of the window to provide more space for socialization in the middle of the room.

Sitting on the other end of the couch was a young man named Mengchao, twenty years old, living in a village close by, often visiting the house to hang out, sometimes staying overnight.

Although not active within the extended family, Gaoming was well known in town for his unique charisma. Unlike the locals, he actually paid attention to his clothes and style. Five feet and eight inches, good looking, dressed in a somewhat Hong Kong style of clothes, and walking at a fast pace with a prominent upright posture, he was easily identifiable in the street. He was also a bit famous for his talents in music. He played accordion in a band for the factory's gala show and even sang solo on stage once. As rumor had it, that was how he and Rulan had started dating in earlier days.

Gaoming also hosted tutoring sessions at home, helping some of the young men in town with math and science. Many of them hardly followed the school subjects as they sought too much fun and strived to reign supreme over the fights among little gangs. Those tutoring sessions often ended with Gaoming showing off and teaching them how to play guitar, chatting about one another's recent experiences. That had gotten Gaoming some younger friends; as Rulan often told Hanwei, "Your father is a king of the young. He feels admired among them and gets to tell them what to do."

"Hanwei." Gaoming said, raising his voice to the direction of the bedroom where Hanwei was in. "We have more friends coming with us this time. Uncle Mengchao will also join us."

#

"Help yourself! Pick your rooms... You are on a trip. So, enjoy yourself," Gaoming happily told the boys. Filled with excitement, shoving one another with laughs and jokes, the boys piled into the three empty rooms along an upstairs corridor in the corner of a residential building. Some residents in Chongqing City lived in this type of residential complex, three or four stories tall, with a courtyard in its center, each floor having a common hangout area with several individual corridors leading to different studios.

Gaoming and Mengchao got a room for themselves. Hanwei and three older boys scattered their stuff in the other two rooms.

In contrast to the quiet and more mature Mengchao, the other three boys were around eighteen years old, outgoing and mischievous. They were from the factory town's vocational school. Although Hanwei might have encountered some of these older boys at Gaoming's house parties, he didn't feel like he had anything in common with them, as he was mostly occupied by his school and his own friends. He saw them as stronger, taller, athletic, loud, and bad. And since they were his father's friends, seemingly knowing things he didn't know and having done things he couldn't do, Hanwei also looked up to them a bit.

The trip was filled with checking out busy districts in the city, eating mouth watering street food, horsing around, and cooling themselves with faucet waters at the common cleaning joint, then enjoying cigarettes and snacks together around the table by their rental rooms. To Hanwei, though, being dragged to different places with those young adults was a bit onerous. He couldn't understand the intricate street affairs the adults talked about, had no playmates of his own, and felt that no one was really paying attention to him. Yet, he had to behave while under his father's surveillance.

One afternoon, Gaoming and Mengchao went out. Hanwei checked around to see what the older boys were up to. He pushed one room's door open. Apparently, two of the older boys were fooling around. One guy, only in his underwear, had one leg on a chair, while the other guy was butt naked sitting in the bed leaning back on the headboard! Seeing Hanwei bump into the room, the two guys looked between each other, then laughed. The naked guy smirked, then teased, "Come in!"

The naked guy's pee-pee was reddish and swollen. *Ouch, he probably got bitten by a bug, poor him.* That didn't surprise Hanwei. Many times in school, he saw seemingly obnoxious guys do silly things, perform dangerous acts, and bully younger fellows. Not wanting to get into any trouble, Hanwei ignored them, backed out, and went on with his day.

The third boy's name was Gang. He wore a pair of glasses and was shrewd and cocky. He was the popular one, often walking around with slippers, humming hip songs. He liked to talk about Hong Kong's pop stars and rave about NBA players' dazzling moves. Lean and athletic, he also showed off his basketball skills in the courtyard on the day of their arrival. Although Hanwei found Gang unpredictable and intimidating, he admired him in a way. After all, Hanwei often learned tricks from his father's friends, then went to his school friends to show off and get the respect he wanted. On this trip, Hanwei shared the same bed with Gang.

Resting in their bed together on a hot afternoon, Gang introduced Hanwei to the comic book, *Legends of God.* They chatted about the characters in it. Although more of a little intellectual, like most boys, Hanwei was fascinated by the wars between strong and powerful characters in the book. When his parents were not around, he liked to play with his toy Transformers, mimicking Autobots and Decepticons, drawing murderous plots and attacking on behalf of one another with imaginary lasers and missiles.

Gang put down the book and said, "Hey. Let's play a guessing game."

"Yes." Hanwei was intrigued.

"But the rule is that you have to reveal your answer by touching the subject and pointing it out to me."

"Okay."

"It has a hole. Somewhat flexible. Everyone has two." Gang smiled at Hanwei.

Knowing he was asked to touch the subject to reveal the answer, Hanwei guessed the answer must be around them in the room. *And if everyone has two, yes!* Hanwei quickly reached out and touched Gang's ear.

Gang smirked. "Not bad." "Hmm… Let's see… It has two holes. Everyone has only one. Some are flat and some are tall."

At this point, Hanwei figured these were easy games and likely he could find answers all around Gang. "It's your nose, right?"

"Well, remember, you have to touch it first."

Hanwei then reached out and gently touched Gang's nose.

"You need to touch for real. That's the rule," Gang emphasized.

Hanwei gave it a more elaborate touch on Gang's nose. He never thought he'd dare to get so close to a bigger, feisty guy like Gang.

"Good boy. Okay. Something elongated, with two nuts attached to it, and like a hose, sometimes water comes out of it."

Hanwei guessed what that might be. However, he couldn't believe Gang actually asked for that. Living in the factory town, little Hanwei had seen naked men when showering with his father in the factory's public bath, grown men with penises and testicles vaguely in sight hanging between their legs in bushes, bodies soaked under water with soapy bubbles, minding their own business, occasionally grunting to one another in the echoing chamber. He thought the grown men looked different from kids like him, but he didn't really know anything about it.

"I think I know. But I am not very sure."

Gang was lying by his side. He could almost hear Gang's breath and heartbeat.

"Show me," Gang commanded, looking at Hanwei with an intimidating gaze through his glasses.

Hanwei nervously extended his arm, wading through their comforter, and found Gang's boxer shorts. Gang had strong thighs. Hanwei was now afraid of what the older guy meant for this. Under the boxers, Hanwei touched something that he thought must be part of Gang's penis, or testicle, although he was not sure. It had thick hairs and was somewhat moist.

"It's okay. You can touch it."

Hanwei listened and touched Gang. He did not know how that body part of a grown man really felt. Now he found out it was indeed much bigger, somehow warm and veiny. *How come it is so different from mine?* Hanwei thought, *Maybe that body part of Gang's is ill, maybe these raucous guys got into trouble after all.*

Gang looked at Hanwei with another smirk, a sense of superiority and pride. "Don't be shy. You can play with it if you like."

Hanwei withdrew his hands, feeling being played and shameful.

"Okay. Let me see yours."

With a sense of defeat, Hanwei could only agree to let Gang examine his penis. At eleven years old, Hanwei was only a boy. It was embarrassing. He now realized there was a clear physical and mental gap between him and a physically grown man like Gang. He thought now he knew why his father often belittled and paid little attention to him, but always groomed and praised these young men at their house parties.

"Have you ever fucked a pussy before? Yours looks like you have done it! Haha!"

"No!" Being laughed at, Hanwei felt inferior and embarrassed; he didn't really understand what Gang was talking about. But whatever that was, he now admired what Gang had and how Gang was and wished one day he could be like him, a proud grown man.

#

The next day, Hanwei's father, Gang, and Hanwei were sharing fruit and tea together in the common area by their rental rooms. Hanwei sat there, listening to his bully and his guardian chatting about things he didn't care much about.

"I asked Hanwei to check out my dick. He seemed to be very shy." *No!* Hanwei couldn't believe Gang just carelessly brought up their secret with his father! *What an asshole! This is mortifying. Now Dad heard this?!* Anxious for his father's reaction, Hanwei wished his father would find a way to smooth it over and get their day back to normal. But he noticed Gaoming only gave a subtle smile, looking straight into his panicked eyes, with only one word coming out of his mouth, "Oh," then looked back to Gang and said, "He-he," as if everything was under control.

Hanwei actually feared his father.

There was a time when Gaoming came home in the middle of his work for errands. Gaoming asked if Hanwei had brushed his teeth. While Hanwei replied yes, he lied, not knowing his father had already checked if his toothbrush was wet. He received a hell of a beating for that, hung in the air with both wrists grabbed by Gaoming's one hand and butt whipped repeatedly by the other.

What triggered Gaoming to react with such rage then was a mystery. But Hanwei had started to feel vaguely that the notion of lying was forbidden within the family. That incident had a lasting effect on him. Not only did he develop a distaste for all lies, he also would panic easily when telling one himself.

Hanwei was also afraid of his father's control in the house, as Gaoming and his friends often gathered and occupied the home, sharing cigarettes, snacks, and beverages. He saw his father joyfully handing those older boys nicely cut watermelon chunks served on plates with toothpicks on top, while his mother washed clothes in the kitchen or knit in the bedroom. Sometimes those boys stayed over throughout the entire weekend, playing guitar and accordion, while Hanwei studied in the bedroom, bearing the loud music and talking. Hanwei once asked Gaoming if he could also teach him guitar. He got his father's answer in front of other boys. "Yes. When you play guitar and girls hear it, their hearts will be touched and they will fall for you." He recalled the laughter upon that exchange and his humiliation. He never got his father to teach him how to play.

Hanwei could not recall any warm interactions between his father and mother. Rulan did complain to Hanwei that Gaoming seemed to indulge his playful single life while giving little attention to Hanwei. There was the one time when Rulan got back from the cinema and she saw Hanwei curled up in the living room corner, playing with his toys while Gaoming was attending to other young guys in the room. When the little boy heard his mother, he reached out his arms in eagerness, letting his mom bring him into her arms.

#

It was the last day of the trip. Hanwei sat on the balcony of the room his father and Mengchao occupied, reading the comic book Gang gave him. Mengchao was a gentle fellow, broad shoulders and strong physique, very quiet. It was said that Gaoming met Mengchao through friends in the village.

Gaoming and Mengchao got back from outside. "It's hot and sweaty," Gaoming said. "Mengchao, you should have a shower. Here, take the towel. Soap should be in the shower room."

As asked, Mengchao went into the shower on the other end of the balcony.

"There is no soap here…"

Hanwei heard Mengchao speaking from the shower room.

"Hanwei, bring this soap to Uncle Mengchao," Gaoming instructed.

Hanwei hated this. *Why does this have to involve me? Plus,*

Uncle Mengchao must be having a shower if I step in.

Hanwei knocked on the door. "Uncle, I got soap here."

The door opened a slit, a hand reached out. Hanwei handed over the soap. It was quick. He then got back to his comic book reading.

"Did you give the soap to Uncle Mengchao?"

"Yes."

"How did you give the soap to him? Did you see Uncle in the shower?"

"Uncle extended his hand out of the shower door and grabbed the soap."

"Hmm… Uncle is still shy," Gaoming said perplexingly.

Luckily, the trip was finally over and Hanwei would be able to see his mom tomorrow at home.

Family

The days back at home after the trip were thankfully peaceful. Several days had passed by without any visitors. Hanwei received good grades in school. Rulan went to work at the factory's pharmacy and came home to raise her son.

The family of three was sitting at the lunch table sharing their meal. "Mengchao is not visiting you these days?" Rulan asked in a careful tone.

Seconds of silence had passed. Gaoming nodded. A sense of sadness floated about. Gaoming almost had tears behind his glasses.

While everyone kept silent, Hanwei thought he could understand why his father had descended into despair. And he knew, even though his father's affection did not belong to the people in this home and those visitors had taken their precious space, his mother still cared for his father's pain.

#

Gaoming often went out to local villages to tutor young men who wanted to apply to the factory's vocational school or prepare for the high school graduation exam. Sometimes, he would make new friends on the road.

A few weeks later, a new guy came home with Gaoming. He was cocky and had friends in the village.

Rulan commented on this to Hanwei, "Your father only knows how to hang out with young guys, so he can be admired and be in charge. In his eyes, Mom knows too little and does not know how to entertain guests. See? Another young guy comes to spend time with him for, who knows, how many days."

One day, Hanwei was working on something in the common area outside his family unit. The common area was where all neighbor adults and kids met one another.

"That Gaoming Zhou is so shameless. Always brings young men home," a middle-aged lady spoke out loud, seemingly to no one.

Knowing what he heard was horrible, Hanwei quickly returned to his unit.

That same week, a neighbor girl, a good friend of Hanwei's, said to him, "The guy your father brought over this time is even cuter than the previous one!"

Hanwei didn't know what to say to his friend, or whether there was anything wrong with his family in contrast to hers.

Hanwei had been a leader among the neighbor kids. When the house was not occupied by adults, he often brought neighbors over to play with his toys, have little boxing matches, and share the latest neighborhood news. But when Gaoming was present, Hanwei would dwindle to a timid boy. He'd rather not have his father around to confuse his friends. Gaoming liked to make derogatory remarks towards women and effeminate men when the kids were hanging out, "Men are superior," "Women have long hair but are short on experiences," "If you guys watch the Animal Channel, you will see that only male peacocks have colorful tail feathers and only male lions have magnificent manes."

Those remarks made a lot of sense to kids at Hanwei's age and were music to the ears of those young, inexperienced guys. But Hanwei always doubted the rigor of such a thesis. *If females are truly inferior in a general sense, why are they so essential? For something that is essential, how can we find a notion of inferiority that is consistent with its essential qualities that have stood the test of practical needs?*

Although Hanwei had acquired a habit of deep thinking at a young age, he was yet to understand nature's law that all matters had a tendency to settle to their lowest energy state and see the universal truth that "beauty is in the eyes of the beholder." In the case of biology, that beholder was the evolutionary pressure. And in some cases, like the birds of prey and many insects and reptiles, nature preferred small males and larger females. Hanwei would have to comprehend these notions later beyond what his father could see.

#

Sunday morning, the new guy and his four buddies descended on Gaoming's home. Rulan would come home late in the afternoon from Grandma's place. While Gaoming and the five guys were hanging out in the living room, Hanwei was doing his homework in the bedroom. He hated overhearing Gaoming's misogynistic preaching to those young men. He was so annoyed that he fantasized a scene where he walked straight to the center of the living room, faced his father, took out a gun and aimed at his father, then said to him in front of all his guys, "You are wrong!" Then, *Bang!* terminated his father.

"Come to the living room, Hanwei," Father summoned.

Gaoming had constructed wood panels and a sliding door at the intersection of the living room, the kitchen, and the bedroom entrance so as to have some privacy for his living room. He also had covered the concrete floor with a patterned floor mat for comfort.

"Hanwei is a gentle boy, smart in school and very talented," Gaoming said to his guys, "Hanwei, take off your clothes and lie on the floor, face down. Father will help open your mind and everyone's for divergent thinking and convergent thinking. Don't be shy."

Following the order, Hanwei took off his clothes, leaving his boxer on, lying down on the floor quietly, with those stronger and taller guys watching. Then he felt his father's hands coming down on him, starting to massage his shoulders and arms.

"We need to engage in divergent thinking," his father said while massaging the little boy from the shoulders to the hands. "There are always multiple angles to look at a problem. Oftentimes, there is more than meets the eye. Once you see outside the box, what was previously incomprehensible would then become comprehensible."

Gaoming continued to touch Hanwei from his upper back to lower back.

"But we also need to engage in convergent thinking." Gaoming moved to massage Hanwei's thighs, then rubbed Hanwei's feet. "Convergent thinking allows you to focus on a practical solution when you have to deal with your matter within your current means."

Why do I have to be called upon to participate in this? While Father's hands massaged his body in front of strangers, Hanwei felt his commanding presence as all the young guys listened. He hated being used as a dummy.

"Okay. It's all done," Gaoming concluded. "Hanwei, now you can go back to your homework. Silly little nerd." His father smiled.

Hanwei quickly got up and walked out of the sight of those men. He then heard his father from his room. "Now it's you guys' turn. Who is next?"

#

That night, Gaoming and the five young guys were still in the living room. Hanwei could hear his father's talk and the music playing from the stereo. In the kitchen, Rulan and Hanwei were sharing a bucket of hot water to warm and clean their feet before going to bed. In those days, a private bathroom was something yet to come for an everyday Chinese family.

Rulan was stressed out that the five guys apparently would stay overnight. She had lived many days like this without complaints, when only one or two visitors were involved. It was too crowded tonight and too loud.

"Women have long hair but are short on experience. One example is Hanwei's mother. She is like Esther, a character in the show *Los Ricos También Lloran*, a jealous, manipulative, and cruel woman. You guys later should only find women from the village to bear kids. They are simpler, and won't interfere with your life much."

Hanwei pretended not to have heard his father, afraid that any reaction could trigger additional demeaning comments from his father and turn this evening into a nightmare.

"Did you hear? Your father said that I am Esther. Did I really do so many wrong things to him? It's terrible that your dad should talk about me like that." Rulan was visibly upset. But she chose not to make a scene. She seemed to have accepted her fate after all these years. She often told Hanwei, "Can you see? Mom is not a capable woman and not pretty. And they say women are the weak ones. Mom could not help you much in your life. So, you have only yourself to rely on. You are a boy. When you grow up, you have to be strong."

#

Gaoming usually slept on the living room's sofa bed. Rulan and Hanwei usually shared the large bed in the bedroom. When Gaoming's friends visited, they slept in the living room. Tonight, the five young guys squeezed among one another on the floor mat in the living room, sharing padding and comforters together.

"It's all because of you!"

"Why do you say that? Can you please clarify?"

"It's what you did! It's because you scared him!"

Startled, Hanwei woke up in a haze from shouting in the middle of the night. He heard loud exchanges coming from the living room and realized mother was not by his side.

"He disappeared in the middle of the night! We don't know where he went! Did you chase him away?! He is such a good young fellow. He must have left because you treated him badly! You, as a wife, have been very unfriendly to my friends, not giving a warm reception to my guests, carrying around a grudged looking face. It must be you who scared him away.

What have you said to him?!"

"In the middle of the night, he chose to leave. We don't know where he is, don't know if he is safe. Poor guy. You go find him and bring him back!!" Hanwei could hear what sounded like his father crying. His voice was filled with anger and despair.

"What did I do wrong? How should I treat guests better? Gaoming, I have not been unfriendly to these young fellows. I didn't say or do anything. Maybe he just wanted to leave." Hanwei heard his mother's voice shaking as she was put on the spot to answer the crowd in the living room.

Then Gaoming continued, "Why would he want to leave?! It's only because of you! Where can we find him?!"

"He is a young adult. He must know his way. It won't be easy for anyone to find him this late. You can check with his family tomorrow." Rulan was trying her best to defend herself with restraint, managing a calm exchange as much as she could through her distress.

"You, Esther, mean and cruel, gave miseries to my life. I could not even have a peaceful time for my visiting friends."

Hanwei trembled in bed, wishing it was only a nightmare that would fade away soon. He feared for his mother's well-being, unsure whether anyone could save him and his mother.

"You have been a bad influence on Hanwei, our nice son. He is such a nice boy but has to be around a terrible mother like you. You should bring him out to us! Bring him to us!"

"Gaoming Zhou, on what ground can you say that? I didn't do anything wrong to Hanwei. He should stay in his bed. We should not be yelling loudly in the middle of the night and waking up neighbors. It only makes our family look bad in others' eyes. I will not give Hanwei to you. You are overthinking. You can try to find your friend in the morning."

Hanwei wished his mother was not alone in the other room fighting for herself and for him. With Gaoming's voice rescinding, he heard Rulan come back to the room. He tucked his head around the comforter, with his back facing the bedroom door, and pretended not to have heard anything. His mother and he lived through another day.

Mother and Son

School was the best playground for Hanwei where he found his pride and comfort. He ranked in the top of class and excelled in math, music, and drawing. That earned him warm attention from teachers. Classmates also gravitated toward him since he was generous in helping them on academic subjects, sociable, and trustworthy.

One morning, Hanwei was on his way to school, holding an umbrella in the rain. The walk from his home to the school was about twenty minutes. The route through town was also where schoolkids, teachers, shop owners, and homeless people brushed shoulders.

"Hanwei," a familiar voice came from behind. It was his Chinese literature teacher. She was a nice lady, who cared for and watched Hanwei's back.

"Hey, Ms. Liu."

Ms. Liu pulled Hanwei under her umbrella and squeezed him together with her while they walked ahead. "Hanwei, I heard that your father brought many young men home and let them stay overnight for days!"

Surprised by the sudden question, Hanwei answered in a timid voice, "Yup."

"How can your father do that? Did your mother say

anything? Who are those people? Do you know? What did they stay at your home for? Tell me…"

For a moment, Hanwei felt as if everyone in the street was asking him that question and everyone could hear his response. His tears came fast and he wished someone somehow could help his family if the truth was told.

Ms. Liu was startled. She now knew the rumor was true, something was wrong. And different from her students' schoolwork, this time it was something that might be beyond her reach.

#

In the factory's pharmacy, Rulan was a likable member of the staff. She grew up in this town, and left for Tibet to work as a nurse for three years. Ever since returning, she had worked in the pharmacy. The pharmacy served all factory workers. Since Hanwei was well known for his outstanding academic performance in school, Rulan often received warm compliments from customers at the medicine pick-up window and even solicitations of advice.

Hanwei sometimes visited the pharmacy after school, enjoying Rulan's company. One afternoon, Hanwei was visiting his mother's office again.

One nurse complained while working her work routines. "Our government is very incompetent, often talks about how we can catch up with Americans and Europeans, but doesn't know what steps to take other than talking about some nonsense policy sketches. Just look at how poor we Chinese are and how messy things are around here."

"But we are only at the early stage of socialism. It takes

time to develop sophisticated mechanisms for a productive society," Hanwei responded.

"Oh, the early stages of socialism, the Communist Party has been saying that for many years. They surely preach that notion well to school kids. While they bash capitalism in the West, we are stuck in that early stage forever."

"But extreme capitalism and its ultimate form, imperialism, induces inequality. Inequality then self-perpetuates by stripping more and more people of fair opportunities. When capitalists eventually capture the state and the world, democracy and freedom would cease to exist. At least our government is able to step in with socialist means to ensure fair opportunities. That is critical to restore the faith and motivation of people. And our free nine-year compulsory education is a good example."

"You think our country has democracy?" she said sarcastically.

One male doctor visiting the office teased Hanwei with a smile. "Young people, nowadays, have aspirations of democracy and freedom."

"Wow. Hanwei, so young, yet talks like an old man already." Hearing the twelve-year-old boy being passionate, the pharmacy's manager commented, "It's good to see our schoolkids believing in our country."

Hanwei veered towards consolidating different ideas into a more sophisticated view. "The West may have done many things right. And we surely have a lot to improve ourselves by learning from a capitalist society like theirs while avoiding their structural issues. But our country can be developed well with the advantageous elements of socialism."

"Overall, we are far behind Americans. I heard their GDP

is ten times ours," Rulan added.

"Exactly," the lady who complained earlier followed. "Every American family has a sedan. When you grow up, you will witness whether Chinese families will have cars. I guarantee it won't happen."

It was hard to blame the lady for being cynical as an adult after seeing and experiencing years of unfairness, setbacks, and injustice. Hanwei, on the other hand, like other youth, still dreamed of something better and, more enviously, had the heart to challenge how things worked. The youths were waiting for their turn when the old guard eventually left the stage.

While the debate fizzled, Hanwei focused on a newspaper he grabbed from the pharmacy desk. A headline noting *Deviant Crimes in Dark Corners Busted by Police* captured his attention.

"Two men under the shadow of the moon glanced around quickly, before hiding themselves into a public restroom. They disappeared into one of the stalls. 'Police! Open the door!' Three undercover policemen rushed in, pulled their People's Police badges up onto their arms, started knocking and kicking onto a stall's door. The two grown men were seen in a panic putting on their clothes and pants. They were committing deviant acts inside the stall. The three policemen quickly subdued the two struggling men in the crime scene.

"Multiple incidents of this deviant type of crime were caught recently, according to the police. In one incident, two men followed by police were found wearing no clothes together in a hotel room bed, rushing to cover themselves under sheets when police burst in. The police department said they will punish such deviant crimes that are recently on the rise."

Instantly, Hanwei felt this had something to do with what he knew about his father. Hanwei had learned from his father's preaching that men were more physically desirable to the general public. Their energy, charm, and ingenuity were what made them interesting and fascinating to passion-loving people, just like a male peacock displaying its astonishing tail feathers, and like a full-maned lion roaring through the African great plains. So, Hanwei thought, while women were gifted for nurturing, inspiring, and sometimes leading the progress of humankind's civilization, everyone was actually fond of men and capable of feeling the pleasure from men's vivid nature. That "everyone" included both women and men, except that, as Hanwei further conjectured, having pleasure was not something productive, hence was culturally discouraged. However, now to Hanwei's shock, this was a crime prosecutable by the organized government of his beloved country and people. *So, men are not allowed to like other men even in private? What my father has been doing is wrong, or sinister like other crimes? And anyone who dares to practice such natural pleasure has to risk ruining his life?!?* Hanwei's head was humming and his heart was racing.

"Hanwei, your mother fainted several days ago in the office. Did you know?" Hanwei heard the pharmacy manager talking to him.

"No." He quickly put the newspaper away.

"Did your father abuse her at home? Your mother is often worried about you. You seem argumentative too. Do both you and your father get together and abuse your mother?" the pharmacy manager said while Hanwei, still in shock, scrambled to correlate the newspaper story with what he knew about his father, mother, and himself.

"Your mom is the nicest mother in the world. You've got to

love your mother back."

#

An earthquake rattled the Chongqing area. A stampede took place in Hanwei's school when students were rushing out of the school's building. Some buildings collapsed, resulting in the authority relocating kids of affected families to the factory town for school. The fear of aftershocks hadn't gone away. Locals were scared. Their worries continued. Hanwei's father hadn't come home for days since then and might have gone to tend to his friend in this unsettling time. One evening after dinner, Rulan and Hanwei had a walk to the river bank.

The thirty-minute walk went past the factory's facilities along a steep cliff, with a vista point illuminated by a large sprawling alder tree overlooking the Yangtze River. The long, flat, sandy river bank was covered with colorful pebbles. From far, one could hear the horns from docking ships and see the busy piers and locals hanging out at the waterfront.

Walking along the waterfront against the wind, Rulan was quiet and seemed to be carrying heavy thoughts. Hanwei stayed quiet, enjoying their time alone.

"Hanwei, your father is terrible. While everyone is afraid of the ongoing earthquake situation, he doesn't come home, not even to comfort you."

Hearing Mom's words, Hanwei understood the situation he was in: a home left with no grown man.

"You may not know what people in the factory have been saying about your father." Rulan seemed to have a need to let it out. "They said, 'Gaoming Zhou puts on a beautiful hat of tutoring young men in this town. But under that beautiful hat, he is conducting filthy acts with naïve young men.' I didn't know how to even respond when I heard it."

Hanwei pretended he was too young to understand what he'd heard and what their life had become.

On the way home, Rulan and Hanwei were silent. They walked and kept walking. By the side of a factory building on top of a cliff, Rulan briefly stopped at a narrow opening to the cliff along the facility's wall. A metal staircase with a handrail went all the way down to the bottom. Hanwei saw the wave below, carried by the wind, submerging the shore, hitting the brick wall one wave after another, chilling. Rulan stood still at the edge of the cliff along with Hanwei. Minutes had passed.

Rulan broke the silence. "Hanwei, if Mom and Dad were to divorce, is there anything you want to take with you if you go with Mom?"

Hanwei thought for a second, numbed between hope and fear, unsure if their problematic life could justify this point of no return. "I want to keep the calendar pamphlet Dad put on my desk, the calendar of knowledge. Every page of it describes something in science and nature. It has many answers to the world around. He would let us have it, right?"

Rulan tried hard to hold back her tears. She could not respond with words to the boy by her side. She felt she couldn't choose to go down the road of a divorce as long as Hanwei needed a family. She had seen much grief in life. In this factory town, there was a transgender woman rumored to have committed suicide, there was a young fellow stabbed to death by a local gang, many blue-collar workers had died of cancer at early ages linked to the pharmaceutical company's chemical hazards. Besides all the miseries around, in Rulan's heart, Hanwei had been a jewel to her in this town and a hope for a happy and meaningful life.

Scuffle

It was the last year of middle school for Hanwei. Now fifteen years old, Hanwei had become the most academically accomplished student in his school, winning awards in special academic contests in his province, in just about every category: physics, mathematics, chemistry, and English. That was unheard of for a rusty factory town four hours away from the city. The factory's TV station dispatched its crew to the school to take video footage of Hanwei for local news, thanks to the Chinese culture rooted in its imperial examination system a thousand years ago. That made Hanwei's family proud.

A patient visiting the pharmacy asked Hanwei's mother, "Rulan, can you tell me how your family raised Hanwei to do so well in school?"

"We don't really push him much. It's probably because he is interested in math and science. His interests may be influenced by his father. We do try accommodating his interests by providing him a decent studying environment, like a designated desk, papers, science books, and magazine subscriptions," Rulan answered. "I also think he is lucky to have good teachers in school. They inspired him."

Gaoming gave his own answer when asked. "We didn't do

anything special. He ranked second in his class the first time he took an exam in his elementary school, not having any notion of an exam or competition. So, I think he is smart to begin with."

Hanwei, however, wasn't so thrilled that the school's system, to some degree, despised students with poor grades. "I think a school that pushes and evaluates all students using the same set of academic subjects could overlook different potentials and talents and end up suppressing some students' growth. Some classmates are athletic, some are handy, some are good in arts, and some are very social. They all can be productive to our society in some way. I hope the school can help them succeed in what they have to offer."

While that answer was a bit awkward to some, especially on camera, the physics teacher standing by Hanwei was not surprised by the ever-confident and outspoken fifteen-year-old Hanwei.

#

After moving to an apartment in a popular location close to the factory's recreational swimming pool, Gaoming started regularly bringing home local guys in their early twenties, promising them friends, cigarettes, and music. They were like street guys, fun, athletic, ripe with hormones.

Gaoming stuffed the wall shelf with books about ancient Rome, telling of its culture, where young men were considered a source of desire, and it was the norm for men to enjoy sex with other men without being perceived as losing masculinity or social status, so long as one assumed the dominant male role. He also supplied some sex education books, where penises were drawn and the benefits and concerns of masturbation were discussed between a Japanese doctor and a boy.

In the corner where Hanwei slept, Gaoming put a poster of a nude ancient Roman male sculpture on the wall. When Rulan told Gaoming the visiting grandma was embarrassed seeing it, he simply replied that it was art.

Gaoming even put a framed picture of one of his young men on the living room wall shelf, and once pointed it to Hanwei and said, "His body is the best among all those guys." As if that was not disturbing enough, he added, "Don't worry. You will one day look like him."

That young man was Yong. It was a day Rulan went for her night shift when Hanwei interacted with him. That day, after other friends had left, Yong stayed in Hanwei's bedroom to play video games upon Gaoming's request.

"Good game," Yong said in excitement, after the two killed the big boss together in the Nintendo game, Contra.

"Yeah," Hanwei responded.

"Not bad. You are a good player," Yong turned to Hanwei and smiled. "I feel like my heart is strong and pumping. I can hear my own heartbeat while sitting here, maybe because of the video game. Wanna check it out?" He pulled Hanwei's hand toward him to touch his masculine chest under the shirt.

When Hanwei felt the warm, solid chest of a fully grown young man, a sense of inferiority rose in him. He wanted to be like Yong in every way.

"It's time for you two to go to bed. Yong, you should have a shower," Gaoming said, while slightly opening Hanwei's bedroom door. "Change your dirty clothes and give them to me."

Yong unbuttoned his shirt, unbuckled his belt, and then took off his clothes, and happily handed them over to Gaoming behind the door.

"Your underwear too."

With a smile, then *shew*! The young man stripped off his underwear, stood completely naked in the middle of the bedroom, exposing his athletic body, hairy bush, nice penis and butt in their full glory.

Dang! Sitting on the floor right behind Yong, Hanwei was so startled, a butterfly feeling rose in his stomach. For the first time, he felt so drawn toward a man.

That night, Yong and Hanwei opened up to each other while in bed. Yong told Hanwei about the physical fights he had in the street. Hanwei told Yong a science fiction story he read from his *Youth's Science* magazine. The weird thing, though, was that Hanwei noticed, how, while they were chatting, his father's face rose behind the bedroom door and appeared on the glass panel at the top, looking at them like a spy. It was creepy. But Hanwei had learned to ignore it. The two then dozed off after a long day.

As days went by, Hanwei continued to grow up. He had already developed a fit build and had an attractive manly voice, well into his puberty.

One day after returning home from the community swimming pool, Hanwei was having a shower. While he was rinsing and rubbing himself with hot water and soap, Gaoming suddenly opened the shower door. He stood there staring at Hanwei with a slightly discerning look. Cornered, Hanwei looked slightly to the side, knowing his entire nude body was now in front of his father's stare, every inch of him being watched. He continued his shower, hoping to avoid any exchange. Gaoming's envious stare lasted for ten seconds or so, before he closed the door without giving a single word of explanation.

The tension between Hanwei and Gaoming started to rise with Hanwei's increasing testosterone level.

On one particularly hot day, while Hanwei walked through the living room towards the kitchen, passing by his father's shirtless young men, Gaoming pointed to his friends and said, "It is really hot. Why are you wearing this much? Look at everyone here. Act like a man. Take off your shirt. You have a nice body. You should feel proud of it."

Feeling insulted, Hanwei defied his father's order in front of the group of grown men. "I don't feel hot right now."

#

Only a few months before his high school entrance exam, Hanwei accidentally fractured his right ankle. He ended up staying home for more than a month and had to sit in bed most of the time. Elevators for apartment buildings didn't exist in those days. Other than home schooling himself, he played Nintendo games his father's friends brought over for him to kill time.

While Hanwei wasn't mobile, Gaoming had to cut down his outing time to share the responsibility with Rulan to take care of their son.

One afternoon, Rulan went to Grandma's place. Gaoming and one of his favorite guys were hanging out with him in the living room.

"This place suffocates me," Gaoming said.

To Hanwei, his father's inflammatory comment meant he

had to live through another episode of stressful times at home.

"This guy's mother has been a terrible thing to my life!" His father continued venting.

"No. Mom hasn't done anything wrong to you." Hanwei mustered the courage he had, and talked back.

For years, Hanwei had been afraid of his father's authority. Even Rulan questioned him more than once, "Why are you so afraid of your father like a mouse sensing an approaching cat?"

Hearing his son's direct challenge, Gaoming came to Hanwei's room in anger. "Your mom has been a terrible wife, very incapable."

"No. That's not true." Hanwei raised his voice, making sure he could also be heard by his father's friend in the living room.

"I have never loved your mother!"

"I know why."

"Huh? What do you know?! I couldn't love your mom because your mother has a very unattractive body!"

"You are making it up," Hanwei angrily replied. His voice trembled in fear and his heart was full of shame.

"You go ask your mom to take off her clothes, reveal herself in front of you! Your mom has pectus carinatum; she is deformed!"

Hearing the unthinkable thing his father said, Hanwei was speechless. He had learned long ago that con artists lied without conscience; they had no problem making things up, so long as it served themselves and the opposite was inconvenient for others to prove. They pretended to be the victim in order to destroy the innocent and productive people standing in their way, and if needed, they would throw out conspiracy theories, preying upon men's weakness that they tended to believe something larger was at play if they couldn't instantly make sense of the matter they were facing.

"You are lying," Hanwei asserted.

"You shut up! You'd become as dumb as your mother, continuing to live this way!"

Bang! Gaoming pushed Hanwei's head against the wall.

Hanwei's tears streamed down his face. He felt he wasn't able to defend his mother in front of outsiders in his home where his father's power reigned. He told himself that he had to do something to stand up for his mom and himself.

Awakening

Grandma Wanqing's birthday was coming again soon. As a tradition, the extended family would gather to celebrate the most beloved figure in the family. Hanwei talked to his two younger cousins about his idea of requesting a song to be played on the factory's radio station for Grandma's birthday. He revealed the plan to his parents at the lunch table.

Gaoming responded, "I don't think you will be able to do that. They wouldn't let you guys just walk in and arrange that. You'd need some sort of connection."

"Why? I heard it is a transparent process. Anyone can place a request at the factory's main office building. It isn't complex."

"I work in that building. It is not what you think."

Rulan added her take to soothe the conversation. "Your father meant you may need some connection to seal the deal."

"I am not sure about that. The people I asked didn't mention anything more to it."

Facing Hanwei's insubordination, Gaoming countered, "You are being stubborn and not trusting what we say. You are still a kid. There are many things you don't know."

Hanwei, however, was convinced the talk of his father was just another lie.

Ever since the time Hanwei was beaten by his father for lying about having brushed his teeth in the morning, Hanwei had theorized that a liar could develop an addictive yet resentful relationship with his past lies. Like his father, someone who lived a lie might desperately try to cover his tracks, sometimes resorting to more seemingly unrelated or unnecessary lies so as to confuse those they lied to, yet at the same time, they would hate to see their own actions in a mirror.

Hanwei backed down in that conversation. But he went ahead with his younger cousins to the factory's radio station the next day, having his aunt wait for them at the security gate.

The kids got the job done. They were received warmly at the radio station. Their grandma would hear their surprise birthday gift.

When they happily walked out of the building, his aunt said the security guard told her that they had received a call earlier that day from someone asking them to look out for some kids coming for trouble to make sure to block them.

#

Returning home, Hanwei joined his father and mother for lunch. The lunch table was a place where this family could feel they lived a normal life as everyone else did; they put food on the table and had each other by their side when no one else would, in a place they could call home.

"We actually ordered the song for Grandma's birthday. It was as simple as what I said earlier." Hanwei pushed for his I-told-you-so moment, overplaying his hand.

"You did?"

"Yeah. So, it's not like what you mentioned to me earlier."

"Don't talk to me like that!"

"I just want to tell the truth, and not do something just because you said so." Hanwei played it out like in a courtroom exchange, knowing he had more damaging info from his aunt.

"You are a homosexual!" Gaoming said loudly, out of nowhere.

The minds in the room went blank. They couldn't understand how the scene had changed in an instant, as if they were transported to an alternative nightmarish reality, only wishing to be pulled back to their normal life.

"No! I am not a homosexual. What are you talking about?" Hanwei collected his thoughts to focus back on the table.

"You are not?!"

"Your father has proof. Remember those drawings you made? Your sketches of naked men and their penises that I found in your school bag?! Those pictures are disgusting, unwatchable, immoral! I already shared those with your mom!"

It was two years ago when Hanwei was once called into the living room by his father. When he arrived, Gaoming was sitting across the couch, kindly talking to him with a smile behind his glasses.

"Hanwei, are these pictures drawn by you?" Hanwei nodded, knowing he was in trouble.

"Do not worry. It's okay. Everyone has a secret. We can have them, as long as others don't know. You know your father is very open minded and knowledgeable. It's actually normal for boys in puberty to experience those thoughts and desires." Gaoming managed to calm the scene, while looking into Hanwei's eyes. "How is the growth of your penis? Have you experienced ejaculation yet?"

Hanwei nodded, balancing between his need for respect and privacy and his need for his father's protection.

"Father will keep these drawings for you. It would not be good if others find out. I will not share these with anyone."

Hanwei had thought that episode was over. Now, his worst fear had come true.

"Today, your father will sear this shock into your life!"

"I also drew women in those pictures. I am not a homosexual."

"You are Gaoming Zhou's son. Your father knows what you are that you are yet to know!"

"Enough. Stop." Rulan rushed away from the lunch table and went to stand against the kitchen sink, facing the wall. Her face turned reddish. Without a sound, her tears ran down over her trembling lips.

Hanwei got up and went for his mom. Standing by her side, he could see in her eyes that she was dead inside and shocked that her life could come to this. To him, this woman in front of him was everything good in the world, and the only thing he must save if it came to an end.

"Mom. I promise I am not a homosexual. Can you see that I am not? Mom, I was just young and curious."

"Stop. If you are not, you are not. No need to explain," Rulan murmured.

After standing in silence with unstoppable tears, Rulan retreated to the family bedroom.

Sitting on the bed, Rulan looked around; the bedroom, its furniture, Hanwei's desk, TV, and closets were the only sanctuary she had to remind her of a normal life. Outside this bedroom were the days of loud parties, thick cigarette smoke, men after men occupying the house, and rumor and laughter behind her back in the street. The only thing she could hold onto was Hanwei, who had been upright since young, and loved her when she was vulnerable.

Hanwei rushed to the bedroom for his mom. "Mom, please. I will always be your good son," Hanwei begged.

Gaoming followed to the bedroom door. "See! You have tortured and crumbled your own mom! Your mom's life has come to this because of you."

"Stay away," Rulan said assertively.

"Dad. Please. Give Mom space." Hanwei stood between his mom and his father, ready to protect her for the first time. He looked into Gaoming's eyes, warning him how far he was willing to go.

Gaoming stopped.

It was the first time Hanwei stood up to his father to the end, protecting his mom. Since the day his father insulted his mother in front of strangers and hit his head against the wall, Hanwei had hidden a knife beneath his pillow. He imagined he had grown up and would not be afraid. He projected that his tormentor could no longer hurt him any longer. If Dad abandoned Mom and him, he could work in mechanic shops, he could sell newspapers, he could clean shoes for others, but he would not let his father torment his mother any longer. If it would come necessary to use the knife beneath his pillow, he thought he would.

Since that day, Hanwei no longer saw his father as the authority. He found his freedom; like prisoners of war, their bodies could be tortured, their endurance and dignity could be crushed, yet some could still find the ultimate freedom of spirit, that no one, not even a bullet, could take away from them. That freedom was knowing what was just and meaningful in their life.

#

Only a few weeks before the province-wide high school entrance exam, Hanwei visited one of his friends. This friend's father was a renowned chief engineer of the factory. Hanwei enjoyed the warm and peaceful atmosphere in his friend's home.

"You two want to go to university one day?" his friend's father asked.

The boys nodded.

The friend's father teased the two boys. "I can give you a problem to work on. Whoever finds the solution in five minutes will be able to go to university. Here are some paper and pens. You may need that. Ready?"

"There are ten balls. One of them weighs different than the rest. Using a balance, how many times do you have to weigh to find that one ball with a different weight?"

The boys quickly started working on it.

"It seems I can find it within four steps," Hanwei murmured.

"A good direction. Give you guys a hint. The minimum number of steps to solve this is actually three. But you need to find out how."

Hanwei then laser focused on finding out what he had missed. His friend was struggling.

"I think I got the answer," Hanwei said with hesitation, as the time ran out. "First split them into three groups, each with three balls, and leave the last one aside. Weigh the first group against the second group. If they have equal weights, the faulty ball must be in the third group. Then weigh between any two balls of the third group. If they have equal weights, the faulty one is either the third one in this group or the one left aside earlier. The third step is to pick either of those two balls to weigh against any of the good ones. If their weights are equal, the remaining one must be the faulty one. Otherwise, the faulty one must be the one we just picked."

"Good job! But what if the first two groups in your first step had unequal weights?"

"In that case, weigh one of the first two groups with the third group. That will tell which of the first two groups have the faulty ball. Also, we'd know if the faulty one is lighter or heavier. The third step is just to weigh any two balls in the faulty group. If they are equal, it'd be the third ball. Otherwise, whichever is heavier or lighter based on what we already know by then would be the faulty one."

The friend's father was surprised but very delighted. He had been almost ready to reveal the answer, thinking the problem might be too complex for teenagers in this factory town.

"Okay. This boy will be able to go to university."

Hanwei looked at the man's hand resting on his shoulder and found he didn't want to move.

#

In the three years that followed, Hanwei studied at the best high school in the city. Living in the dormitory, he met many bright classmates who became his close friends. From them, he learned lessons that would stay with him—there will always be someone stronger or wiser, one must still defend what is rightfully his, and among one's peers, alliances must be tended with care.

Each weekend he visited his uncle for warmth; every few months he returned to the factory town and its river wind that reminded him of his beginnings.

Whenever work brought Rulan into the city, she stopped by the school to see the son she missed. Sitting across from the boy now stepping into adulthood, she repeated the principle she hoped would steady him: never looking up in fear, nor looking down in pride.

University

Yang, lying on the upper deck of the bunk bed, turned over and greeted the others: "Good morning…"

"You too…"

"Good morning…"

"Too busy yesterday with moving in. We should introduce ourselves to each other." Yang broke the ice. "Duan, how about starting from you?"

"Sure, I am from Chengdu. My parents are middle school teachers. It still feels surreal to be admitted into this prestigious university."

Yang agreed. "Totally. We are very lucky. And for a guy like me from the capital city, we get to be admitted with a lower bar. I might need help from you guys on academic work later."

"Well, we definitely would seek your help for navigating around this big city," Hanwei commented.

"Yeah. Speaking in Mandarin all day long feels weird for southern guys like Hanwei and me," Duan added. "Hanwei, maybe it's your turn?"

"I grew up in a factory town in Chongqing. Like Duan, speaking in Mandarin feels like acting in a movie to me." Everyone laughed. "Lu, it's your turn."

"Okay. I am from Xi'an. My family is from the aerospace

industry. I grew up in the town of Xi'an Satellite Control Center…"

It was a dorm at Beijing University, a small space with the essentials, a desk and chairs, storage cabinet, and bookshelf. Through the window, the four roommates could see trees that grew to their third-floor room, small shops, and students walking and biking in the street.

The four young men were energized and chatting with each other, excited about their new life.

"As they say," Yang added, "once you enter this university, you can dream big—but not without hard work."

#

Hanwei spent his time on the weekend exploring different corners of the university. He walked along the shore of Weiming Lake and stepped onto the stone vessel on the central island, enjoying from a distance the calming view of Boya Tower rising above the willow trees beneath it. He walked among academic buildings, appreciating their bold architectural design that blended traditional Chinese chamber-style with ancient west-style stone walls. It was pleasant to be accompanied by the chirping birds dashing across roof edges and see people biking along the alleys, with the jubilant crowd at the nearby basketball courts and soccer field cheering in the background.

Besides its beauty and academic prominence, this university was well known for its openness to diverse and critical ideas. Curious, Hanwei walked into the Triangle Field, an iconic site on campus, once a cultural phenomenon in the nation, where students and faculty members used to gather and express their different political opinions and ideas. While its time had passed, it was still a hot place for student associations and affiliated organizations to set up desks for recruiting and marketing.

Hanwei noticed a station set up by a tall female student. She wore thick glasses, and looked tough and serious. Her station had few visitors. A sign by her side read, "Stop the unnecessary daily flag raising ceremony."

That is odd but interesting, Hanwei thought. *People are usually raised with a strong sense of patriotism and nationalism. Challenging flag raising ceremonies is contentious, if not deemed disloyal.*

"Hi. What is your reason for opposing the campus's daily national flag raising ceremony?"

"Because the ceremony is just a form of preaching national-ism," the woman quickly responded.

"But isn't it legitimate for the government to encourage patriotism among its people?"

"Nationalism is not patriotism. It asks for loyalty without intellect. It demands obedience by power and peer pressure. And it dismisses people of other countries and ethnicity without reasoning."

"But isn't it valuable for people to have a forum to express their sentiment of loving their country?"

"Yes, but not by government coercion. What is loving your country? Is it standing by your country regardless of its actions being right or wrong? We need to go beyond that and see loving our country as more about loving our people and being willing to challenge and improve what we do. We won't truly love our country unless we produce real values instead of building walls."

The eighteen-year-old Hanwei was mesmerized by her

words and courage.

A booth several yards away was a lot busier. It was selling an affiliated MBA program, decorated with business management and economics books. Unlike in the 1950s, the concept of market-oriented economy was now trendy in China under the term of socialism with Chinese characteristics, coined by the party leader.

"Free market works best when all individuals look for their own best interests," a student spoke to another in the crowd.

"Does that mean everyone needs to act purely selfishly, though?" someone asked.

"The term 'being selfish' may be uncomfortable to some. But when it comes to optimizing the economic outcome of a system, individuals looking for their maximum returns will lead to the best outcome."

"That is too simplistic," a skinny guy with glasses commented inquisitively. "What you referred to is actually well studied in game theory. It can be mathematically shown that a player making their best move without any regard to another player's return can lead them to a lose-lose outcome."

"That player should not have chosen the move that will get everyone in a lose-lose situation then," the guy countered.

"But however smart that selfish player is, he won't be able to trust the other player not to choose his best selfish move, right? And that's exactly where an organization should come to collectively represent all players and reconfigure the game properly. The game configuration should incentivize players to engage in some seemingly selfless moves that will lead to a better win-win outcome."

What a refreshing debate! That makes a lot of sense, Hanwei thought. A sense of pride and humbleness arose within him.

#

"How many of you have heard of these two famous quotes? One is 'Common sense is the collection of prejudices acquired by age eighteen.' And the other is 'Truth is what stands the test of experience.'" The professor spoke to a room full of electrical engineering students.

A few students raised their hands. Among them was Hanwei.

"Great. Do you know who those quotes are from?"

"Einstein," someone in the crowd murmured.

"Correct. And Einstein did exactly that when he came to the shocking discovery of special relativity. When experiments in early twentieth century showed that light travels at a constant speed regardless of its observer's movement, Einstein had the wisdom to abandon the long, unquestioned assumption that the absolute speed of a moving object on a moving platform was a simple arithmetic addition of the speed of the platform and the relative speed between the two. Today we will look into his discovery, mathematically."

That is exciting, Hanwei thought to himself. Gaoming had a book about this subject on their bookshelf back home. While Hanwei felt chronically distraught under his father's tyranny, he knew his vanished father had nurtured his love of science. He was mesmerized by a picture in that book: a person, hastily riding a bicycle, looked over his shoulder, noticing the buildings and people around him all being squeezed thin, and even stranger, all frozen in time! A caption below it read: "When traveling close to the speed of light."

"Imagine a woman on a moving train watching a beam of light travel vertically to the ceiling and back. She measures one duration. A man on the ground sees the light travel a longer diagonal path as he also sees the train travel horizontally. Since light's speed is constant, he must experience more time passing." The professor laid out the thought experiment that would lead to Einstein's theory of special relativity.

That's crazy! That means the man on the ground experiences his time passing faster than what the lady in the train does! Not only Hanwei, at that moment every student in the room was trying to wrap his or her head around this deceptively simple but shocking revelation.

"So, from the gentleman's perspective, the clock of the woman runs slower than his, and things in the train appear to be in slow motion. This aspect of reality is hard to see in our everyday experience, only because our train moves relatively slow. Nowadays, this phenomenon is confirmed by advanced measurement tools in experiments with high-speed objects every time."

"Question." A student raised her hand. "If his time passes faster than hers, wouldn't she see him age faster? When they meet, would she be younger than him?"

The professor smiled. "Yes."

"Well, since the laws of physics apply equally to both of them, wouldn't she see the man younger than her when she arrives? Which version is true?"

Seeing the paradox, the whole room went silent.

"Excellent question. Anyone?"

Hanwei recalled the notion his professor highlighted earlier: "If a logical conclusion does not match the experience, some part of the assumption must be wrong."

"Someone raised his hand. Please." The professor pointed to Hanwei.

"Could it be that the lady was actually a little girl and saw that the gentleman was already an old man when she started traveling? That seems to be the only way to make them observe the same thing when they meet."

"Exactly! What they each saw when they were apart were not the same!"

That's insane! Hanwei thought. *This means, contrary to our naive daily experience, two people in two different locations don't see the exact same thing happening. The nature of our reality is indeed more profound and unassuming than our daily experiences.*

The teacher commented, "And you know, ironically, Einstein was a Jew living during the rise of Nazis, deemed by them as inferior. Yet, his ingenuity in modern physics had helped defeat them in World War II."

Riding on the watershed moment, Hanwei reminded himself of the recent startling scientific finding that all modern humans were descendants of early humans from Africa. *Now that also makes perfect sense. Apparently, the commonalities of different human races are much more likely to have originated from a common root than conspicuously converged from different origins.*

While his mind was racing, Hanwei further realized that his earlier suspicion that all men were secretly attracted to men and the opposite assumption others seemed to have had that all men were attracted only to women were both flawed. *Obviously, the least arbitrary and most resilient assumption would be that genetics and biological mechanics are flexible for different sexuality, since evolution doesn't serve any arbitrary purpose other than being a process augmented by the environment.*

In the following days, Hanwei learned many more things from his classmates and teachers. An English teacher inspired him when she paused in the middle of her class on the Nanjing Massacre Memorial Day, reminding her students to contemplate what had led to one group of humans committing atrocity against another. One of his socially awkward classmates showed him what it meant to be thinking outside the box by demonstrating how to trap more than thirty atoms in the Jezzball video game.

#

One afternoon, the building manager dropped a letter on Hanwei's desk: "Mail for you."

It was his mother's handwriting.

> *Hanwei,*
>
> *This is Mom. How have you been? I hope the school is going well with you. Beijing is very far. Mom could not go see you. But Mom can see the big and prosperous city on TV. Local news sometimes reports on your university. They showed the beautiful footage of Weiming Lake and Boya Tower. Many young men and women wish to study in your university. Hope you cherish what you have and learn knowledge and skills. Mom doesn't have much education, and could not help you much in your journey. So, watch out for yourself, be safe, and do well.*
>
> *Hanwei, Mom has not received your phone call or letter for a couple of months. Did you reply to my previous mail or call me? Mom doesn't know if you are well there, doesn't know if you still remember Mom at home. Sometimes, Mom really misses you. Mom is worried about you. When you have time, can you call*

or write to Mom? Mom would be happy.
Mom

Holding the letter, Hanwei was hit with tremendous guilt. He just realized he forgot to reply to Rulan's previous letter and two months had passed.

In the mid-nineties, the university didn't have telephones in student dorms. They had to find local shops that offered long-distance call services to talk to their remote families. But Hanwei knew he should have called. Instead, he was enthralled by his new-found life, while his mom was still in that remote factory town.

The House Has No Man

During winter break, Hanwei joined millions of students who traveled from where they attended school to their homes. From Beijing to Chongqing, it was a two-and-half-day journey by train.

The train was packed with college students and migrant workers. Hanwei was lucky. He got a window seat surrounded by other college students on this trip. They could rest their arms and heads on the tables through the nights. Those migrant workers weren't as lucky. They curled up on the floor and leaned on one another, exhausted. Their compartment was so packed that they had to plow through the crowd in the aisle and tiptoe across those on the floor in order to get to the toilet.

Hanwei and his fellow students talked to one another to kill boredom and gain spiritual support. A girl described the horror movie *Child's Play* to Hanwei and others, giving them thrills and making them laugh. Another fellow brought up the subject of whether there were other intelligent beings in the universe. After an elaborate debate, they agreed among themselves that intelligent beings likely existed somewhere else in the universe, drawing parallels to the fact that it was only a few hundred years ago when the Chinese emperor was visited by the British colonists for the first time, and citing the circumstance that it was only a couple years ago when an exoplanet was first detected.

Those conversations were not as exciting, though, to their travel pals on the floor. The migrant workers, clothes tainted by dirt from their journeys, bodies labored by their work, had accepted their fate. To them, visiting their loved ones, bringing the money they had earned and food they bought, once in a year during Chinese New Year, had become the meaning of their life.

These passengers felt as if they had become friends until some of them reached their destination and bid farewell to each other. Each stop, watching familiar faces rush their way out and new faces come in was a reminder that they were one step closer to home.

After two days and two nights, the train was finally approaching Chongqing's main train station. Soothing music was playing on the train speakers to congratulate the passengers for reaching the end of a long journey. Many already stood up with their luggage in their hands, looking for a sign of their loved ones outside the window.

"Hanwei!" "Hey!" "He is there." "I saw him." Hanwei's aunt and uncle's families who lived in the city were waving toward him.

"Hey, aunts and uncles!"

Hanwei's uncle took his luggage and gave him an approving look.

Aunt gave Hanwei a lavish smile. "Hanwei, it's been another year! You look good, stronger, and grown up!"

Uncle-in-law chimed in too. "Hanwei, your mom is over there, still walking, a little slower behind us. You haven't seen her face. She was so emotional that she was holding her tears."

Looking in that direction, he saw Rulan. She was walking over in a quick but steady pace, carrying that familiar cautious and illuminating smile.

"Mom!" The nineteen-year-old son she had been waiting for now stood before her, confident and warm.

#

Back in the factory home, Hanwei enjoyed the reunion with his extended family members. They held their traditional Chinese New Year's banquet and heard Hanwei's exciting stories in Beijing.

One day, at Hanwei's uncle's home, Grandma Wanqing checked out a book of Hanwei's, *Programming with Pascal*.

"Whoa!" Grandma exhaled in surprise while browsing it, "How do you read this?" The programming instruction lines in the book were beyond her imagination of what university textbooks would be. But her hope and happiness were written all over her smiling face.

Another day, Hanwei's uncle accidentally ruined a floppy disk Hanwei had brought back from school in the washer. The floppy disk fell apart, exposing the thin black colored disk inside.

"These scientists indeed have their tricks. How can such a thin disk show images on TV?!" Uncle held the disk, looking at it left and right, with a puzzled face, drawing laughter from Hanwei and his younger cousin.

#

At night, the workers' residential compound lay in its familiar quiet. Returning to a home he had not seen for so long, Hanwei closed the windows, shutting the winter cold outside. While, his mother was in the bedroom watching television, Hanwei walked past the dim living room and stepped into the small cubicle his father had once built for him.

He switched on the desk lamp. Its warm glow made the room feel close again. Against the bookshelf rested Gaoming's brown guitar. But the house no longer carried any trace of his father or the young men who used to gather here—no bursts of music, no drifting smoke, no tense silences after arguments.

Gaoming had left the factory town when Hanwei was seventeen.

Before that final disappearance, he had vanished several times—first for months on a supposed assignment near Suzhou; then for nearly a year on medical leave. By then Hanwei was living at his city high school. In his rebellious years, he barely asked where his father had gone, hearing only that he was recuperating in Guizhou.

Hanwei reached toward the bookshelf beside the guitar, running his fingers across the books and manuals his father once arranged neatly. One slim booklet caught his eye—his father's medical record. A faint unease rose as he opened it.

"Diagnosis: Patient, Gaoming, suffers from a psychiatric condition requiring long-term counseling and convalescence."

Inside the booklet was a folded piece of paper. He opened it and recognized his father's handwriting at once:

"I, Gaoming, due to mental and psychological illness, am unable to manage daily life or work responsibilities. I request unpaid leave for convalescence. I extend my apologies to the factory and leadership and ask for approval."

Staring at the letter, Hanwei's face remained still, but a thin tension drew behind his eyes. Through those lines, he seemed to get a glimpse of a man he had known all his life—proud, forceful, unwilling to bend—now forced to bow his head before the organization that shaped his existence. Suddenly and with clarity, he saw the humiliation his father must have endured, the pity he must have accepted in silence.

His thoughts drifted to the afternoon his father last came to his high school dormitory.

"Dad will be away for a while. This time, it will be long. Dad feels sorry for everything. All the savings have been left for you and your mother. Take good care of yourself. Your mother has your uncle's family—Dad won't worry." Standing among other students, Gaoming looked stripped of the sharp pride Hanwei once feared. "I hope you learn from my mistakes, and grow into a decent and useful man."

That was the last time Hanwei saw him. No one knew where he'd gone—not even Rulan. Some said he had gone out to make money for his family. Others whispered he had started anew elsewhere. Many believed he had fled to escape the rumors about him and the young men.

His disappearance left a hole in the household and became gossip across the factory town. But it also brought Rulan a long-needed quiet and gave Hanwei a sense of release. For the first time, he felt no longer caged—freed from the shadow that had followed him through childhood. He felt he could finally choose his own fate. After his father left, Rulan often went to her brother's home for dinner, where he received her kindly without asking what had happened. Life remained difficult, but she had Hanwei—and with him, she kept her hope.

Hearing the television in the background, Hanwei walked into the bedroom. Rulan sat at the head of the bed, legs tucked under the blanket, the glow of the TV washing softly over her face.

"Mom," he asked, eyes still on the screen, "how do you usually spend your evenings when you're here by yourself?"

Rulan gave a small, knowing smile. "I sit here and watch TV. What else is there for me to do?"

At that moment, Hanwei understood she had endured far more than he had known—facing her nights alone, unsure if anyone would think of her, unsure if her son would still come back to her. No words felt right; any attempt might brush against old wounds. So he eased himself beside her, quietly, letting his presence be the gentlest comfort he could offer.

#

One afternoon, Rulan had gone to work. Wanqing came to see her grandson. She brought fruits for him. They sat side by side on the couch while she gently held his hand, and chatted with him about his life in the university. Hanwei told her what he saw in Beijing and his favorite places, like the Summer Palace and the Great Wall.

"Hanwei, your mom missed you a lot when you were in Beijing. She once told me you hadn't written to her or called her for months. She said, 'Mom, Hanwei does not want me anymore.' She felt bad. You know your mom likes to cry sometimes. I told her not to overthink. I told her, 'Hanwei is a good son and a good person. He will come to you.' So, you remember to call her and write to her, then she knows you also miss her and she won't feel lonely."

"Yes, Grandma."

"Your mom earns about nine hundred yuan a month. She splits it in half. One half for her own expense, the other half she sends to you. She has nothing left after that. So, caring for her and doing well in school would make her happy, right?"

"Yes, Grandma." Hanwei struggled to hold back his emotions.

For a moment, Hanwei looked outside the window. The sun was about to set. Hanwei could hear the people outside running their errands, families and kids talking among one another in the courtyard. Mother was still at work.

A sudden panic arose in Hanwei. *This house has no man.*

He had no father. But there was this woman, this innocent and vulnerable lady, who went to work every day to earn an honest living to support him, and hold their life together. While the life inside that remote and prestigious ivory tower was dignifying and enjoyable, Hanwei's roots back home were humble. He could rely on no one but himself. He had to survive and build a decent life, so this woman's effort would not be in vain; he must one day bring her a peaceful life.

The Dorm

As they began their senior year, Hanwei and his classmates started to develop their own interests. Some spent time networking with entrepreneurial-minded peers and took on freelance jobs, determined to have an early taste of financial success. Some attended seminars from neural networks and game theory to astrophysics, quenching their thirst for the deeper secrets of nature. Some were more laid back, playing plenty of sports, going to disco bars, or reading books of others' intriguing life stories.

Although already in their early twenties, these young men and women were yet to engage in the dating life. They felt mostly content in a communal environment with little romantic stimuli. When sparks flew occasionally, they often felt more confusing than settling.

On a summer night, the dorm was very hot, as it had no ceiling fans or air conditioners. Hanwei walked to the common cleaning room with a hand towel, a bucket, toothbrush and toothpaste to clean himself before going to bed.

The cleaning room was packed. The guys had to face one another to use the faucet stalls separated in two rows in the center. The thirst for cooling themselves lured some young men to strip themselves naked and poured buckets of water over their heads and shoulders.

After getting a faucet stall, Hanwei took off his tank top, exposed his fit and toned body, and started cleaning himself. He could see the torsos of many shirtless young men under the dim light. It was hard for him to resist the temptation of a quick glance at them, especially the good-looking athletic ones. When he took the opportunity to take a quick look around while he brushed his teeth, he was caught off guard. Haodong, one of his classmates, was completely naked, facing him using a faucet stall on the right in the opposite row with a couple of classmates on his side.

Haodong was square jawed and handsome, with a great smile. He was skillful in basketball, friendly, and funny. Many classmates were fond of him.

Hanwei was startled by the full display of Haodong's athletic body, his beautiful arms and strong legs, soaped up and glistening in down-pouring water. While his heart pumped faster and his face turned reddish, Hanwei instinctively turned his eyes away from Haodong's direction, especially his private parts, hoping no one noticed.

"What's up, Hanwei?" Haodong said while he scrubbed his back and legs with a wet towel, not minding exposing his nice penis and furry, manly bush.

"What's up? How are you? It's really hot today, huh?" Hanwei turned his head up.

"Yes. Nice frame and biceps, Hanwei." Haodong nodded with a grin.

Hanwei smiled back without a word, doing his best to remain cool.

"Wow, you are really sexy. Look at your vest line and happy

trail there." Haodong made sure others also could hear his tease.

"Hanwei, you may not know, Haodong is a pervert! He is probably horny seeing you shirtless right now!" Others burst into laughter.

"That I am not sure. He is packed with more muscles himself."

"Indeed. He is showing off. Look at this body. It's like gold." A classmate on the side circled his hand around Haodong's torso, expressing with an envious tone.

Hanwei nodded, not giving away his true feelings.

Regarded as a model student among his classmates, wise and dependable, he took seriously the image of others' expectations of him, rarely engaging in any mischief or crude jokes. While he suppressed his desire to reciprocate in such flirtation, by now he was well aware that he was drawn toward male beauty, just like his estranged father.

#

Men in their twenties often felt a compelling need for building bigger biceps. One summer evening, Hanwei and his classmates came to the gymnastic bar area, and took turns on the bar.

Haodong stirred up the crowd, pointing to Xin who was working on pull-ups. "Xin, your butt looks round and nice," he said, drawing laughter from the crowd.

"Haodong, no wonder people say you are a pervert." Xin clinched on the bar, straining to hold tightly.

Another guy pushed it further. "You'd better watch out. He may harass you tonight."

"Are you gay?" Xin giggled and dropped off to the ground.

"He may not be gay, but definitely has some fetish," another guy added. The crowd laughed more.

Xin followed, "I was in Professor Qiu's psychology class, 'Origin of Morality and Its Instrumentality in a Civilization'. He argued that homosexuality or sexuality itself should not be subject to moral judgement and is likely an innate biological condition. So, I won't take issue if Haodong has such an innate biological condition, or a fetish."

"Professor Qiu said that?" a guy commented. "This university indeed has a liberal culture."

"Yeah. And homosexual acts were only decriminalized in 1997," Xin said.

Hanwei injected himself into it. "Good, the university was ahead of the curve."

A classmate, Liang, suggested, "But if homosexuality is normalized and everyone becomes homosexual, the human race won't reproduce anymore. Wouldn't society collapse?"

"That premise doesn't hold water, though," Hanwei replied. "The attraction between male and female is essential for the reproductive process. So, human's heterosexual tendency will be naturally retained among offspring through natural selection."

Liang shared his thoughts. "It's odd that homosexuality still exists today after tens of thousands of years of evolution. Don't you think? I wonder whether it is just a glitch."

"Don't begin with discrimination, Liang," a short guy jokingly commented.

"Or, more objectively, an outlier. But that is part of the statistical distribution in nature," Hanwei commented. "Assigning a social connotation to it would require a proper moral compass for the subject first. To me, it doesn't seem to hurt anyone." Hanwei then walked up to the bar. He looked up, ready to grab it.

"How about for the human race as a whole?" Liang questioned.

Hanwei turned, his head lowered and hands on his hip, "That I am not sure. It may have its evolutionary utility. Otherwise, it might have disappeared long ago. Maybe it is part of the greater mechanics of love and affection that keeps members of a species together."

"Yeah. Maybe that's why we all love you, Hanwei," Haodong interrupted.

"Thanks. I hope I am as popular as you are."

"Okay, save the love and affection between you two for another day. Hanwei, finish your turn."

Hanwei jumped up and grabbed the bar. He pulled himself up, tilted himself upside down until his waist cleared the bar and his legs reached the highest point, then flipped himself with an arc over the bar until his body glided back to the original position.

"Awesome."

Hanwei then started doing pull-ups.

"Twelve, thirteen, fourteen…" Xin counted along. "Try reaching your birthday. Yeah. The muscles grow most when it is most difficult."

"Twenty-four, twenty-five, twenty-six!" *Yes, done.* Hanwei dropped himself and landed on the ground.

#

Before calling it a night, some classmates gathered in the

dorm's corridor for chats. Others passed by hastily carrying their buckets, towels, and cleaning gear.

All lights were dimmed right at eleven o'clock, and everyone started leaving for their rooms. While Hanwei was turning around a corner, someone accidentally bumped into him in the dark.

It was Haodong. He was returning after his shower.

While their eyes met under the dim light, Hanwei saw Haodong only in his underwear. He could feel the moisture from his body. Haodong smiled at Hanwei, looking straight into his face. Excited and nervous, Hanwei looked away from Haodong's stare. *Damn. Maybe Haodong can tell I am attracted to him? Maybe Haodong is indeed also into guys?*

"He-he." Haodong expressed his joy in the confidence that he always had. Maybe Hanwei's silence and reservation had given it away. Haodong leaned his face towards Hanwei's, locking his eyes onto his.

Only inches away, Hanwei could feel Haodong's warmth and manly scents. His heart was beating faster.

With a smirk, Haodong moved onto Hanwei, seemingly about to lay his lips onto his.

That absolutely cannot happen! Hanwei instinctively deemed Haodong's move as an act of dominance and assertion of attraction. Accepting any form of sexuality was not an issue to Hanwei in a cerebral sense. He had heard the stories his father indoctrinated him with about those gladiators in ancient Rome who fought one another fully naked, exposing their genitals, glorifying the appreciation and arousal of male beauty. He had heard stories in his mother's pharmacy that an attractive, middle-aged married woman attempted suicide twice after being shamed by everyone for her affair with a much younger guy. But subjecting himself to a macho man's advance was somehow still a threat. Hanwei moved himself out of Haodong's way in anger, not giving up his own sense of masculinity and influence, leaving the guy he had always found romantically attractive on the spot.

Laying in his bed, cooled down, Hanwei contemplated what he had done. He realized the fear of failing the rigid gender roles defined by others had led to the insecurity and anxiety of his and many others, causing him unable to express himself, instead exerting aggression to guard what he truly felt inside, and his father had done better.

#

Sitting at the edge of the bunker bed by the window in a friend's dorm room, Hanwei enthusiastically explained the technology he used on the software program he and three other friends had built for the university's bookstore.

"Are these testicles?" A playful classmate sitting on the same bed put his toe into Hanwei's revealing boxers.

Feeling the toe, Hanwei turned to look at his classmate, returning the favor with an animated expression of surprise and delight.

"Ha-ha. You may not know, Mingwen is a freak. We, as roommates, were already traumatized by his sexual harassment."

Indeed, many guys are attracted to guys, but never dare to do anything for real, Hanwei thought to himself.

. . .

"Nice chat, guys. I need to leave for studying now."

While Hanwei was turning around the corner going downstairs, he bumped into Haodong again. This time, he saw Haodong with another guy, walking upstairs, covered in sweat, with a basketball in hand. They apparently had just finished playing basketball together. Haodong's arm was around his buddy's neck and shoulder. And the other guy was cute. The two were almost cuddling, excited, indulging in their own world!

Seeing Hanwei, Haodong's face turned reddish. He quickly removed his arm from his friend and looked in a different direction, avoiding any awkward interpretation.

For a moment, Hanwei was jealous and surprised, feeling like a loser. He thought maybe Haodong, a handsome macho man, was indeed also into guys, and there could be many more like him. However, unlike the rest, Haodong was more genuine and audacious. He was free.

Next morning, Hanwei put a book he had been reading onto the bookshelf of his dorm room, *Subculture of Homosexuality*, written by the famous social scientist Yinhe Li. He trusted the bright young men and women in this university to accept this tabooed subject in a positive light and challenged them to come to a better understanding of the nature of living beings.

And they did. Hanwei was elected by his fellow classmates to be their class president the same year, thanks to his academic performance, his friendship, and a confident, inspirational speech he gave to a room full of classmates on the election day.

Young Hearts

The last year of undergraduate school required every student to finish a final year project. Some students chose to join the research lab in their school. Some students chose to work as an intern in tech companies. Hanwei joined a small start-up as an intern and biked there every day.

Hanwei established himself quickly with his engineering sense and programming skills. His full-time colleagues sometimes sought help from him. The company even sent him on a business trip to bring back guidance on what he'd learned on the trip. Having had his first taste of being a contributing member of society, Hanwei grew confident each day, even becoming a bit cocky.

#

Xiong was a new full-time hire, recently graduated from a renowned university. He was tall and gentle, quiet and shy, and always dressed neatly. He was calm and appropriate when speaking to others. He was also handsome with his fine look and steady, piercing eyes. Through his glasses, he radiated a sense of friendliness and intellect, inviting decency and respect from even the crudest thugs. Like many other new college grads arriving in Beijing, bolstered by their education, youth, and aspiration, Xiong was seeking his own place and a promising future in this vast and vibrant city.

Hanwei had noticed this new colleague often resting his head and arms on the desk during lunch break. One day during lunch, Hanwei walked up to his desk.

"Hi. I am Hanwei. I noticed you the last couple of days. Did you recently join?"

"Yes. I am Xiong. I joined this past Monday," Xiong responded in perfect Mandarin with a warm smile.

"Welcome aboard. And nice meeting you."

"Thank you. Nice meeting you too."

This was the first time Xiong met Hanwei. Xiong saw this southern Chinese-looking guy in his early twenties, standing confidently in front of him, wearing a t-shirt and jeans, shorter, but fit and energetic, speaking friendly in a masculine voice and engaging eye contact, mixing boyishness and maturity.

The boss happened to be walking by following this exchange. "Oh, Xiong, I forgot to introduce you to Hanwei. He is our intern from Beijing University. Looks like you two are already talking to each other. By the way, Hanwei is familiar with both GUI and network programming. If you have any questions, he'd be happy to help."

"Certainly," Hanwei responded.

In the following days, Xiong went through his task with Hanwei and Hanwei looked into the steps needed to get Xiong's job done.

To Xiong, staring at a screen full of code and playing with a jargon of unfamiliar programming tools wasn't very inspirational. It felt like being stuck in the woods, distant from social and economic prestige and comfort. To Hanwei, the work was worthy and exciting, like a chef preparing a banquet of taste and style.

Nevertheless, the two grew closer. They teamed up in sports during company outings. Hanwei often gave technical tips for Xiong's projects and Xiong sometimes took Hanwei to places he had never been to and offered his mature takes on social and economic subjects. They felt like a complement to each other, having each other's backs in their transitions to a new life.

#

"Any plans this weekend? Would you like to go out for fun and maybe have dinner together?" Hanwei asked.

"Any suggestions?"

"I am okay with anything. A park or mall would be nice."

"Have you tried roller coaster rides? There is a big amusement park not far from where I live."

...

Beijing was big. It took Hanwei more than forty minutes on the bus and another forty minutes on the subway to reach Shi Jing Shan station. When Hanwei arrived, Xiong was there waiting for him.

"The park is nearby. We'll bike there. You can sit on the back." Xiong had come prepared.

"Cool. Let's go."

The weather was wonderful for biking. The summer breeze was soothing. The streets were colorful with their shops and trees under the sunlight, while groups of pedestrians wandered around for a relaxing weekend.

The park was larger than Hanwei had expected. It was packed with thrilling rides like swinging boats, rotating spaceships, and freefall elevators. Hanwei joined others screaming on the falling elevator, and shared good laughs with Xiong riding the bumping car.

The trail toward the roller coaster was beautiful and full of happy people.

"Will you be afraid of the roller coaster ride?" Xiong teased.

"Nah. I have motion sickness, but as long as the ride is not swinging too much, I should be okay."

"You have motion sickness? Ha. I thought Beijing University students like you should have no weaknesses. So, what does it feel like being in Beijing University? Everyone is smart?"

"Many are. But their skills and aptitudes diverge with their aspirations over the years."

"Which type do you belong to over there?"

"I ranked in the top three of my class. Can you tell?" Hanwei proudly told Xiong.

"Wow. That I couldn't tell. You don't look like an intellectual." Xiong laughed, alluding to Hanwei's crude and street tough side.

"I know. I've heard that before. But my dad looked like one. He once visited me in my high school dorm. After he left the room, all my roommates were laughing. They said I looked like a construction worker while my dad was like an intellectual gentleman."

"Yeah? Maybe I should give you a quiz."

"Sure. Let me try." Hanwei really enjoyed Xiong's interest in him.

"Okay. Assume you have ten cigarettes. Once you smoke three cigarettes, you can return the cigarette heads to get a new cigarette. How many cigarettes can you manage to smoke?"

"Is it fifteen?" Hanwei responded quickly but cautiously.

Xiong was instantly surprised and confused. "That is the right answer. But I couldn't recall why. How did you figure it out?"

"I first assume this person can smoke X number of extra cigarettes in addition to the original ten cigarettes. If he returns all ten plus X cigarette heads, the number of extra cigarettes he can get would only be one-third of the original ten plus the extra X. So, I just need to solve the equation $X = (10+X)/3$. Solving the equation, you get X is equal to five. So, he can smoke up to ten plus five, fifteen cigarettes."

"Wow. That's cool. I am baffled by how anyone could actually do that in concrete steps."

"Let me think. If you smoke the first nine and return all cigarette heads, then you can get three additional cigarettes. Now with four cigarettes in your hand, if you smoke three of them, you then would get another new cigarette. So you will end with two cigarettes. Okay. Now I know."

The two both spoke at the same time. "Borrow one cigarette!"

"Yes. Then you can return three cigarette heads after smoking them." Hanwei proudly smiled.

The two had just arrived at the roller coaster. The rail twisted and turned, spreading itself on top of giant supporting columns, with a full loop midair. When the approaching train stopped, the two quickly climbed into a car. In no time, the train steered out of the station, and the sun shone onto their faces and cars, illuminating the colorful park under the blue sky. They looked at each other in excitement.

Seeing Xiong's beautiful eyes and smile behind his glasses, a tremendous joy and energy arose in Hanwei's heart.

Life felt wonderful with each other by their sides. They screamed and laughed, while the train roared forward, falling and rising, twisting and flipping with the ecstatic passengers and crowd.

Away from the loud park center, the two came to the quiet garden of decorative mammals. A pack of deer was inside the fence. Their slender bodies were suited for their delicate agile moves. With their distinct subtle patterns on their back and a gracious and solemn look, their natural beauty was luring.

"They are so beautiful that they are almost erotic," Hanwei said.

Caught by such a comment, Xiong smiled while facing the garden.

"Do you feel the same?" Hanwei peeked at Xiong to his side.

Xiong turned to Hanwei and nodded with a smile, giving his approval. While their eyes met, Hanwei could see how comfortable Xiong was with him.

The two were tireless. They bought snacks and drinks and hopped over different parts of the park until dinnertime.

"Where should we go for dinner?" Hanwei asked.

"We can get some takeout and go to my place," Xiong suggested.

\#

Xiong's place was in the basement of a concrete apartment building. Walking through a dim corridor and passing through a communal toilet room and a wet common cleaning room, the two reached Xiong's room at one dead end of the basement.

"It is a bit shabby. Hope you don't mind. It is temporary though," Xiong was a bit concerned about letting Hanwei see this.

"Not at all." Hanwei didn't mind. He was happy to be around this gracious charming man.

The place was quiet and cool, not bad in a hot summer. There weren't many items. A desk and a chair were placed along the wall on one side of the room, a wood-framed single bed next to it. On the opposite side of the room, a mattress was on the floor with a couple of suitcases. At the end of the room, a small window was opened to the outside on the upper section of the wall, allowing cool air to flow down from the ground above. A small table and a dining chair resided under the small window. On the entrance side, several sneakers were stacked up on the back of the door, all displaying logos like Nike and New Balance. They were for young guys, like Hanwei, to envy.

Hanwei could see Xiong had made this place tidy and clean. To Hanwei, at least Xiong had his own place.

"Are you bothered by how shabby this place is now?"

"Nope. It's comfortable. And you can always look for a change later."

The two grabbed chairs and started their dinner. Xiong bought roasted duck, Chinese pancakes, and a big box of milk, a luxury for a poor student.

"Thanks for getting the takeout."

"My pleasure. It is not expensive. So, what's the plan?" Xiong asked.

"You mean for my life ahead?"

"Yeah. What's the plan after your graduation? Going abroad, getting a job, or going to grad school?"

"Maybe joining the grad school in Beijing University. With my grades, I can get into the electrical engineering department waiving any exam, pursuing any research project I like."

"Not bad. You are good at that. You don't feel engineering subjects are boring? I guess science and technology interest you."

"How about you? You seemed to be overwhelmed by your software work."

"It's okay. We have to start somewhere. My dad is a principal engineer in the Harbin Airplane Manufacturing firm. He works hard. I want to do something different, like finance and business. Do you know the book *Rich Dad Poor Dad*? It is interesting. It says that the way one thinks of how to make money determines how wealthy one would be. If you haven't read it yet, I have a copy for you to read. You are smart. Maybe you'd come up with fresh perspectives."

"Sure. While many people want to be wealthy, many among us still aspire to contribute raw values to society and create useful means to human civilization."

"But finance and business also create values and means," Xiong responded.

"Certainly, like politics, they are essential for optimizing resource allocation, identifying proper demands and supplies, organizing talents and means. It's just that sometimes I hope those fields have more rigorous processes and less fraudulent practices."

Hanwei looked at his watch. "It's late. Can I stay over for the night?"

"Of course. Just stay here, if you don't loathe my place. You can sleep in the bed. I'll use the mattress."

"No. I will use the mattress. You should stay in your bed."

That night, the two kept each other company. While the basement was shabby, it gave Hanwei a sense of belonging.

#

Hanwei's work in the firm started bearing fruit. The software on the board could now communicate to its connected metering devices. Data coming from the cable could now be displayed on the LCD screen. Hanwei now could have more time for fun, knowing his final year project was in good shape.

Xiong's work, however, wasn't going smoothly. He felt he was drowned in software programming. His reserved personality also hindered any opportunity to strengthen his connections with colleagues. To him, the pathway to success wasn't to labor himself with complex and competitive work. He'd rather devote his time to investing. Troubled by the stark contrast between his aspiration and harsh reality, Xiong felt he was nobody in this fast-developing city. The only one who gave him appreciation, warmth, and joy was Hanwei, an energetic student who upheld an idealistic vision, unfazed by an unforgiving world that relentlessly tested its citizens, willing to march forward with his shrewdness, toughness, and defiance.

One weekend, after playing badminton at the gym, Xiong and Hanwei got back to Xiong's place with their takeout food to have a relaxing evening together.

"Xiong, I want to ask you about something," Hanwei said

while they were about to finish their plates.

"Yeah? What is it?"

"I got an opportunity to go to Hong Kong for graduate school. It is a special program. In total, about seventy students were picked for it, no tests needed, not even TOEFL or GRE."

Xiong raised his head, looked at Hanwei, shocked. "Are you going to take it?"

"What do you think?"

"Going to Hong Kong could be eye-opening. But is the university good? The Beijing University you are in right now is world renowned, you know?"

"The university is well connected to the international academic community. They have many renowned veteran professors from the United States. And they will cover my tuition, my lodging, and my living expenses. It would relieve my mom's burden. She has done everything she could to support me financially up to now."

"That doesn't sound bad. It is probably a good opportunity for you. You will see the world. Maybe you will find that many things we were taught in the past are not true." Xiong smiled.

"But I'd need to leave Beijing," Hanwei murmured.

The two shared a few seconds of silence.

Xiong broke the icy atmosphere. "You can always choose to come back if you find a better career here. Sometimes, you need to look out for yourself."

"If I go there, I'd come back often to see you."

"Don't overthink now. Maybe do a bit more research and see if it would really work for you. We should have a shower. We sweat a lot playing sports today."

Hanwei finished his shower first. While Xiong was having his shower, Hanwei browsed through the books on Xiong's table. To him, looking at them felt like looking into Xiong. Many of the books were about biography, finance, entrepreneurship, social skills, and temperament coaching.

"Ah. Feeling much better now." Xiong got back to the room. "Did you find anything interesting?" Xiong sat down on the chair in front of Hanwei.

"Yeah. They are all interesting, although quite different from what I have. I have *A Brief History of Time* and *Man's Search for Meaning.*"

"I can imagine, probably science and technology related, or philosophy. You always like abstract notions. We have some differences in taste."

"But we have more in common," Hanwei said earnestly.

Sitting in front of Hanwei right out of the shower, Xiong looked rather fresh and handsome. Only in his underwear, Xiong's defined chest and arms, tight waist, flat abdomen, and toned muscular thighs were on full display. While having been emotionally connected to Xiong, Hanwei now felt an irresistible attraction towards his beautiful, masculine body.

"Wow. You have a nice body. It's really sexy."

"You have nice muscles too. How did you get them?" Xiong smiled while he used his hand to nudge Hanwei's arm before putting on his glasses.

The two looked at each other for a brief moment. Xiong's gaze pierced through his glasses. Hanwei reached out to Xiong's glasses and said, "Can I see your face again with the glasses off?"

Xiong took off his glasses with a confident and sweet smile.

"Whoa. You are remarkably handsome." Hanwei couldn't move his eyes; he looked at Xiong in awe, and wanted every bit of him.

Hearing that, Xiong couldn't hide his pride and joy. "You aren't bad either, manly good looks and nice body too."

That felt like a breakthrough and was hard to believe. "You think so? Can I touch your face?"

"You also have that kind of fetish?" Xiong proudly smiled while locking his eyes to Hanwei's, showing no sign of unease.

"I like you, your gentle soul. I have always found you attractive," Hanwei confessed. "May I?" Hanwei asked, then reached his hand out to Xiong. Seeing no sign of rejection, he touched Xiong's cheek. Xiong looked at Hanwei with a sense of curiosity, calm, and comfort. Hanwei's hand then slid down to Xiong's arm, cautiously threading across the territory of this unoffendable man. "Are you feeling okay?"

"Yeah."

Their breathing became heavier.

"Do you mind?" Hanwei stared at Xiong and asked with all the courage he had. He gave it up to this friend he trusted.

"What. Do. You. Want?" Xiong asked word by word, in a slow and intense tone, gazing into Hanwei's eyes.

"I want you."

Hanwei then took Xiong's hands, pulled him toward the mattress on the floor. Xiong didn't resist. The two landed on the mattress, instinctively tussled against each other trying to assert dominance. While Xiong was grabbing Hanwei's arms, Hanwei managed to push his core, tilted his balance, and landed on top of Xiong.

"Got some strength, huh?" Xiong breathed heavily while resting his head on the bed.

With a brief look at Xiong under him, Hanwei removed his t-shirt. Xiong watched while Hanwei unclothed his athletic body on top of him. Feeling the touch and warmth of Hanwei's body, a sense of arousal and excitement arose in him.

Looking into Xiong's eyes, Hanwei reached to Xiong's lower body.

Xiong opened up his most secretive and intimate presence to his fellow man. He appeared shy at first, yet couldn't resist but touch and look at Hanwei in excitement. Every inch of his body was magnetic to Hanwei. His beautiful physique and gradual descent to euphoria filled Hanwei's senses and emotions.

Not long after grappling and kissing in bed, caressing and stroking each other in their sensitive parts, both men came in ecstasy. For the first time in his life, Hanwei felt he and another human being physically and emotionally belonged together.

The two laid side by side, looking at each other inquisitively after catching a breath.

"It was nice," Hanwei said, still in euphoria.

After a moment of silence, Xiong asked, "Are you still into girls with all this?"

"Girls sometimes come to my fantasies and dreams, too, but not often. I feel much more attracted to men. There is a sense of belonging."

Hearing what Hanwei said, Xiong's eyes were wide open. "Maybe you haven't met the right girl yet."

"I am comfortable with my own sexuality, or human sexuality in general, after all of my growing up experiences. I didn't tell you. My dad is gay. He struggled a lot and it almost ruined my family."

"Your dad is gay? How did you know?"

"He brought young guys home, all the time. Some stayed

in our house for weeks. We couldn't have peace. He ignored my mom and me. We were an inconvenience to him. He psychologically abused us for years so we don't have the spirit to speak up."

"Did your mom do anything?"

"She was in denial. That's how she managed to pull through and raise me."

"I am so sorry. How is your dad now? Is he still living with your mom?"

"No. He left. The last time I saw him was when I was seventeen. He left many times before that, for three months, then for a year, and then gone. We don't know where he went. I don't want to know either. I hate him. He is a monster to me. He once told me in front of my mom that I was his son, so I had to be gay and I would never marry a girl; he wanted that notion to be my life. I guess he succeeded."

"That's terrible. Could it be that you are into men because of his influence?"

"I don't think so… Well, it is possible. Maybe I got his genes, maybe I picked up cues from him. But do we have one gene that tells us how to walk? Do we have one gene that tells us what type of food we crave? I really think not. Most likely, we are all predisposed to be sexually attracted to either gender. But, to be honest, none of that really matters to me, nor should it matter. There is no reason to root for one or another. I think people being attracted to each other and falling in love is the greatest thing."

The two men laid in silence for a moment.

"How about you? Have you dated girls in the past?" Hanwei asked.

"I haven't dated girls yet. But I don't think I am gay. I

thought gays were those feminine guys."

"Are you fascinated by girls?"

"Not by all of them."

"How about men? You were pretty excited just now. You don't have to answer, though."

"I didn't think like that." Xiong's answer was confusing to Hanwei. "Wow. What a story of yours. I am sorry to hear. But it's amazing you still grew up well and made it into the best university."

"Now you know me."

That night, the two slept together on the same mattress.

#

Spring was beautiful in Beijing. The streets were green after a cold winter. Hanwei had accepted the offer of the university in Hong Kong. Xiong was still struggling with his project and had started seriously looking into changing his career.

One morning, the two woke up on the mattress at Xiong's place under the sun's rays coming through the window. They glanced at each other, their bodies and scents reminding them how they had spent their last night together.

Hanwei extended his arm toward Xiong beneath the comforter. While Hanwei's hand touched Xiong's abdomen, Xiong grabbed his hand and stopped him.

"What's the matter?"

"Am I also gay?" Xiong looked to the ceiling.

Hanwei was startled by the sudden question. "You may not be."

"After what we did, you don't think I am gay?" Xiong exhaled a deep breath, his expression turned serious and sober.

"That doesn't mean you are gay," Hanwei thought at least such an answer would make Xiong feel better. "The fact of the matter is you are a manly man. You are shy and introverted, but not feminine as those you previously referred to as gay men. For convenience, people like to apply simple labels to things that are much richer in reality. You can call feminine men who are into men gay, or you can call all men who are into men gay, or not gay because they are still somehow attracted to women. It does not matter. You are what you are. If you are sexually attracted to men's anatomy but feel you are different from feminine men, then that's your own nature. Don't worry about what to call it."

"But men who fall for one another will not have a family, not have children. Life would be over."

"Having children is definitely an immensely intense love experience. Not having one would be a loss. But, living with your loved one is also a tremendously intense love experience. And more so, I think living truthfully to yourself, having a deeper understanding of life, love, and the world is equally meaningful, if not more at a fundamental level." Hanwei sat up from the bed and looked to see if Xiong was okay.

"What you said is just so abstract," Xiong closed his eyes.

"And you don't need to be worried about being alone, 'cause I'd be with you."

"You are leaving for Hong Kong."

That gave Hanwei a pause. "I'd live with you if you allow me to. I didn't say this before, because I don't know how you really feel about me. But I have fallen in love with you…Xiong, I do love you."

Xiong lay in bed, eyes still closed. His face turned reddish and emotional.

"But are you into men?" Hanwei pleaded to know how Xiong really felt.

"If not, why would I have done what I have done?" Tears burst through Xiong's closed eyes. He trembled while turning to Hanwei's lap.

Seeing the man he loved in pain, hit Hanwei hard. He realized what he had felt with ease was much harder for Xiong, and what he got Xiong into might have altered his life forever.

"Once I finish my study abroad, I'll come back. We can find a way to live together."

"Two men living together is not possible. People will talk. There will never be peace again."

"I know me. I would do anything to be with you."

"It won't work. I have my parents to take care of, a lot of responsibilities. Maybe your situation is different, it is easier for your mom to accept you since she already had experience with your dad."

It was hurtful for Hanwei to hear that last comment from Xiong. Hanwei laid down on the mattress and turned to the other side, holding his emotions. He always knew Xiong was a pragmatic person, security oriented. That was partly why he had not been up front with Xiong. But he knew he would do anything for this man, if he gave him the chance.

#

For the first time in his life, Hanwei saw people of many different ethnicities at one place when he stepped into Hong Kong's busy subway station. It was an eye-opening experience.

The vibrant and dazzling street scenes of Hong Kong gave

him a first-hand experience of life under a strikingly different political and economic system from that of mainland China. The university's administrative processes were so streamlined and transparent that they just worked without soviet style entities like class president, head teacher, or party secretary with which Hanwei had been familiar.

While the university was located by the breathtakingly beautiful Clear Water Bay on Kowloon peninsula, Hanwei didn't spend any of his time there. He trained himself in rock climbing and kayaking, frequented the gym and the swimming pool, and ventured out for sightseeing, movies, and even nightclubs.

Far in the north, Xiong had quit his previous job. He joined another start-up, rented an apartment, and started teaching himself economics and finance, wishing one day to be a financial service industry professional. Hanwei flew to Beijing whenever he saved enough money. Every time Hanwei walked into the reception hall of the capitol's airport with his luggage, seeing Xiong standing there waiting for him, perfectly manicured and dressed, with hopeful eyes and subtly romantic smiles, it was homecoming all over again.

As they spent time together in Beijing, the two young men grew more sexually adventurous and uninhibited. They learned it from the Internet. Yet, they still could not give up their own sense of masculinity, wasting time debating on who should lean on whose lap while watching TV together on the couch. The two visited as many places as they could during their limited time together. They even went to the old apartment building with the basement where they had their first taste of passion to connect to their old memories.

One night in the fall, they walked together in a quiet

residential street nearby. The wind was cold, and the hazy residential lights behind trees rendered the neighborhood like a painting. They walked and walked, side by side, like brothers, lovers and a family. This was when they felt like life was kind, and the peace and warmth were everlasting.

"We should live together once I finish my PhD in Hong Kong," Hanwei suggested, knowing it was a thorny topic.

Xiong exhaled deeply. "It is not very realistic."

"Why? If this is right for us, we should do it. There will be difficulties. But we can overcome them."

"We each have plenty of things on our plates. You graduated from the most renowned university in China with a stellar resume. You may be able to live above the fray, setting an ideal example. But, I still need to establish myself in society. I may lose my social standing. There would be no peace."

"The world is changing though. It could be very different in another ten years," Hanwei argued.

"Not as fast as you think. And even if we could survive others' opinions and alienation, what about our parents? We wouldn't be able to shield them. And they want grandchildren for themselves too."

"I think they will accept us one day. Having seen the suffering of my father and my mother, I just think there is a greater course for our shared humanity. People in the past had struggled and sacrificed for a better world. Without their brave work, we wouldn't have the rights and civility we enjoy today."

"You sound like you are doing it for the sake of an ideal world."

"But I do love you. It's with you that I feel I can do it."

"Maybe you do. But did you think about how I feel?"

"Do you mean you don't really love me?" Hanwei was getting upset.

"That's not what I meant."

"If you don't, should we stop seeing each other? Maybe we should cut our tie!" Hanwei's temper flared.

Xiong paused, looked at Hanwei, and then moved his head to the side. Tears wetted his glasses.

"I am sorry. I shouldn't have said that. You know I won't leave you. You mean everything to me." Hanwei pulled Xiong's jacket, standing in front of him.

"I don't want to leave you either," Xiong answered in a cracked voice. "Let's just do it one step at a time, okay?"

The two cuddled together for another night before Hanwei flew back to Hong Kong. They both knew they now had someone important to them in life.

I Still Miss You

Back in Hong Kong, Hanwei started working on his research paper on fair resource allocation in distributed wireless networks. The subject fascinated him, as he saw its parallel in human society, where when there is not a centralized policy to prevent better positioned players from taking all the resources, poorly positioned players suffer to a degree that it could cause a system to collapse. In the meanwhile, he often called Xiong, checking on how he was doing and planning for their next reunion.

One Friday evening, Hanwei called Xiong again. This time, no answer. In two hours, he tried again. Still, no answer. *That is odd*, he thought.

It was already eleven o'clock. Hanwei decided to call it a night and go to bed. At that moment, his cell phone rang.

"Hey, Hanwei." It was Xiong, with a warm but fuzzy voice. He sounded sad and impaired.

"I called you twice earlier. Are you doing okay?" Hanwei asked anxiously.

"Yes, I am fine. I am sorry," Xiong murmured on the other side of the line.

"What do you mean? Where are you? Were you drinking?"

"Yes. I did."

"What happened? Why are you drinking? Where are you?"

"I am sorry. Okay?" Xiong continued in a depressed tone.

"Sorry for what? I certainly hoped you would answer my call or call me back earlier. But what is going on?"

An attractive female voice came through the phone. "Xiong was with me. We were together. Ha-ha!"

Hanwei's heart stopped. He felt like a freight train had hit him.

Xiong's voice intercepted the woman's. "I am sorry. I drank too much tonight."

Then the woman's voice came through again, giggling, drunk. "We are truly in love. He is not gay. He is in love with me. We'll be together forever!"

"I am sorry. She drank a lot."

"I love him and he loves me. He-he."

"Don't, please," Xiong said as he seemed to grab the phone back.

Shocked, Hanwei spoke into the phone, "Can I speak to you solely, Xiong?"

"Yes. I am sorry, Hanwei."

"Is that true? Have you been with her?" Hanwei asked through a bleak sense of hope. There was no answer from the other side. "Why did you call me at this time? I loved you." Tears ran down Hanwei's face.

"I don't know. I didn't mean to hurt you. I wanted to call you."

The woman then spoke loudly behind Xiong. "He is not like you. He likes women. We are truly in love."

"No!" Xiong's voice came through. Hanwei could hear the woman sobbing on the other side.

"You don't need to listen to what she says. She drank a lot.

It's my fault."

"So, you have been with her all these days when I am here. You were sleeping with her, weren't you?"

Xiong didn't respond.

"And you don't really love me, do you?" Hanwei asked. Days he had had with Xiong over the last two years flashed one after another, from the day Xiong smiled at Hanwei at his desk when they first met to the evening Xiong bought the box of milk and poured it into Hanwei's cup in his basement. From the train station where Xiong dressed up and waited for Hanwei's returning to school from his home in Chongqing to the night when Xiong, naked, reached his ecstasy under Hanwei's body. From the time Xiong was pissed and jabbed Hanwei when Hanwei screwed up an installation of a newly bought lamp to the moment Xiong laughed out loud with all the joy in the world as he looked at Hanwei when their roller coaster shot up in the air.

"I love you both," Xiong answered.

"Why did you do this to me?" Hanwei's heart was aching with sadness and pain.

"I am sorry. Okay? You are too far away. I needed someone, then I met her."

"I thought we would be with each other forever. I loved you with every bit of my heart. I didn't know this is what you would have for me in the end."

The woman's tearful voice came through. "Hanwei, I heard your story. I told Xiong you are the one who truly loves him. And I told him he's got to love you back."

"I still love you, Hanwei." Xiong's voice came through.

Hanwei put down his phone, heartbroken.

That night, Hanwei cried hard. He told himself that one

day, Xiong would come back to him, or at least that would be a wish he would always keep inside.

#

"Hey, Hanwei. I've been thinking. Would you like to go to the United States for a PhD degree instead?" Hanwei's best friend turned to Hanwei from his classroom desk. "We can convert our PhD program here to a master's program, prepare for the GRE exam together, and apply to universities in the U.S."

"Yeah?" Hanwei was intrigued with the thought of a PhD degree from the States and having a life-altering experience living abroad. After all, the past had been something hard for Hanwei to hold onto, something he felt had punched a hole in his heart, something that had led him to spend numerous nights talking to himself, wishing the one he loved would come back. If the past was a shadow he had to muster his strength to walk out of, that strength would have to come from his aspiration of intellectual pursuit and fulfillment of his intellectual prowess.

In the following days, Hanwei devoted his energy to his research work, solved the complex fair resource allocation problem, published it as a research paper, completed the TOEFL and GRE exams, and eventually got an offer for enrollment into a PhD program from the university he had dreamed of in the city of angels.

One evening, Hanwei's cell phone rang. The caller ID showed "Xiong." It had been more than seven months since that fateful night.

Hanwei's heart was pumping hard as he answered.

"Xiong?"

"Yes. It's me." Xiong's voice came through with kindness and humility.

"It's been a while. How are you?"

"Yeah. It's been a long time. I wasn't sure you would answer my call."

"Of course," Hanwei said. "How is your work, life, and everything?"

"After all the things I have done? Well, I missed you," Xiong said in a soft voice.

"I miss you every day. Where are you? I can hear cars around you."

"On a bridge above the traffic, on the way home after work. Yeah. I can see a lot of cars below."

"Is everything okay? How is your relationship with the girl?"

"We separated."

"I am sorry."

"That's alright. I am working for a futures brokerage firm now."

"Awesome! You wanted to switch to finance a while ago. How is it?"

"The job is tough. I am still on their IT support side, not yet on their financial service team." Xiong sighed, "I feel tired after the day. My boss is pushy and rude. Sometimes, life feels like it's crushing down on me."

Hanwei tried to soothe Xiong. "Bosses sometimes have a hard time themselves. You don't have to take what they say to heart. Things will work out, or you will find a way elsewhere. I root for you."

"Yes. None of these things probably will matter when I look back one day."

"Right. I wish I was there with you right now."

"Yeah?" Xiong sounded touched. "It's cold and windy up here. But the city lights are beautiful. How about you? How is your PhD program?"

"I… I accepted an offer from a university in the United States."

"Wow. Going to the United States! Congratulations! I am happy for you."

"I'm happy you called," Hanwei said. "You can call me anytime. I'll call you too."

…

Hanwei visited his mom in Chongqing before he packed up for his journey to Los Angeles. He would always remember the moment when Rulan held her tears and suggested he should kowtow three times for her before his leave if it were for tradition. After that, he got on the flight toward the country on the other side of the globe.

Life sometimes felt strange to Hanwei. When he made a move on his journey, familiar things became memories, and unfamiliar things became his real life. He felt he had lost so much and wondered if he was digging himself into a ditch. But he reminded himself what others had said: *When trees are moved, they die; when people are moved, they come alive.* So, he hoped it would be worth it. He believed that, in the end, pains and sorrows would be a distant memory, but he would understand life better and know how to love back those who had cared for him.

Fresh off the Boat, Los Angeles

"Who wants some ice cream?" A South American looking guy spoke loudly, looking back at the group of young men and women. "We've got a Ben & Jerry's here!" The guy's name was Carlos. He was from Brazil and was volunteering for the university's orientation program for newly arrived graduate students.

Looking across the crowd in the direction of Carlos, Hanwei saw a colorful sign: "Ben & Jerry's." The exterior of the shop was painted in white, with a colorful bench, a pair of chairs, and a couple of adorable mini-cow mannequins stationed outside its window. The group of young men and women happily walked into the shop. The busy shop was beautiful inside. The staff serving the ice cream was upbeat and full of smiles.

A beautiful lady behind the counter came to Hanwei. "Hi, how are you today?"

"Doing great. Thanks."

"Yeah. Such a beautiful day. What would you like? You can pick any two flavors you like."

"Vanilla and strawberry."

"That's my favorite," the lady commented with an amazing smile.

"Thank you."

The ice cream was delicious, especially on a warm summer afternoon at the famous Venice Beach of Los Angeles.

Hanwei had just arrived in L.A. a week ago. He rented a room from a Chinese family and took the bus to school. The university was located at Westwood, one of the most affluent districts in this mega city. The California sunshine, vibrant and beautiful street scenes, convenient access to local amenities, and warm and friendly daily encounters in and out of campus all impressed Hanwei.

As they left the ice cream shop, the student group emerged onto the busy Venice Beach walkway. The street was full of artists who were selling and showcasing their musical talents, handcrafts and magic tricks. The locals were proud of their athleticism and style, shirtless or in bold garments. They played competitively in the basketball courts, mini-tennis courts, and beach volleyball courts by the walkway. Occasionally, groups of skater boys and girls sailed through the crowd, with pop or rap songs playing on pocket stereos latched to their hips.

Passing through beautiful palm trees and lawns, Hanwei and the group arrived at the roller-skating park at the center of Venice Beach. Spectators surrounded the skating pit. The scene was metaphoric to what they call a melting pot: African Americans, white folks, Latinos, and Asians were together showing off their skills, exchanging tips and giving one another high fives. Hanwei loved their jumps, dashes, and dances to the upbeat hip-hop music coming from the stereo on the ground.

Across the cycling trail were the sand beach and the Pacific Ocean. It was the first time Hanwei had seen the oceanfront of the Pacific Coast. The sun warmed and comforted the colorful crowd on the beach. The ocean breeze brought cool moist air with a delightful scent of seaweed and fish. The ocean was radiant with its blue waves. Everyone — young and old, men and women—was having a good time.

On the way back, Hanwei and the group were drawn to a crowd of bystanders in a circle. The crowd was watching a team of shirtless young men doing a street stunt. The team consisted of a black guy, a white guy, a Latino guy, and an Asian guy. They reached out to a young boy and a young girl in the crowd.

"Where do you come from?"

"I'm from Colorado," the young girl answered with a smile.

"Colorado. Nice! Good to meet you. And I am from California!"

The crowd laughed.

He then reached out to the young boy. "Where do you come from?"

"Ocala. Ocala, Florida."

"Wow, that's far, isn't it? My parents live in Miami, Florida. We all come from different places. And now, you two can join my buddies in the middle." The black guy led the young boy and girl to the middle and lined them up with the Asian guy and the Latino guy on either side.

The white guy told the boy and girl, "Now you are part of our family. Watch our stunt. After this, I'd like you to remember we are together, and we are one race, the human race, okay?"

"Let's go!" the black guy announced.

The Asian guy and the Latino guy held the hands of the boy and girl, squatting together in a line with their backs hunched and heads lowered. The white guy stomped his feet then sprinted towards the line formed by his buddies. With a forward flip, he jumped across the four and landed on the other side, then quickly squatted down and joined the line. While the crowd burst into applause, the black guy dashed across from the opposite side. Then with a forward flip, he passed the line of five and landed on the other side.

"How was it?" the black guy asked the girl and boy.

"Yes!" Excitement illuminated their faces.

"Do you remember what I told you earlier? Yeah?"

The boy and girl nodded.

The three guys then walked up front with the young girl and the young boy. "There is only one race. We are of black, white, Latino, Asian, and others. That is the human race."

Los Angeles, a massive metropolis on the west coast of America, with rich cultures from around the world, and people whose lives intersect one another by enacting daring activities as free spirits at different corners, was the true melting pot for this fresh-off-the-boat Chinese guy to come of age in.

#

The university campus was beautiful and pleasant. It had warm, colorful buildings of Romanesque Revival design, immersed among trees, connected by stairs and pedestrian walkways. Walking on campus, Hanwei saw a diverse community, full of vibrant young men and women, students and faculty members, all of different ethnicities. Situated near Hollywood, the students here were trendy. They kept themselves in great shape, perfectly manicured, and culturally tuned. It was refreshing to bump into a stream of stylish students on the university's famous Bruin Walk, a pedestrian route connecting residential and academic buildings. Some called it "The Red Carpet."

The university town, Westwood, hosted many high-tech firms and offered a variety of restaurants, gyms, and movie theaters to students within walking distance. Walking in the neighborhood, Hanwei could see many decorative flags and flowers around buildings, people focusing on their laptops in coffee shops, and shoppers hanging out in groups.

Hanwei enjoyed his new life, shuffling among the graduate student research office, PhD lab, his advisor's office, and classrooms, while making new friends with fellow Chinese students and American locals.

Ordering food from perplexing, unfamiliar menus in local restaurants was a challenge. Once while visiting a restaurant with his Filipino-American friend, Hanwei had great difficulty understanding the various side options. His friend once teased him, "You have a long way to go."

Communicating with locals was also hard. Once in a sushi restaurant when Hanwei and his black friend finished their meal, he waved his hands to the waitress to ask for the check with an accurately descriptive but awfully clumsy question: "Can you please get the bill over for us so we can pay?" His black friend smiled and helped, "Just wait and say, 'Check, please.'"

Going to the hair salon was another level. He had to learn phrases that GRE never taught him, such as "tapered" or "one and half or two." Otherwise, he might have to suffer an awful look for weeks. It took him a while to master asking for a short, manly, and sharp hairstyle that looked good on him.

Those challenges didn't faze the open-minded Hanwei. He was eager to connect to different people of different lives.

The most refreshing thing Hanwei found in this new place was that the university offered strong support for LGBT rights. Its student and faculty LGBT association routinely hosted events to advocate LGBT rights and help them connect with one another. The association's website compiled information related to sexually transmitted diseases, local LGBT-friendly bars and clubs, and progress in LGBT rights. The association also assigned mentors to help international students become accustomed to their life in Los Angeles.

Hanwei's mentor was Nick, an all American man, outgoing and humorous, who was happy to show Hanwei the locals' way.

#

"Hanwei. It's Nick. We are here."

"Cool. I'll be right there." Hanwei put down his cell phone, grabbed his jacket, put on his Nike sneakers, and went for the door.

It was late afternoon on Thanksgiving Day. The streets were empty. People were already in their homes for the holiday. The school encouraged mentors to take their international LGBT students to their family gatherings, the best the university could offer for the international students on such an important American holiday.

"Come in." Nick waved from the passenger seat of a sedan parked at the curb. An Asian guy was in the driver seat.

"Hi, Nick. Thanks for picking me up."

"Welcome. This is my boyfriend, Jake. Jake, this is Hanwei."

The Asian guy turned and smiled at Hanwei. "Nice meeting you."

"Nice meeting you, too." It was the first time Hanwei had met a same-sex couple who openly greeted him in public.

While Nick worked as a manager in the university's facility management department, Jake was a successful interior designer. In LA, where the rich and famous routinely renovated their homes with the latest style and luxury taste, it paid to be in this profession. Their home was in Hollywood Hills.

"You guys are supposed to be enemies. Jake is from Taiwan," Nick joked with a challenge.

"Not exactly. We have many things in common," Jake replied.

"Yes." Hanwei followed.

"Should China invade Taiwan? Hanwei, what do you think? And don't worry about Jake."

"Events in the past had led to the separation and hostility between these two groups of people of common ancestry. Some may feel winner-takes-all is a fair game, especially when they are in power. But I prefer everyday people like us not to assume it is in our right to supersede others' wishes using ours."

"He is smart." Nick raised his voice with a laugh.

"I told you, we have a lot more in common. There are thinkers in every corner of the Earth," Jake commented.

Hanwei looked out the window. The wide street was decorated with many rainbow flags. Shops displayed posters of seductive half-naked men on their windows. A billboard sign stated, "We connected gay refugees with safe houses," and was subtitled, "That's our kind of hookup," humor that Hanwei got immediately, referring to the fact that people in gay communities did not only know about hookups, but also provided humanitarian relief to gay refugees.

"What is this place?" Hanwei asked.

"Ah. You have not been here yet, right?" Nick answered in an exciting tone. "It's West Hollywood. It's all gay people here. You are lucky, Hanwei."

"We can bring him here after Thanksgiving dinner," Jake followed.

Hanwei heard about gay towns in America. But when he actually traveled through one, it felt exciting.

…

The three reached Nick and Jake's house. The house was a modern two-story home hanging on a cliff of the Hollywood Hills. When the door opened, two big dogs rushed over, jumped up to Hanwei's chest, and greeted him.

Inside the stylish and comfortable house, a big, flat TV on the wall was playing a hip-hop music video. Hanwei recognized some of his favorite pop stars featured in it: Usher, Nelly, and Mary J. Blige. They were inescapable in this entertainment capital of the world.

Two friends of Nick and Jake's, Darren and Zack, also arrived. They brought wine and plants as gifts.

"This is Hanwei. A new graduate student, recently joined UCLA from China," Nick introduced.

The first guy greeted him with a feminine tone and gesture. "Oh, nice. Fresh off the boat. Nice meeting you, Hanwei. I am Darren. Did I pronounce your name, right?"

"Yes, nice meeting you, Darren," Hanwei responded warmly, a bit unsure of the meaning of the term "fresh off the boat".

Darren smiled. "Are you also gay? 'Cause I couldn't tell."

"Yes."

"It's okay. We love macho guys. Especially hot ones like you."

"Don't scare our new boy in town," Jake said.

"Please, Hanwei isn't uptight like you. Right, honey?" Darren responded.

Hanwei was happy in the middle of everyone. He had always been comfortable with more feminine men. There was once a flamboyant high school kid in the dorm. He had a high-pitched voice, and mannerisms that were unabashedly feminine and flamboyant. Many called him "fancy" and some kept a distance from him. Hanwei, however, made sure he was on his side and rooted for him. He admired his classmate's courage to be himself and appreciated how his presence challenged himself and other men to be in touch with their feminine side. And, since his father loathed feminine men, being in solidarity with them gave him another pleasure in his rebellion against his father's bigotry.

"Yeah. Hanwei is not that gay. I haven't seen him checking out guys in the street yet," Nick added.

"Well, maybe he has a standard, not as slutty as you." Darren kept joking with his sharp tongue. "Honey, hope you are not scared by our incendiary comments. We are just making life more fun for everyone."

The five soon seated themselves at the table and started their Thanksgiving dinner.

Darren expressed his gratitude. "Thanks for inviting us, Nick and Jake. It's so nice of you to host us for a wonderful Thanksgiving dinner."

"You are welcome. For gays like us, friends are our family," Jake kindly replied.

"You two are like the perfect match," Darren complimented.

"Thanks. We fight too."

"All couples fight. And that's okay. Look what a lovely life you two have built together," Darren commented.

"How long have you been together?" Zack asked.

"Five years already," Nick replied.

"That's nice," Zack quietly commented.

"How's your love life?" Nick asked Zack.

'Love life,' that's an interesting notion, Hanwei thought.

"It's okay," Zack replied.

"Just okay? When was the last time you got laid?" Nick went after Zack.

"Like last night?" Darren interrupted.

Zack smirked.

"Lucky you," Nick joked.

"Guys. What's next, top or bottom? You guys are scaring Hanwei," Jake said.

"Hanwei wouldn't mind. He is smart, no hang-ups," Nick said.

"Look at the guy on TV." Darren turned to the TV screen on the wall. It was a movie scene, in which two guys in torn ancient clothes were fighting on a muddy ground, a typical American action flick, men half naked exposing their muscles fighting for dominance.

"That guy is hot," Darren commented on what everyone in the room was probably thinking.

"But they are really dirty and muddy," Jake followed.

"I wouldn't care. I would fuck him anyway," Nick replied.

"Nick! Jake, should you punish him tonight?" Darren commented.

"Punish," Zack murmured, emphasizing its sexual connotation.

"Zack is getting horny." Darren laughed.

"I thought Zack was just versatile, didn't know he is also into S&M," Nick commented. Everyone started laughing except Hanwei. His head was spinning trying to pick up every cue.

When the five finished dinner, the world outside the window had grown dark.

"Let's check out the view," Darren suggested.

The group followed Jake to the deck extended from the top floor of the house.

"Amazing," Darren gasped.

Holy moly, Hanwei thought. *It's truly a breathtaking sight to behold from the Hollywood Hills.* The vast land of Los Angeles stretched the entire view on the outlook from the cliff, with innumerous city lights spread across the ever-stretching land under the dark sky. The downtown Los Angeles skyscrapers abruptly rose above from the center of the vista.

"Guys, it's ten o'clock. Let's go check out West Hollywood."

#

West Hollywood, one of the most prominent gay towns in America, had a high concentration of upscale hotels, restaurants, shops, and night-clubs. In daytime, the city exhibited a typical laid-back California tourist scene with locals and tourists filling the outdoor patios of coffee shops and restaurants. At night, the city turned itself into a vibrant nightlife scene.

Hanwei, Nick, Jake, Darren, and Zack arrived in West Hollywood shortly after ten o'clock. The street, full of night clubs and bars, pumped with hormones, looked glamorous under the city lights. The people on the patios took care of their appearance, enjoyed their drinks, and engaged with one another with ecstatic conversations in intricate social etiquette. Through the glass wall of some night-clubs, Hanwei saw handsome, athletic men in their underwear standing on top of the bar tables, teasing patrons with engaging eye contact and smiles, occasionally flexing their arms and squatting down with their strong thighs in front of their admirers. The crowd on the dance floor moved along with the strong music beats and bold video depictions of male and female beauty.

"Do you like what you see?" Nick asked.

Hanwei smiled and nodded.

Nick laughed. "You are sick."

"Let's check out the store."

It was a spacious adult store. Facing the wide French door, books with artsy depictions of male bodies were laid on top of an exhibition desk. Hanwei turned a few pages of a book. Beautiful male models with their large penises were revealed in full pages. Inside the store, t-shirts with graphic slogans were on sale for rebellious-minded youth. Some slogans were provocative and funny like, "I am not gay, but my boyfriend is." While some others, Hanwei thought, had much poorer taste: "Fuck you. I have enough friends." *What an attitude from a modern gay culture*, Hanwei thought to himself. Along the wall, Hanwei could see many adult items like porn videos, poppers, condoms, lubricants, and realistic dildos.

Getting back to the street and passing by a busy patio, Nick pointed Hanwei to the nightclub and said, "This is the one with the least attitude and no cover charge until eleven." The neon light on the nightclub's sign said "MICKY'S." The men on its patio were mixed in age, not particularly dressed in fashion, giving a less pretentious feel. The crowd was racially diverse.

Hanwei noticed some men in the crowd were checking him out. Seeing the joyful faces and vivid moves of many men and women, Hanwei thought, *This may be the happiest place on Earth.*

Walking across the street, Nick pointed to the nightclub by the side. "This is Rage. They have an Asian night every Friday. You should come."

"Asian night?" Hanwei asked.

"Yes. You'd find lots of fun," Zack said.

"He is not into Asian," Darren said. "Maybe you guys should also introduce something else to him, like the club Tiger Heat."

"Tiger Heat? 'Where beautiful people meet' as they advertised. That one has the worst attitude," Zack commented.

"Rage's Asian night also has many rice queens. Maybe Hanwei will find his dates here," Nick commented.

"'Rice queen'?" Hanwei asked.

"Means white guys who are into Asians," Zack answered. "You can come by yourself later," Zack encouraged.

At a traffic stop, the five joined the crowd moving across the street toward the boisterous other side. Alongside attractive men, beautiful girls among them loved their limelight walking on the pedestrian crosswalk in front of the standstill traffic, holding onto arms of their trusted male guardians, making fashionable swings, occasionally turning around making sure their voices were heard by their friends.

The five finally arrived at Abby, a large club with a long line of socialites which they said Madonna once visited. In the club, Hanwei found himself surrounded by many tall men. Go-go boys in their boots and underwear moved their bodies along the music on elevated beams among the crowd, occasionally jumping onto the iron bar hinged to the ceiling, doing flip overs to demonstrate their athleticism, landing back on the beams, then hunching down and hugging their cheering admirers.

"What drink do you want?" Nick asked Hanwei loudly over the music.

"I don't need anything."

"What?!"

"I am okay with Coke. Or a beer is also good. I can't drink much alcohol," Hanwei put his chin close to Nick's ear and explained.

"Okay!" Nick squeezed himself into a vacant spot in front of the bar. Hanwei could see the shirtless bartender swiftly moving across the bar counter, shuffling himself between patrons and cashiers, tirelessly pouring and handing out drinks.

Behind the go-go boys, large crowds of men and women were dancing. The crowd was ecstatic, gazing at one another, bodies touching one another. Their clothes were glittering under the laser beams. Their movements were filled with beastly hormones.

Hanwei joined his friends in the dancing crowd. He had inherited a good sense of rhythm from his mother and father, and moved along with the beats, high and relaxed.

"The boy fresh off the boat wasn't shy or nervous at all!" Nick commented.

"I told you Hanwei is open minded!" Darren followed.

"And he got a good rhythm!" Zack added.

Nick, Jake, Zack, and Darren didn't know Hanwei got part of his temperament from his father, bold and envelope-pushing, and he had been long familiar with homoerotic scenes among many men, except this time, in this new world, it was his turn to do it right, and it felt like homecoming.

New Home

On Saturday evening, the people of Los Angeles were at parties, from the bonfires at El Segundo Beach to the nightclubs on Sunset Boulevard, or the midnight restaurants in Koreatown to the many poolside parties at home.

Hanwei drove to West Hollywood by himself one Saturday night, shedding off a busy week of research work. Dressed in a soft blue t-shirt and a pair of brown jeans, he walked into Micky's nightclub, the one with the least attitude as Nick told him.

Surrounded by men who were looking for men, there was pressure in this place to prove a man's worth. And that was not a man's checkbook. Hanwei quickly got a beer and walked through the crowd surely and steadily, with his vision focused ahead while occasionally checking out guys on the side. At this moment, he felt himself return to a very basic human being, without intricate mathematics or theories, without tribalistic or materialistic needs.

While Hanwei stood at the edge of the dance floor watching the electrified crowd, he noticed a man a few feet away staring at him. He was a good-looking Caucasian man in his early thirties, with macho features and short hair. While he kept his composure, his prying eyes and mysterious facial expression had given away his intent. Hanwei looked straight at the man and guessed the man wanted him.

In this place, every man was the predator and the prey at the same time.

"How are you doing?" A voice said into Hanwei's right ear. A Latino man smiled at him. He looked a bit chubby wearing a tight t-shirt, apparently with friends by his side.

"Doing good. How are you?" Hanwei replied while quickly glancing back at the direction where the white man stood. The handsome man had disappeared.

"I am doing great. You are so cute. I am Luis, by the way. Where are your friends?"

"I came by myself. Nice meeting you. I am Hanwei. Did you guys come together?"

"Yes. This is my friend, Alex. And this is Miguel."

"Nice meeting you, Alex and Miguel."

"Do you come here often? Where do you live?"

"Sometimes. I live about twenty minutes away."

"Lucky you. It must be nice to live so close to WeHo. We came from San Diego."

"Oh cool. Haven't been to San Diego yet. Heard it's nice there."

"You definitely should go there for a visit."

"Yes. Cheers." Hanwei raised the beer for the group.

Hanwei moved on after a couple of minutes. That mysterious handsome man was on his mind.

Walking through the crowded floor and patio, there were hot guys who were enjoying hugs with their admirers, and there were middle-aged men who laid their eyes on Hanwei's face and body. But there was no sign of the man whose thirst was met by Hanwei's.

It was disappointing. Hanwei left the club after chugging down a glass of Coca-Cola to wane off the alcohol.

Just as Hanwei was about to walk across the street, he spotted the Caucasian man. He was standing by the crosswalk, chatting with an Asian guy.

The man looked at Hanwei.

Hanwei stopped and greeted the two. "Hey, how are you guys?"

The white man nodded, looking unwaveringly towards Hanwei.

"Doing good. How are you? I am James. My friend Matt wants to meet you," the Asian boy boldly answered.

What an introduction! Hanwei thought, then walked towards them. "Yeah? I am Hanwei. Are you two boyfriends?"

"No. We are not boyfriends. He is just someone who fucks me."

"I'd be glad to meet your friend if that is okay," Hanwei replied while looking at the white man.

"You guys have fun. I'll talk to you later, Matt. Bye." The Asian boy walked away, leaving the white man and Hanwei on the spot. His confidence and grace in the street were rather impressive.

"Hey. I am Matt."

"Nice meeting you, Matt. Would you like to have a walk?"

"Sure," Matt nodded and replied with a soft and low voice.

The two walked along a residential street by Santa Monica Boulevard. While Matt had very few words, Hanwei could feel the mutual attraction.

"You look very cute," Hanwei complimented.

"You too."

After a few minutes, Matt stopped in front of the gate of an apartment complex.

"Where are you going?" Hanwei was perplexed.

"Going in. I live here." Matt slightly tilted his head towards the gate, hinting Hanwei to follow. It surprised Hanwei.

It was a one-bedroom apartment, furnished in good taste, simple and contemporary. A long couch faced a flat TV mounted on the wall, accompanied by a slender wooden coffee table. An inviting white round table was situated in the dining spot of a modern kitchen.

"Nice apartment. You live here by yourself?"

"Yes. You go to school here?" Matt asked, then turned to face Hanwei, looking straight into his eyes while Hanwei stood in the middle of the living room.

"Yes. UCLA. I came from China half a year ago," Hanwei replied, then subtly shifted his sight away from Matt's stare. "Do you wanna sit and chat?" he mumbled while trying to distract himself from the sudden irresistible intimacy.

"You are so Chinese."

Hanwei looked back at Matt, seeing himself being stared at intensely and sexually. Matt's manly and sensual face was intimidating, and at the same time trustworthy and warm.

Flattered, Hanwei smiled.

Matt reached out and held Hanwei's left hand firmly then turned toward the direction of the bedroom.

"What are we doing?"

"The bedroom."

Inside Matt's bedroom, under the dim light, Hanwei saw a pair of jeans, rugged style, sprawling out flat on the floor.

In no time, he was standing by Matt's bed, a contemporary style bed with a rusty metal frame and a wood headboard.

"I like your taste," Hanwei complimented.

Matt had already cornered Hanwei. With the bed behind Hanwei's back, Matt stood in front of Hanwei, reaching out to Hanwei's waist.

While Hanwei felt embarrassed and excited, Matt pulled Hanwei's t-shirt off from above his head, exposing his upper body, and pushed him onto the bed. Then he reached out to his zipper and pulled it open.

"You have a nice body," Matt commented. He got on top of Hanwei and started to remove his own clothes.

Hanwei pushed himself up against the bed instinctively, yet failed to overcome Matt's strength. Under the dim light, he saw Matt's body. It was as beautiful as his face.

Matt pulled Hanwei's pants off and let Hanwei lay completely bare under him. "Wow. You are so sexy," Matt said.

"You are too."

"Thanks." Matt then took off his pants.

"Whoa, you are big," Hanwei exhaled in admiration.

Matt smiled. He then overpowered Hanwei beneath himself and went for the lower body. Hanwei tried to reach Matt's arms to conceal his own desire, only to be denied by Matt's aggressive stance. Matt rubbed his body part against Hanwei's then stroked him until he got close. While Hanwei was engulfed in Matt's intense and sensual presence, Matt was excited by Hanwei's feisty intimacy.

"Please," Hanwei pleaded in an intense moment before the two finally relieved. It was the first time Hanwei had sex with a man of a different race. It felt novel, fun, and addictive.

The next morning, before they set out, Hanwei checked out the books on Matt's bookshelf. He noticed a book with a remarkably beautiful cover page titled *Buddhism*.

"What is this book about?" Hanwei didn't yet know the English word in the book title.

"You don't know? It's from your country, your religion. No?"

Hanwei now guessed what it was. While he opened the first page, a beautiful golden-colored art of Buddha came into his view. *Interesting, apparently in the West, one can be promiscuous and love the spirit of Buddhism at the same time.*

"Should we meet again another time?" Hanwei asked when Matt dropped him off at his parking location.

"Sure," Matt replied.

Hanwei then drove away to continue his sunny California weekend.

#

On weekdays, Hanwei shuffled himself between classrooms and office cubicles. He was fascinated by the subjects he came across in his classes and research work, such as the trade off between collective and individual gains in distributing resources among diverse users, and the intuitive geometric perspective of optimization problems. He felt lucky that he now lived an academic life where his intellectual curiosity and talents were well suited, incubated since his childhood from the factory town.

During lunch at school, Hanwei sat at a picnic table surrounded by students and opportunistic squirrels and pigeons. While he was about to finish his lunch one day, Matt came to his mind again. It had been a few days since they met. Hanwei called him a couple of times and left voice messages. So far, there was no reply. He felt puzzled.

Is he not really interested? No. Matt's passion toward him was quite evident that night. After all, Matt gave the number to him.

Is he actually irresponsible, not even bothering to return a call? No. Matt didn't seem like a jerk.

Is he occupied by his work or out of town? That doesn't make sense. Could Matt have gotten into an accident? Nevertheless, Hanwei wanted to give him another call, hoping that wouldn't disturb him.

Again, no answer. The ringing stopped eventually and went to voicemail. Hanwei had no choice but to get back to finishing his lunch.

Then, his cell phone vibrated.

It was Matt's text. "Sorry I didn't call you back yet. From the calls you made, I guess you want something more than what I am looking for. Hope you will find someone nice. Take care."

Every young man wants to believe he would be among those lucky ones favored by love and passion. This time, Hanwei learned he wasn't always going to be lucky.

#

"Let's move closer to the stage!" Hanwei raised his voice under the loud pop music on the crowded dance floor, speaking to his Sri Lankan friend, Sidharth, and American friend, Bob. It was Friday night in Club Rage.

The three pushed themselves through until they got a good spot in front of the stage. Hanwei met Sidharth and Bob online. Sidharth came to America from a rich family in Sri Lanka as a foreign student to study agriculture. However he changed his major to hotel management after he got here so he could work as an intern and make more money in the famous Four Seasons Hotel. Bob was a local white American, who grew up in Riverside, a rural place in East Los Angeles. He was a sharp, self-taught IT professional. Considering the poverty and challenges he experienced in his childhood—raised by a father with a gambling addiction and a mother who struggled with alcohol and drugs—it was remarkable he had made it this far. The three had ever since become loyal friends, especially since both Sidharth and Bob had a crush on Hanwei at the beginning.

"Hey, Hanwei!"

Hanwei turned around. It was Duan smiling at him, and among other familiar faces were Ming, Andrew, Chao, Fan, and the gorgeous lady, Wanshu. It was Hanwei's Asian gang. He had mingled with this group of friends since the third year of his LA life. Duan was a Chinese student who came recently looking for opportunities in this new world. Ming and Fan were professionals in the tech industry, living a comfortable life. Andrew, Chao and Wanshu were well off business people and loved to host house parties. Hanwei and his Asian gang often hung out together in East LA, a sprawling new Chinese area with fine restaurants and upscale malls, spread across multiple freeway exits.

"You guys all came out tonight!" Hanwei greeted his friends.

"Whoa. Look at you, looking hot tonight," Chao commented, accompanied by Wanshu who gave Hanwei a soul-snatching smile.

"Are those two your friends?" Duan asked.

"Fuck buddies," Ming interrupted with his joke.

"Yes, they are my friends. Let me introduce them."

The two groups merged and then immersed into the surreal atmosphere of Club Rage.

Soon after eleven o'clock, guys on the dance floor started taking off their shirts following their implicit tradition. Hanwei had long become conformable with such a scene. He took off his shirt among his raucous friends, revealing his sexy body, inviting the touches of strangers around him.

Ming, Hanwei's close friend, grabbed his left hand to pull him outside the dance pool. "Come with me."

Just like that, Hanwei was pulled by Ming walking in front of him, like a rent boy, parading across the night club, through the hallway and the stairs, shirtless in a pair of low-rise jeans saddled around his butt below his waist, exposing his six-pack abs and masculine happy trail. Hanwei could see the attention he was receiving from hungry eyes illuminated by the street lights coming through the patio. He didn't care; if anything, he was confident and pleased to entertain his fellow men.

After showing off with Ming, Hanwei put on his t-shirt and joined his friends around the patio. They joked and chatted about their life, ideas and plans.

With his friends in LA, Hanwei felt a sense of belonging. This foreign land had become his new home.

"Hanwei, a guy is checking you out," Andrew notified Hanwei. He then saw this handsome Hispanic looking guy, younger, with a nice frame, smiling at him.

"What are you waiting for? He is cute." Andrew nudged Hanwei.

…

That night, Hanwei had a steamy encounter with the Latino guy at home. His friends joked afterwards, asking him how he managed to get on with the Latino on his small bed. He told his friends that they did it on the floor.

Hormone-fueled time aside, Hanwei did not develop a deeper relationship with the men in the club. In this hedonistic home, young men could hardly figure out what they wanted and what they needed in their life to come.

Immigrant

Hanwei had been working under Professor Haddad for almost three years and had passed the PhD qualification exam. It was high time for him to find a concrete research topic for his PhD dissertation. If anything, he learned that a PhD was not about getting a high-paying job but rather involved a cold and hard intellectual pursuit of a proper understanding of nature. Professor Haddad once told him, "If you believe in something, write a theorem and prove it so that nobody can argue with you. If you can't, you know you must have missed something."

"This is not English! Nobody will buy it." Professor Haddad wasn't impressed with the slides Hanwei summarized for his research work. He was always harsh in his criticism of work he deemed lousy. A fellow Chinese student already gave up his PhD under him after years of struggling. Another Iranian student had to switch to work for another professor after, as the story was told, Professor Haddad said to her, "Students work for me. And I don't pay."

To be fair, Professor Haddad was a brilliant man. He was said to be one of the early pioneers in academia who worked on the genesis of the Internet. But in his late sixties, his drive and energy were diluted, often a common problem for students who went to work for renowned professors who had significant success in their early career. Hanwei respected him and admired his toughness, rigor, and brilliant mind.

"I will go back and do some modifications. I'll rethink my approach and come back to you next week," Hanwei said.

"Sure. What's your plan for the next quarter?"

"I plan to enroll in the last two courses I need for my minor discipline credits, then use the remaining time for research work."

"I don't know how you would find time for research if you take two courses." Professor Haddad was unhappy.

"If I finish all my courses early, I will be able to fully focus on my research work. But if you think I should take only one course per quarter, I can do that."

"Okay. That's better. But if you enroll in courses, I cannot pay you."

"I will focus on research work. The workload of one course should be light enough. Professor, my family won't be able to financially support me living in Los Angeles. And I cannot work off campus except for internships as a foreign student. So, I really need your help on the research work stipend."

Professor Haddad didn't like his students to do internships, since some students quickly quit the PhD program after they had a taste of their financial prospects working in high-tech companies.

"I don't have money." He was about to step out of his office.

Hanwei knew this might be his only chance to secure his PhD program and the consequence would be so catastrophic for him that the professor might not even know. With a quick thought that came out of nowhere, he took one big step towards the professor right at the door, looked at the professor in his eyes, and said in a candid voice, "Professor, I can do anything for you, anything."

Stunned, Professor Haddad paused and then responded, "Okay. You can convert my lecture manuscripts into Power-Point slides. I need that done for four courses. I will pay half of your hours."

"Okay. I will do that. Thank you, Professor."

Hanwei drove back to his dorm feeling stressed out after the meeting. He cried at home. He had always excelled in school and ranked in the top of his class. The research paper he wrote years ago had been cited more than a hundred times. He didn't want to lose before the finish line for financial reasons. He recalled how his mother had split her income in half to support his study at Beijing University, telling him she would look for help and borrow money if she had to. He recalled some family friend had told his mom that she should be proud to have a smart and loving son. And he recalled that some relative had told his mom that he should go to work as soon as he could to make money instead of wasting time in school. He also knew he was twenty-seven years old, while at the same age, many of his childhood classmates had been working for years, supporting themselves and even helping their parents.

That afternoon, Hanwei took a long nap to clear his mind for his next move.

"Hi, Mom. How is your day?"

"Mom is fine, just doing things as usual. How is your day?" Rulan's voice came through the phone.

"My day is okay. I've been busy with my research work."

"How is your research work? Made any good progress?"

"It's been tough lately, but not bad. Professor has quite high standards."

"While being busy with your research, make sure you eat well and sleep well. Health is still the most important."

"Mom, sometimes I think about quitting my PhD program and getting a job with my master's degree. Financially, it wouldn't be a bad choice. I don't know what you would think. I can still continue my PhD, although it would take another couple of years." Hanwei couldn't help but check with his mom before making his decision.

"Mom is not a well-educated person, may not be able to grasp your situation or know what is best for you. But you do not need to be worried about me. Mom's health is good. Uncles and aunts are around me. They would help if I need any. You should think about what is best for you and fulfill your dream. Since young, you have shown talent in academics, fascinated by mathematics and science. Not many local young men and women in our town could go to study at a renowned research institute in the United States like you do. So, cherish your opportunity and work hard on where your passion is. If a PhD is not meant to be, Mom wouldn't blame you. But you also shouldn't give up due to obstacles that you can overcome."

"I got it, Mom. Take care of yourself when I am not there with you. I will look out for the best for me."

That night, Hanwei decided to work on lecture notes of the four courses for his professor and get some under-the-table jobs to survive at the same time.

#

"South Linden Drive, south on McCarthy Drive ..." Hanwei looked for the right intersection while driving towards the east along Olympic Boulevard in Beverly Hills. *Here it is,*

Bedford Drive. The summer afternoon was beautiful and peaceful, with flourishing trees, blossoming flowers, and multi-million dollar homes lining the boulevard.

This should be the one. Hanwei parked his car outside a large and beautiful house.

"Hi, how are you? I am Sandra. And you are Hanwei?" A blonde fifty-something-year-old woman, white, with tanned skin, perfect makeup, wearing an expensive dress opened the wood-framed glass door and greeted Hanwei. She had a strong presence, carrying a confident and commanding smile.

"Yes." Hanwei nodded and smiled. "Nice meeting you."

"Nice meeting you. I'm glad you came. Come on in."

It was a two-story home with an open floor plan. It boasted glass walls, lavish interior design, and beautiful decorations.

"Let me introduce my son upstairs. As I told you earlier, his lower body was paralyzed in a car accident. But he is strong and doing well." Sandra led Hanwei to the stairs.

Sandra talked to a Mexican maid in the kitchen as she led the way. "Ana, I wrote the grocery items we need on the note by the fridge. Thank you."

"Sophia, this is Hanwei. He's here to help Joseph. Hanwei, this is my daughter Sophia." A high-school-age girl was standing by a bedroom working on her manicure while they approached the second floor. She smiled briefly before getting back to her own business. Hanwei could already hear the noise from several kids talking.

Entering a bedroom, Hanwei saw three boys with toys on the floor. One with short brown hair, about eight years old, looked agile and inquisitive. Another was younger, probably four to five years old, smiley and jubilant. Then a blond-haired boy on the floor; he looked confident and uninterrupted.

"Joseph. Let me introduce you to Hanwei. He will hang out with you often this summer."

"Hi, Joseph." Hanwei smiled.

"Hi," the boy responded before getting back to his toys.

"Joseph usually plays with his friends in his bedroom. He is able to crawl around without help. When he needs to get on the bed or go downstairs or to the backyard, he will need you to carry him. There is a powered chair latched onto the rail of the stair you can use to bring him safely up and down. He has a wheelchair downstairs. I will show you in a minute."

"Sure," Hanwei said.

Another middle-aged Hispanic woman walked into the bedroom and started to quickly put clothes in a basket.

"This is Maria," Sandra said. "She is Joseph's nanny, helping him with the bathroom, clothes, and food, so you don't have to worry about those things. Just notify her when Joseph has needs. You will help Joseph be mobile, help him when he plays with his friends in the backyard sandbox, bring him tools, join him swimming in the pool, and watch out for him," Sandra explained. "And ask Maria to give you swimming trunks when you guys use the pool."

"Got it." Hanwei nodded. *Basically, I am a playmate and a lifeguard,* Hanwei thought to himself.

"I will leave you here to play with them now. Have a good time." Sandra walked out to attend to her own business.

Staring at the three kids, Hanwei felt awkward. He had no experience with kids. He thought maybe he could pretend to be interested in the games the kids were playing or try having some conversation with them, but they would probably find him dull and boring anyway.

The afternoon was filled with chasing Joseph and his friends around the house. Joseph often crawled around the floor to reach what he needed, refusing Hanwei's help. He was quick to put his wheelchair into motion once Hanwei put him in it. He was focused when using his tools in the backyard sandbox, and he liked to command the other two, apparently a mastermind from a young age.

He reminded Hanwei of himself when he was little.

Later in the afternoon, all the kids wanted to hit the pool. In no time, the brown-haired kid, Jason, jumped into the pool. Hanwei helped the younger boy, Matthew, Joseph's younger cousin put on his life jacket, and then he helped Joseph into the water. The kids instantly came to life in the water, laughing and screaming about every little thing that they found interesting. Joseph was quite capable of swimming; he pedaled using his arms, while the water supported his weight.

"Jump! Jump!" the kids shouted. Answering the kids' call, Hanwei stepped back from the edge of the pool and jumped with a splash.

"You are an amazing man…" Sandra said as she returned to the house, walking upstairs with a smile, while Hanwei was waiting in the second-floor loft for Maria to finish cleaning Joseph. "I placed your check on the staircase. I will see you on Thursday, same time."

Inside the envelope was a check for seventy dollars. That wasn't bad to Hanwei, since he got paid less than nine hundred dollars a month this summer for his research work.

\#

Hanwei filled his summer schedule with his research work,

creating course materials for Professor Haddad, babysitting Joseph, and tutoring high school kids for cash. To save money, he cooked his meals or ate at McDonald's and Subway when he had no time. Although an immigrant, he was starting to feel like a local.

While tutoring kids around Los Angeles, Hanwei saw first-hand the family's impact on a kid's performance in school.

He tutored a high school African American boy in a poor school district who had a single mom. Their apartment was disorganized and filled with random things. The family had three hyperactive dogs to tend to as well. The boy was energetic and polite, but had such a difficult time learning how to calculate the area of a trapezoid even in his last year of high school.

Hanwei also tutored a high school black girl from a rich African American neighborhood. The girl already grasped preliminary calculus pretty well and asked Hanwei to train her on difficult advanced placement exam problems for applying to universities. Her house was organized and her parents spoke and behaved in a refined manner. "Are you getting your doctorate degree? You are a PhD student, right?" they once asked Hanwei, "We will wait for your book."

...

"Hanwei, as I mentioned last time, we are going to our family's vacation house in Malibu beach this afternoon. Maria, Sophia, Joseph, and Jason will go in my van. You can help Maria get our household items into the van. Here is the address. I will see you there."

"Sure."

It wasn't an easy feat to own properties on Malibu Beach and Beverly Hills. Hanwei admired how Sandra was able to become so financially successful and raise her handicapped son, as a single mother.

As he entered the Malibu beach house, Hanwei could see that some family members were already there. In the living room, a gray-haired lady in her eighties was sitting on a long white couch with a couple.

"This is my mother." Sandra introduced the gray-haired woman.

"Hi, ma'am," Hanwei greeted her.

The elderly woman switched from her conversation with the couple and greeted Hanwei. "Hi, young man."

"And this is Jason's parents." Sandra introduced the couple. "This is Hanwei, a PhD student from UCLA. He is helping Joseph these days."

"Nice meeting you." Hanwei reached out to Jason's parents, while Jason went over and hugged his mother.

"Nice meeting you. How was the movie? I heard you guys went to the theater this morning," Jason's mother asked.

"It was pretty good. It's nice to take them out."

"It's so nice to have Jason come over and hang out with Joseph. And it is impressive how Jason won the sprint competition in school that day," Sandra complimented Jason's parents.

"Thank you."

"We read your book about psychology. Such a wonderful book." Hanwei could hear the two guests giving compliments to the grandma, while he moved on to follow Sandra.

"My mom was a psychology professor," Sandra explained while they were escorting Joseph and Jason to the kids' room. "The man over there in the kitchen is my stepfather. He was on the board of directors of UCLA."

Walking behind Sandra, Hanwei could see the beautiful courtyard in the center of the house and the beautiful decorations and family pictures on the white wall of the large corridor.

"You may want to change into your swim trunks soon. We will go to the beach in a few minutes," Sandra said while they got into the kid's room. The kids were already playing in the room; their Legos, playing cards, and mini robots were scattered around the floor.

Coming out of the bedroom in his swim trunks and t-shirt, Hanwei bumped into Joseph rolling his wheelchair towards the gate of the house, while Maria was trying to get a hold of him to finish getting ready.

"No!" Joseph's grandma yelled as she stopped in front of his wheelchair. "You idiot! You cannot go out looking bad!"

"Clean your face and hands, change your clothes in your room first, then you can go to the beach," the grandmother commanded.

"Joseph, listen to your grandmother," Sandra said. Hanwei could see her uncomfortable expression.

The family definitely raised their kids with a tough standard, Hanwei thought to himself.

Sandra, Joseph, Jason, Matthew, and Hanwei walked out of the house towards the beach. The community's narrow residential streets were very private. Many entrances to the street and passages to the beach were put up with gates and misleading signs claiming the rights of private properties to warn and block average beach goers.

"Hi, David." Sandra smiled at a shirtless guy in his trunks and his gal in a bikini passing by.

"Oh. Hi, Sandra, how arc you? You guys are also going to

the beach?"

"Yes. How's it going?"

"It's wonderful. You guys have fun," the man said.

Apparently, families living in the neighborhood know each other well, Hanwei thought.

"You don't have to wear a t-shirt. It's okay to go shirtless. And you look very fit." Sandra smiled at Hanwei while he carried the beach umbrella and chairs on his shoulder while holding a bucket of toys in his hands.

Hearing her compliment, Hanwei noticed how different he could be in different situations. One day, he could go shirtless among a large crowd, jump into a car and hump with a guy, and join loud conversations with his buddies at a party. On other days, he didn't feel comfortable taking off his shirt in front of a family or speaking his mind freely around an uber rich family.

The family reached Malibu Beach. The beautiful Pacific Ocean filled their view with blue waves with white foam tops. The beach had almost no people, except some folks who occasionally walked along the waterfront. Sandra settled herself into a beach chair, sitting comfortably reading her book.

The three kids started digging in the sand with tools. Joseph was the one who got the most ideas and called the other two into action. Jason was the athletic and strong one, who worked swiftly to build the castle. Matthew, the little one, couldn't get his hands properly around the project, as his effort often fell out of alignment and was snubbed by Joseph.

While working on their little projects, the kids sometimes became distracted by the coming waves and went to chase the waterfront. Joseph sometimes crawled to the edge of the water. Hanwei would immediately get near the kids to make sure they were safe. He also needed to pick up the toys the kids threw around to make sure they didn't get washed away by waves.

Once the kids returned to their sandcastle project, Hanwei would return to the beach chair by Sandra's side and carefully watch the kids from a distance.

Sandra was dressed in a beautiful white gown, matching perfectly with her fashionable waterfall hair, a silver blond color, as she read her novel through a pair of stylish sunglasses. Hanwei took off his shirt and started enjoying his first time on Malibu Beach. The California sun shone onto Hanwei's chest and six-pack.

"It's a wonderful day." Sandra turned her head over to Hanwei and smiled through her sunglasses.

"Yes. It's beautiful."

"So, how was it?" Hanwei suddenly felt Sandra's hand on his thigh. He saw her confident smile and command. For a brief moment, he was stunned and embarrassed. He had never had a woman touch him like that. *The question must be about babysitting*, Hanwei thought.

"It was pretty good. Joseph is smart. Jason and Matthew are fun to be around too." Hanwei conveyed his appreciation, although he actually felt it was strenuous and awkward to take care of the kids. The kids probably looked at him as a servant. Joseph rarely listened to him anyway, and probably thought of him as a nuisance, dull and alien-like. The family was rich, white, and blond and had nothing in common with him.

"You are quite an amazing man," Sandra responded. "Taking care of the kids is not easy. I gave birth to Joseph and Sophia without ever being married to a man."

Hanwei was a bit shocked to hear Sandra's comments. There were many questions in his mind. *It must take a determined personality to give birth to two children and raise them alone.* He could see this woman had "it", intelligence, grace, grit, and most of all, the aspiration to live a successful and meaningful life in her own way.

But Hanwei didn't follow up with any questions or comments after Sandra gave him a peek into her personal life. He didn't feel he was at her level and didn't want to make himself look like a fool asking silly questions to such a remarkable lady. This was probably one of Hanwei's weaknesses, an unnecessary pride and reservation from a yet-to-be mature intellectual. While he was a good listener and was determined to learn and figure it all out by himself, Hanwei had not yet mastered the art of reaching out to people who had far excelled in different fields to ask for help that could fast-track him to a new altitude. He hadn't yet learned to build connections that would otherwise magnify his potential instead of limiting himself to a one-man pursuit.

"You are probably shy. But you know? I admire you. I could not travel thousands of miles away to survive in another country, learn from a different culture, speak a different language, build everything from scratch, and experience a journey on my own at my own risk. That was something my grandparents did when they brought my parents over here while they were still young, escaping from Poland in the middle of World War II. Most of the people in this city are transplants. We have been considered locals ever since my grandparents settled here in the forties. I could only imagine and admire the work and spirit of my grandparents and new immigrants like yourself. This country was built by immigrants. So, I am sure you will do well." Sandra smiled at Hanwei before she returned to her book.

Hanwei was mesmerized by Sandra's words.

"Hanwei, look!" Hanwei heard Joseph shouting from where the boys were digging. "There are crabs! Come over here!"

Hanwei rushed toward the kids. Jason was using his plastic shovel to dig the muddy sand away to expose the escaping crabs. Matthew was giggling around and goofing around, while Joseph was laser focused on where the crabs were going.

"There's one here!" Joseph shouted loudly.

Jason couldn't wait. He threw his shovel into the air to use his bare hands. The shovel flew straight in Hanwei's direction.

Clunk! The plastic shovel hit Hanwei's head right above his left eye. Feeling the pain, he instinctively covered his eyes and forehead. Jason quickly ran over to Hanwei.

"I'm sorry!" the eight-year-old kid said to Hanwei.

Hanwei realized he was only hit on the ridge bone above the eye. Since the impact angle was right on, it did not cause laceration, just a swollen bump.

"It's okay. It's okay. We are lucky it didn't hit the eye," Hanwei said to Jason.

Jason still looked worried. He stood by Hanwei's side, catering toward him closely.

"We've got to be careful," Hanwei said to Jason. He could tell Jason was a good kid. Although raised in a privileged family, Jason remained a responsible and honest boy, and had the capacity to care for others.

Hanwei walked over to the kids' sand project and started helping. *It is my lucky day*, Hanwei thought. *I could have lost an eye just trying to make ends meet.*

#

"Anyone have anything to add?" the project lead, a female PhD student, asked, looking at a room full of PhD students in the lab. This was the group of students with a wireless network research background from both the electrical engineering department and computer science department in UCLA that were working jointly on a technology demo funded by the U.S. government.

"Okay. We're done here. Let's proceed with our plan," the lead said. The group of students then walked out of the lab toward their office cubicles.

"Hanwei." Ahmed, a Mid-Eastern student who worked in the same lab as Hanwei walked closer to him and said with a sly smile, "I think the Chinese girl sitting on the opposite side likes you."

"Yeah?" Hanwei replied.

"She was sending you signals," Ahmed said seriously with eyes wide open.

Hanwei blushed a little. He knew the girl. Her name was Huiling. She had beautiful eyes and a sensual smile. With a petite and delicate figure, she radiated a fine sense of femininity and grace. Hanwei had found the girl very special. They lived on the same floor in the same student apartment building. They had bumped into each other a couple of times before, said hi to each other, and briefly chatted about their PhD programs. Hanwei was energized every time he saw her, and he wished to spend more time getting to know her. But up to now, it had become unimaginable for him to think about having encounters with girls, not with the gay life he was living in West Hollywood.

#

"Is my car ready?" Hanwei walked into the mechanic shop with Sidharth and talked to the staff standing outside. A skinny brown Labrador walked away with his head hung low. The mechanic shop was only a block away from Hanwei's graduate student housing, a rather convenient location. And Hanwei was not a new customer.

"The Ford Escort?"

"Yes."

"Check with Miguel over there." The staff pointed to the Hispanic looking guy around the car lifts.

"Yes. It's a piece of junk, man. You can throw it away. But it's ready," Miguel said sarcastically.

Hanwei knew his car had years on it. Besides living with many of its mechanical problems, he once spun his car out of control with a one-eighty degree turn and hit the wall of Freeway No. 10, right around downtown Los Angeles.

Hanwei paid two hundred bucks for the repairs and then drove with Sidharth into the McDonald's parking lot around the corner. It was Saturday. They had planned to meet Bob for lunch before they would go fishing at the Manhattan Beach Pier.

"My classmates in Beijing University are making a good living now in China, bought their homes, and are helping their parents. And here I am with a broken car, struggling with my PhD program, and can only afford to go to a formal restaurant once a week in Chinatown," Hanwei said while biting into the ice cream he bought from McDonald's.

"You shouldn't think like that. Once you graduate with your PhD, you can make a good living," Sidharth said.

Bob added, "Hanwei, like you said before, a PhD is less about making money, more about the type of work it would open to you. You'll have a better chance to work on high-tech and research work you are interested in."

"My professor is too tough. He often trashes my proposal, tells me what he thinks I should do, then a week later, trashes what he proposed I should do. It's been really difficult. Sometimes I want to argue back. But my future lies in his hands, so I just swallow my pride and keep my mouth shut."

"Hanwei, my father once told me, 'It is easier to do bad things, much harder to do right things.' You've got to think carefully about your next best move; do not react with your temper. Finishing your PhD is really important, you know?" Sidharth tried.

"Hanwei, you are very intelligent. I played video games with you. The way you play is way above me. I am a director in a small IT firm. I see many people. I know you can make it. It takes time. Sometimes it can be really hard. But you can do it," Bob said. "And no matter which way you go, your future lies in your hands, not others.'"

"Thank you both. I am lucky to have you as my friends. I love LA. I will do my best to stay."

It Has To Be Another Life

Oh, shit. I left my keys at home, Hanwei thought to himself as he stood outside his apartment after returning home from the university via the school shuttle. His roommate was out.

What should I do? Maybe I can push the window above the kitchen wall open. He just needed a chair to stand on to reach it.

Then he thought of Huiling.

She lived a few doors down. They had worked together on a project a year earlier, and some classmates had teased that she seemed to have a crush on him. He hadn't really bothered her since then.

To Hanwei, Huiling felt like a character lifted from a romantic movie—soft, familiar, and unexpectedly magnetic. He even confessed to his gay friends that he couldn't explain why he was drawn to her. One friend teased that it was because her tender expressions and quiet grace reminded him of his mother, but Hanwei sensed the pull came from somewhere more complicated within himself.

...

Hanwei knocked. The door opened.

"Hi. How are you?" he said, and felt something brighten

inside him.

"How are you?" Huiling answered, her smile quiet but disarming—bright eyes, silky black hair tucked casually behind her ear. She radiated a homey romance Hanwei wasn't prepared for.

"Sorry to bother you," he said. "I forgot my keys. I was wondering… if I could borrow a chair to climb in through the kitchen window."

"Not at all. Sure, I can get a chair for you," Huiling responded in delight. She left him and returned with a chair shortly. "Would this work?"

"I think so."

They walked back together to Hanwei's apartment with the chair. Stepping onto the chair, he could reach the window. He pulled the screen off first, and then pushed the window open. He used one hand to grab the wall, and the other hand to push onto the window ledge. Then he lifted himself up. Dust flew from the window frame. "Uh, it's dirty."

Hanwei stood back on the chair. Without thinking, he took off his t-shirt—partly to keep it clean, partly because something inside him wanted to feel her eyes on him.

As Huiling was right next to him, Hanwei felt a bit awkward. But that might be why a man with a crush is adorable. Hanwei managed to squeeze himself through the window and climbed in successfully.

Moments later, he opened the door from inside.

"Thank you," he said, stepping toward her, still warm from the climb.

"Good that you got in," Huiling said. Hanwei's athletic physique was inches from her. He grabbed his t-shirt and backpack from the chair, dusted the dirt off the chair and his body, and quickly put his t-shirt back on.

"Let me return your chair. And… um… I should treat you to dinner after I finish my work."

She hesitated—only for a breath—before her smile broadened.

"I'm actually cooking now. If you don't mind, join me around six? It's been a while."

Hanwei felt a small spark light inside him.

"I'd love to, if that's okay."

#

At six, Hanwei rang her doorbell. He had showered, styled his hair, and chosen the thin blue t-shirt and brown jeans his friends said looked best on him. He didn't usually think so much about getting ready for meeting a girl—except tonight, thinking of her, he had.

While people say you may be totally straight until you gobble down several beers with your best buddy, Hanwei thought it might also be true that you may be totally gay until you meet a pretty girl.

"Hey, you came." Huiling opened the door. Her smile warmed the entire room. Her black hair framed her face softly, her eyes bright in a way that made him feel calm and alert.

"Thanks for inviting me. I brought wine."

The apartment smelled of spices and simmering soup. The room was tidy and inviting—an Impressionist painting above the fireplace, a plant catching the late sun. She moved around the kitchen with practiced grace, her gestures small and fluid.

"The food smells nice," he said.

"That helps my confidence," she laughed lightly. "Take a seat."

Scrambled eggs with leek. Steamed tilapia. Mapo tofu. A fragrant pot of pork bone and lotus root soup. It was a dinner that came from someone who cared enough to prepare something real.

"It looks delicious," Hanwei said, genuinely touched.

"Simple dishes. Do you cook?"

"I do. I grew up in Chongqing. And people there say, 'A Chongqing guy who can't cook is going to have trouble finding a wife.'"

"That's funny. I thought it was the other way around." They both laughed and their eyes met—this time, longer.

"Let's start while the food is warm." They began eating, the steam from the dishes drifting softly between them.

"Where did you grow up?" Hanwei asked.

"I'm from Nanjing."

"Nice. I visited there once with my parents. One of my aunts still lives there."

"Oh. You have relatives in the Jiang Zhe area."

"Yeah. My father's family is from there. He never really got used to living in Chongqing."

"But I always heard good things about Chongqing, like the city is hilly and fun, guys are raw and candid. Girls there are especially known to be beautiful and spicy."

"Yeah. They have a reputation."

"Your dad must be proud of you, having a son, nice and talented like you."

"Thank you. I am not so sure about that myself. Hopefully he is," Hanwei commented, and then shifted the conversation after a pause, "How is your research work going? I remember you were working on pattern recognition."

"It's going well. My dissertation is on that."

"That's a very promising field."

"How about you?" Huiling asked. "I remember you were working on wireless networks. It's a hot area too."

"Still working on it. But I think your research area has a brighter future. It's related to machine learning. Research aside, what do you do in your spare time?"

"Mostly hang out with my girlfriends. Sometimes sightseeing. Sometimes window shopping."

"Only girls? No guys?" Hanwei asked, glancing at her before looking back down.

"Sometimes, my friends' boyfriends join."

"Do you bring your boyfriend?" His voice tried to sound casual but weren't able to hide the curiosity.

"Me?" She shook her head lightly, her hair brushing her cheek. "I'm on my own these days. Research occupies me."

Hanwei swallowed. "I thought… I mean, you're pretty. I figured you'd have someone by now."

She looked at him—directly, softly. "Thanks. You're good-looking yourself. I'd think you'd have plenty of dates."

Their eyes held. Something moved between them—quiet, warm, and unmistakably alive.

"What do you do in your spare time?" she asked, her tone gentler.

"Mostly research too. And sometimes I hang out with my friends." He hesitated. "We should hang out more."

Hanwei felt he had never gotten a chance to express his fondness for Huiling. Huiling also felt she had never gotten a chance to know Hanwei, although she always liked him during their brief collaboration on the project.

"Sure," She said.

"Do you know the Thai restaurant two blocks away down on Venice Boulevard? We could meet there this weekend."

"Sounds good. Like a date?"

"Yes." The word came out steady. And as she smiled back, Hanwei felt a warmth rise through him—soothing, exciting, close enough to feel like another version of himself he had forgotten how to be.

#

"Wow. You called. Where have you been?" Xiong spoke over the phone in sarcasm.

"He-he. I was busy last week."

"Busy having fun with lots of guys, right?"

"Yeah. Met some hot guys. But they can't replace you."

"Ha. I could imagine. You probably had so many dicks there that you forgot about me."

Since Hanwei came to America, he always called Xiong once every few days. He also visited Xiong whenever he flew back to see his mom.

Hanwei often told Xiong what he had seen and done in Los Angeles. Xiong often asked Hanwei about his mom and discussed financial affairs in China and around the world, and talked about his latest career moves.

Xiong had finished the transition he had always dreamed of, becoming a financial industry professional after obtaining his finance degree from an after-hours program. Hanwei had a part in it. Since economics was in principle applied mathematics, it wasn't difficult for Hanwei to grasp. He helped Xiong on his course materials and sample exams when he visited Beijing. Sometimes the two studied late into the night and then they jumped into bed together. Those were the days the two could lie down side by side and skin to skin, looking into each other's eyes to feel the moment they had been familiar with, knowing they both had to progress with their own lives, while still believing they always had each other's backs.

Now Xiong lives in Shanghai, the financial center of China; he had joined the remarkable rise of China in the twenty-first century. Over the last few years, Hanwei suggested Xiong should come to the United States to be with him as he still hoped they could live a life together forever. But Xiong always told Hanwei that there was no easy way for him to go there, it wasn't realistic for two men to live together, and he had his parents to care for at home. Instead, he suggested they wait and see and figure that part out later.

"So, how is it going?" Xiong asked.

"It's going well. The PhD work is tough. But life is fun."

"How is your mom doing?"

"She is doing fine. My uncle's family is nice to her. They all get together for lunch and dinner. Although my mother's relatives are not that educated, they are kind. Oh, and she will retire in a year."

"How old is she now?"

"Fifty-six."

"Still young."

"Yeah. She is active. She plays ping pong and still beats her colleagues."

"Wow. Is she worried about you in America? Asking if you have a girlfriend?"

"Nah, she didn't ask after I told her about you and me. But

she still hopes that I will marry a girl and have a conventional life. She liked you though. So, if one day we live together, I think she will accept it and will be happy," Hanwei said.

Hanwei came out to his mom two years ago when he visited China. It wasn't easy for Rulan, a traditional lady living in a Chinese factory town, especially after having gone through the humiliation and suffering of being married to a homosexual man. The day Hanwei told Rulan at her bedside that he was into men and had been in love with Xiong, Rulan cried. She told him she didn't think he was gay, it was just that he had been influenced by his father. Once he met the right girl, he would fall in love with her.

While Rulan's theory could still be sound, life had configured Hanwei to be the man he was today. He'd had a crush on a girl he met in a village during his stay when he was in elementary school. He'd had a crush on a nerdy girl in his middle school class. And now he had feelings for Huiling, the girl next door. But he'd had many more crushes on guys since middle school. Perhaps all his biological motors were functional, but with a bias. Now living only a twenty-minute drive away from a gay mecca, fully experienced with men, Hanwei was sexually matured.

"How are things going with you and your girlfriend?" Hanwei asked, knowing that finding a smart girl to marry and moving up toward a life of comfort and wealth had always been Xiong's pursuit.

"We are doing okay. And to tell you my news," Xiong said, "we will get married this fall."

"Whoa." For an instant, Hanwei didn't know what to feel.

"I am not young anymore. My parents have been pressing hard for years."

This is now real. Hanwei thought. *After all, this is what is for me in the end. What we had is all there is.* "So, I should give up my hope for you."

"You also didn't stop and rest these years, right?"

"But you know I love you." Hanwei felt the pain of his breaking heart.

"I know." Xiong always knew Hanwei was crazy for him and loved him. He knew the boy he saw walking out of the reception gate at the airport with luggage and a big smile every year, the boy he argued vehemently with after being caught peeking into his diary without permission, the boy he made out with in bed and almost got caught when his father returned to the apartment earlier than expected, and the boy he lived with in the basement for months when he first stepped foot in the big world of Beijing.

"Is what we had real?" Hanwei asked through his sadness.

"Yes. It was," Xiong answered in a sober voice.

"A peaceful traditional life is what you have always wanted. Congratulations. I hope you will do well," Hanwei said, knowing that life would never be the same without Xiong, a man whom he could never forget.

#

Walking across the corner mall at Venice Boulevard and Vinton Avenue and the climbing stairs, Hanwei arrived at the Tree House Thai restaurant.

He picked a window seat. The restaurant was elegant, and the street outside was calm, covered in a layer of golden sunlight that ran toward the Pacific Ocean.

Huiling stepped in, wearing a patterned blouse and a soft

blue skirt that framed her waves of black hair. Walking over to the table, she could see Hanwei's calm and passionate look. He had freshened up with a shower and gelled hair.

"Hi," she greeted.

"Hi. Thanks for coming."

The waitress brought menus. They ordered. They talked easily—Hanwei learned that Huiling's father was a music teacher; she was influenced by music from a young age, played piano and was into literature. Huiling learned that Hanwei was into art and science; his parents had been divorced. Hanwei learned Huiling loved comedy and drama, like *Friends*, *American Beauty*, and *Frida*. Huiling found Hanwei's taste to be more intense, like 24-hour news networks, *Monster*, and *Terminator*. Hanwei enjoyed her presence more than he expected. Sitting across from her, he felt calm, seen, and strangely safe.

"It took a while but I am glad you finally asked me out," she said while the two ordered some apple cider and paid the check.

"Yeah. It took a while. I should have talked to you earlier." Her eyes sparkled.

"But I have something I want to tell you, something I've been thinking over for the last two days." Hanwei lowered his head before he looked back at Huiling.

Huiling tilted her head, inviting honesty.

"I think I am gay." Hanwei looked down.

Hanwei was heartbroken the night Xiong told him he was getting married. It was a moment seven years in the making. Xiong was the one Hanwei had always wanted to bring home and grow old with. At that moment, he understood the heart of another human being who fell in love with him was never something to take lightly. *I really like Huiling. But for how long?* He had thought to himself. Seeing the pain his mother had experienced in her life, Hanwei knew he had to come clean.

He saw the slightest shift in her expression—surprise, not hurt.

"I have been with men many times. There was also a guy I loved. But the first time we met in the lab… I liked you. I thought maybe I could build something with you. It confused me about my sexuality. But I should not hide anything from you."

"I'm sorry," Huiling said. "I wouldn't have known."

"I am still the same person. And I like you. But I know that I would be problematic when it comes to being with girls."

Huiling took a breath.

"Don't worry about me," she said. "But if you decide to live as your truest self, you'll need a lot of strength."

Hanwei lifted his eyes to hers.

"And I think you can," Huiling added. "Thanks for telling me. I did like you, from the beginning. But I'm glad you're an honest man.

She rose gently. "I should head home. I still have work tonight."

That night, lying in bed, Hanwei felt a bit lost. *In this limited lifetime, we often try to understand who we are, eager to fulfill the highest and truest expression of ourselves. Yet, our truest selves may be more than those rigid boxes the world wants us to fit in. At the end of the day, many of us have to make hard choices, pick honest fights, and stay in touch with our alter ego and the good things we otherwise could have become.*

This was the last time Hanwei saw Huiling. He heard that she passed her PhD defense the same year and moved to

Silicon Valley.

The Pride

Dear Sir or Madam,

After years in UCLA's PhD program and living in Los Angeles, I am finally graduating this summer. To celebrate this joyful moment, I am inviting my mom, Rulan Xu, to visit me in the United States and join us for my graduation ceremony. I plan to take her for sightseeing in California. Her visit and our travel would be one of our most precious memories to come. I will provide financial support for her trip. I appreciate your help on her tourist visa application.

Yours sincerely,

Hanwei Zhou

The visa officer behind the counter read the letter on his desk, double-checked the passport, and took a second look at the woman outside the interview window.

"Welcome to America. Please come back in the afternoon to get your visa."

#

After saying goodbye to her brothers and sisters at the security gate of Chongqing's Jiang Bei Airport, Rulan adjusted herself back and forth in her seat and tried to get some sleep on the fourteen-hour flight. She stood in a long line for customs, carefully answered questions from the tall officer with other worldly features, and then finally walked into LAX's international terminal reception hall.

She anxiously searched for the sign of the Chinese boy she was familiar with. In her hand was her son's phone number and Chinese to English translation notes in case of emergencies.

"Hey, Mom!" Hanwei walked swiftly toward the end of the handrail.

"Hey!" She smiled.

With her son standing in front of her taking her luggage in excitement, she knew she was safe now.

Besides it being the first time Rulan had traveled this far, there would be many firsts for her on this trip. It was the first time she sat in her son's car, the first time she stayed in her son's place, and the first time she used an ironing board. That had surprised and saddened Hanwei, as he realized how different his mom's life had been from that of other women, having been married to a homosexual man then living by herself.

Her stay in Los Angeles was eventful and surprisingly homey. She found that Americans in Los Angeles looked brown. Hanwei told her there were Mexican immigrants who came from the south and white people who loved trendy tanned skin. She also found that Panda Express was a nice escape from burgers and salads, locals were outgoing and friendly, and the air felt fresh and clean. And then, most joyfully, she found a large Chinese population that had settled in East Los Angeles, covering miles and miles of malls, shops, restaurants, banks, and residences where they had grown roots on this side of the Pacific Ocean.

#

Rulan sat on the bed, knitting by the bedroom window, while Hanwei was on his computer.

"Mom, the annual Los Angeles Gay Pride is coming up in a week. Let's go see it. It's a vivid and uplifting event. Many people will go there, gays, straights, police, firefighters, even the mayor. You'd find it fun there." Hanwei turned to Rulan while he was browsing the West Hollywood Gay Pride webpage.

Rulan nodded her head slightly, while she continued knitting.

"Why will police and firefighters go? They are also gay?"

"Most of them are not. They show up on behalf of their communities to support gay rights."

"Hard to understand. These westerners…" Rulan slightly shook her head. "In China, to most people, homosexuals are sexual deviants or human scum. Yet here, people are celebrating them."

Not really a surprise to hear anyone in the general population give such comments, Hanwei thought. "It's natural that people's sexual orientations are not all the same. Like everything else, it has its own statistical distribution."

"It can't be natural." Rulan shook her head. "Nature created male and female, yin and yang, complementing each other, giving them the most magical and riveting experience when they combine. Two people of the same sex exploiting each other for physical excitement is a misalignment of such natural mechanics." Rulan paused her knitting and used hand gestures to heighten the atmosphere and give meaning to her words.

"I can see why people could arrive at that conclusion by only looking at things on the surface, the complementary anatomies and the complementary personalities. But such mechanics is only a product, or more precisely a byproduct, of evolution. Biological evolution doesn't have a preset goal. It is a process. Whatever traits humans have developed along that process, including different sexual orientations, as long as they are stable without arbitrary intervention, would be by definition natural, and may even have their own merit. It's just that people may not be aware of more of their own fundamental natures, but rather just recognize and worship easily identifiable ones."

"I am not able to debate you in sophisticated terms. But humans evolved from animals. They are more in touch with their nature. Do animals exhibit homosexual behaviors?"

"They do. In fact, from worms to mammals, from insects to birds, each species has members that practice homosexual behaviors and some exclusively so," Hanwei eagerly told Rulan.

"I don't know," Rulan sighed. "You have been such a wonderful boy in the factory town when you were young. Everyone praised you, your demeanor, integrity, and performance in school. Friends often say to me, 'You are so lucky to have such a good son. Having him would be equivalent to others having ten sons.' But if people know you are gay, it would be another ground-shaking scandal to the factory town after your father.

The respect you earned by getting a PhD degree from a top U.S. university would be tarnished. Mom's life was ruined by your dad, and you."

Hanwei toned down. "Mom, it's not like that."

"Mom gave birth to you. So, Mom doesn't have a choice, can't blame you, but must accept you."

#

"Mom, here is a spot for us."

Rulan stepped into a spot among the crowd. She now had an unobstructed view of Santa Monica Boulevard.

Jubilant men, women, children, and seniors packed along the sidewalk. Colorful shops along the street were decorated with rainbow flags and festival banners. Riveting music and beats rose from far and near and spectators moved their bodies along the rhythm. It was the first time Rulan saw in person ordinary citizens self-organize a festival and movement of this scale, joined by residents, private firms, and government officials, supporting the rights and well-being of fellow humans. When she saw two shirtless handsome men in rugged jeans walking up to the crowd pulling two horses in front of a bus load of guests who were waving rainbow flags behind a balloon combination hat spelled L.O.V.E., she knew she was now watching a gay parade.

"Mom, wait here. I will get some beverages for us."

"Okay." Rulan smiled and turned her attention back to the parade.

The parade was a feast for the eyes. Cheerleader squads moved in perfect unison, tossing their flyers high into the air — a breathless flip — before catching them safely in waiting arms. The crowd erupted. Rulan clapped along, swept up in the joy of it.

Then came a fire truck with the city's firefighters hanging on its sides. These firefighters were strong and calm, drawing the ecstatic crowd to wave at them and pour affection on them for their masculine male beauty.

There were thunderous motorcycle squads of hairy men and tough women roaming along the street. They swirled in front of the audience in circles, touting their style and spirit.

There was a busload of seniors on the upper deck of a tourist bus, dressed in colorful clothes, waving signs like, "I love my gay son." "Make love, not war," and, "Love your neighbor."

Seeing those moms and dads of gay children, Rulan thought, *While I am not sure if I could judge whether being gay is normal, for the brief life I could have in this world, heaven knows how much I have loved my own son.*

"Mom, here is your Frappuccino. Try it," Hanwei said as he returned.

"Hmm… It tastes so sweet." Rulan cringed after taking a sip. It was the first time Rulan tried such a beverage. For a woman born around the same year of the founding of the new China, who worked honestly in a pharmacy for once as little as ten U.S. dollars a month, a Starbucks drink was neither a craving nor a necessity. "I will only drink a little. You can help with the rest."

"Hanwei!" They turned around to see an Indian man and a white man moving toward them.

"Finally found you!" the two men said "This must be your mom!"

"Mom, these are my friends, Sidharth and Bob."

Rulan couldn't speak English. But she nodded her head

with a constant smile, expressing her happiness to see her son's friends.

"Did your mom enjoy it?" Sidharth asked.

"She looks like she did."

"Now she knows what you have been up to, huh?" Bob joked.

"Is your mom now okay with you being gay?" Sidharth followed.

"Not much yet. But she is being nice about it."

Hanwei's phone vibrated.

"Hello? Is that Chao? I can hardly hear you! I am on the north side of the street, in front of Trader Joe's. Hello? I can't hear you! Will text you!"

"My Chinese friends want to come over to say hi. Mom, see," Hanwei said, while a truck full of shirtless men approached, accompanied by pop songs blasting from the truck's mounted speakers.

While Rulan was waving toward them, one of the men escorting the float ran toward where Rulan and Hanwei stood, and randomly handed over fliers and packages to the audience. Rulan took a look at what Hanwei got from the man. The package had a couple of condoms, and the flyer said, "America, Grow Up. Use a Condom."

"Here he is. I found him." A small group of guys were heard talking to one another. Hanwei turned around. It was his Chinese gang.

"This must be your mom. Hey, ma'am. How are you?"

"Hi. I am well. Thank you. Nice to meet you. So many of you came here today?"

"Yes. We still have some friends several blocks away over there. We heard Hanwei's mom was here, so we wanted to say hi. Hope you are having a good time." Chao was always the smoothest among Hanwei's gang.

All of a sudden, the crowd burst into cheers. A convertible car was slowly moving up. A middle-aged man in the car waved at the people lining the street. With the encouragement from the crowd, he jumped off the car and walked along the street to shake hands with the crowd.

"It is Antonio, Los Angeles mayor!" Hanwei recognized the Latino-looking man.

"Really?" Rulan could not hide her astonishment.

No. This isn't happening. He is going to shake hands with mom. Before Hanwei could get ready, the mayor saw the kind-looking middle-aged Asian woman. He ran to where Rulan and Hanwei stood, gave Rulan a firm handshake and a warm, passionate smile.

"Thank you, Antonio!" Hanwei called out as the mayor moved on.

The parade carried on with many different groups before it concluded. There were religious groups who were advocating the spirit of inclusivity. There were Asian and Pacific Island groups who were pitching for racial diversity and unity. There were gay families who were pushing their baby strollers and holding their kids high over their shoulders.

Standing by the side of her son and her son's friends, Rulan thought of Gaoming. *He had always wanted to leave the factory town, looking for a place where he could find a passionate life and be happy.* She did not know where he was now or if he was doing okay. But she knew her son might have a chance to find happiness.

#

As planned, Rulan and Hanwei traveled to three-world famous cities in California.

Rulan was caught up in absolute awe when the magnificent red Golden Gate Bridge suddenly appeared from nowhere over the deck of their ferry and pierced through the thick fog hovering above the San Francisco Bay.

She was amazed by the marvelous Getty Museum on top of the hills of Los Angeles, overseeing the UCLA campus, the affluent Century City, the laidback Santa Monica and its backyard, the vast Pacific Ocean.

While Hanwei led her up to the deck of the Griffith Observatory after sunset, Rulan was not prepared for what she was about to see: the breathtaking view of downtown Los Angeles standing in the middle of the endless Greater Los Angeles, inlaid with countless lights, streets, and communities.

She enjoyed her walk with Hanwei along the seaport village in San Diego, watching locals fly their beautiful kites, checking out souvenir stores, watching street artists pull their tricks, and taking a big bite of Hanwei's favorite treat, Ben & Jerry's ice cream.

And Rulan enjoyed the most important day of her trip, Hanwei's doctoral graduation ceremony at UCLA. She was on high alert while holding the camera tight in her palm waiting for Hanwei to step out of his group, walk up the stage, and see the faculty representative place the doctoral hood over his head. She made sure she captured that moment—a sendoff moment for her son, a moment in which she knew she had done everything that she could, after which the son grew up and would stand on his own two feet.

#

"I am in deep trouble," Sidharth nervously said to Hanwei.

"What happened?" As close as he was to Sidharth, Hanwei knew something must be wrong.

"I think I fucked up."

Hanwei's heart started beating faster. "What is it?"

"The CIS sent me a letter requiring me to leave the U.S. within thirty days," Sidharth said.

"What?!"

"They say I am not eligible to renew my H1-B visa."

Hanwei couldn't believe his ears. He could see the panic and desperation in Sidharth's eyes and face. "What did your lawyer say?"

"He said it would be a very tough case if I wanted to pursue it. The CIS said the income report that the company provided for my H1-B was fraudulent."

"I thought you worked for the Four Seasons Hotel. That is a prestigious hotel. They must have provided valid papers for you."

"I got the employment authorization card with a consulting firm, then used it to work in a Four Seasons Hotel. The consulting firm inflated my expected income on the application. Four Seasons Hotel can't pay that much, you know? I thought the lawyer would help me get a green card in time first," Sidharth explained, then dropped onto Hanwei's bed and lay facing the ceiling.

"Oh my God." Hanwei was dumbfounded by what he just heard. He knew how serious the CIS was with this type of case.

"How about your nursing school? Would you still finish it?" Sidharth had paid and joined a good nursing school so he could become a nurse in this country. As warm, caring, and trustworthy as Sidharth was, Hanwei knew he would succeed and become a good one, fulfilling his American dream.

"I am already an illegal immigrant." Tears ran out of Sidharth's eyes.

"Let's think. You may finish and get your nurse's degree. A nursing degree in the U.S. is solid. Then see if a lawyer can help you stay."

"And the worst thing is that I will lose you if I leave." Sidharth burst into deep sob.

Sidharth always loved Hanwei. They had sex. While that might not mean much to gay men living around a gay town, he was among Hanwei's most trusted friends. He approached Hanwei about dating earlier to no avail, then accepted their relationship as close friends ever since. That time Hanwei told Sidharth the story of himself and Xiong, Sidharth covered his head with both hands and sighed, "I feel so sad now. You are like an Angel baby to me. But I can see how much you still love Xiong in your eyes. And you probably would never look at me that way."

"I am a loser," Sidharth said through his sobs.

Not long after that day, Hanwei accepted an offer of a high paying job in a high-tech startup in San Diego. Shortly after that, Sidharth left the country in order to avoid further violation of U.S. immigration laws to retain a chance to return in the future.

Hanwei cried in his car as he drove to see Sidharth for the last time. He recalled the days they went fishing with their friends, the days Sidharth drove him to school in his SUV, the night on a camping trip when Sidharth turned to him in the bed in the dark tent, and the day Sidharth handed over a bouquet to Hanwei's mom.

We never know when the hardest moment will strike in our life. Before it strikes, life is full of color. When it hits, we fall like a burnt down tree. The best thing in life is love. The hardest thing in life is to live.

Pretense of Strength

"Are you guys going to the happy hour?" asked James, Hanwei's manager at the high-tech start-up.

"I am going."

"I am going too. Where is it? Do we drive in separate cars?"

"It's in the Doubletree Hotel in Carmel Valley. I can drive. My car can take four people," Hanwei told them.

Hanwei, James, Andrew, and Florence got into Hanwei's car.

"This is your new car?" James asked, buckling in.

"Yeah," Hanwei said.

"So clean," Florence commented. "Your mom would be proud."

While Hanwei started the car, 50 Cents' hit "In Da Club" came through the stereo with riveting beats. The car was not expensive. But its sound system was something Hanwei didn't forget to upgrade.

"Excuse me." Hanwei switched the audio to the NPR radio station so as not to offend anyone.

"No, leave it," Andrew laughed. "It's happy hour."

"So you're into hip-hop," James said. "You're American now."

...

Happy hour was in the bar and patio section of the hotel.

Refreshments and snacks were passed around. Some colleagues gathered around the couch and in chairs in the bar section. Others scattered in the patio around plants and the water feature, bathing under the afternoon sun, occasionally bursting into laughter from someone's joke.

After sharing a conversation with a few colleagues, Hanwei walked up to a group of engineers around his age. They came from different countries, and almost everyone had a PhD.

"Oh, here it is, the wireless network expert," said Omar, a Mid-Eastern guy on Hanwei's team.

"I thought signal processing experts were more critical at this stage of our product development. Network operation can catch up later," Hanwei responded.

"Do you guys think we will make it?" one fellow asked.

This start-up was deemed the hottest kid on the block at that point. Getting into a high-tech start-up and making it rich on stock options was the dream of many young engineers.

"I have some concerns. I mean we still have not finalized the design of many key operations," Hanwei said.

Another fellow expressed his optimism. "Nah. Don't worry. They are throwing a hundred million at it. With that amount of money, something's got to come out of it."

"Nice haircut, by the way," someone added. "So, Hanwei, how many girlfriends now?"

"I prefer things to be simpler," Hanwei said.

"So, algorithms and simulations are not complex for Hanwei. But girls are." The group laughed together again.

Feeling the vibration of his cell phone, Hanwei stepped out of the circle. "Excuse me."

It was a missed call from Rulan. "Hanwei, it's Mom. Just giving you a call. Nothing special. You can call me back later.

No hurry."

#

That evening, Hanwei returned to his apartment. He dropped his backpack on the floor and turned on the TV. Some guests on CNN were debating about the seemingly conflicting trends of the unstoppable housing boom and the increase of the subprime mortgage delinquency rate. It seemed to be a big deal, telling from the serious facial expressions and high-tempered exchanges among the CNN guests.

Hanwei lowered the TV volume and dialed his mother.

"Hey, Mom."

"Hanwei?"

"Yeah. How is your day?"

"Mom is doing fine. Hanwei, your dad came back."

"What?!" Hanwei was shocked. It had been thirteen years. His father wouldn't even know he had made it to college. Fear and hope arose in his heart.

"Where is he now? What is he doing?"

"He came back to the factory town, claimed to the factory's officials that his mental issues had caused him to leave his job earlier. He threatened to commit suicide on the factory's premises if his demand was not met."

"Unbelievable. What does he want? What did the factory say?"

"He wants the factory to accept him back, basically work out a deal for him, like retirement with mental disability. He said he resided somewhere in Guizhou these years. Apparently, it did not work out for him. So, I helped him with his claim. He also had some good friends in the factory's higher ups.

He was lucky. They approved his case and granted him the retiree's benefit."

"Where is he staying? He cannot come to you anymore. You two are legally divorced. Thank God that I urged you to divorce him earlier. Don't let him stay with you. It's not safe to be with him."

"Hanwei, you are using such harsh words about your father. He loves you, although he has his problems. But no, he is not staying with me. He has actually been living in the city somewhere before he came to the factory. He apparently knew that you are now in the United States," Rulan said. "What can we do? This is our fate."

Fate, it was something Hanwei felt had never been fair to his mom and him, something he always had complete contempt for.

"Do you have his number?"

"You want his number?"

"Yes. I can talk to him."

Hanging up the phone, Hanwei read the number and with his heart pumping, he dialed his father, a man he had feared and hated since young. *I will try to make the best of it*, he thought to himself.

"Hello. Who is this?" It was his father's voice.

"Hi, Dad. This is Hanwei."

"Oh. Hanwei. Yes, it's Dad. Dad is very happy you called. He-he. How are you doing over there? I know you are in America. And you went to Beijing University." Without giving any pause, Gaoming continued. "You see? Dad knows everything. Dad has many leads in the town. Right? You say something."

"Yes."

"Do you have a girlfriend now? You are not young anymore. Once you have a girl, you can have a family. Father will feel more settled."

Hanwei stayed silent. He couldn't trust anything his father said.

"You must have become a grown man, should be quite attractive. How tall are you? I remember you were very fit."

"No. I am just so-so. Not tall."

"When are you coming back? Dad wants to see you."

"Where have you been all these years?" Hanwei cut to the main subject.

"Oh. Dad is doing very well. There are many things and many stories Dad can tell you later. I know I have not been a good husband for your mother. But rather expecting Dad to be a good husband in a heterosexual marriage, I'd say your father is probably better suited for same-sex marriage."

And where did this man learn the hip term "same sex marriage"? And what about the part of being a good father? Hanwei was surprised by the way his father revealed the gay part. It wasn't a subject they could touch upon in the past. And it wouldn't be prudent to immediately exchange such info with his father now, as he knew his father was good at setting traps. There was too much at stake.

"But you are always Dad's son." Before Hanwei could inject any comment, Gaoming continued. "You can help Dad, right?"

"We should get to know each other first. It's been many years."

"Dad raised you for many years. Why don't you think about that? Those years don't count?!"

"I am just saying I need to…"

"I worked hard for years to provide for this family. What

did you do? You just hung around in school with the money I left earlier and the money your mom sent! If Dad cannot live well now, you won't live well either!"

"Don't say that." Hanwei started trembling.

"Although it did not work out, your mom and I were still once husband and wife. When she needs something, Dad would still help her; it also reduces your burden." Gaoming seemed to be able to change his personality in a second. It was hard for Hanwei to tell if his father had a clinical mental issue or was just plain manipulative.

"Please, let Mom do her own thing for now. It takes time for you guys to get to know each other again. I will help you if you are in need," Hanwei said.

"Your mom is a nice woman. Dad will not bother her," Gaoming spoke in a kind tone. "That's all, right? Call me often, okay? Can you give me your email address, so Dad can write to you? It's not easy for me to call you in the U.S."

Hanwei gave Gaoming his email address and then they hung up the phone. He took a deep breath. *It is not good.*

Hanwei took a long hot shower. He let the warm water run through his hair and face and flow over his body. For moments, he cried.

At the beginning of the last thirteen years, he wished that monster would never come back. As the days passed, he had told himself to forgive, telling himself people learned from pain and love. If one day his father returned, he'd wish his father had become a responsible and loving man so there could be a happy ending. His mom and he could have a home they never had. Maybe life would be enjoyable and sweet again. Maybe he would be fine living with a girl, having a family, and never having to reveal to anyone that a gay life could be a happy one. But when reality set in, he could see the family he had wished for was never there and would never be.

#

Looking around Rulan's new apartment in Chongqing's bustling Jiangbei district, Hanwei felt quietly proud. His part-time earnings before graduation had helped the mother buy this small one-bedroom unit. Though modest, the corner high-rise apartment—with its floor-to-ceiling windows and balcony off the kitchen—was filled with light and felt open and warm. The simple, fresh décor made it cozy. And beyond the glass, the lively streets of Jiangbei stretched out in every direction.

Hanwei's aunt, who often looked after Rulan, had come to see Hanwei now that he was back.

"Do you plan to visit your father?" Rulan asked.

"Yes. I'll go tomorrow."

"You should," the aunt added. "Your mother is getting older, and you're not home most of the time. We've told her to find a companion—maybe not as charming as your father once was, but better than living alone. Yet she's stayed by herself all these years. Now that he's back… yes, his temper is strange, but they were once husband and wife. If he's truly changed, maybe the two of them could still look after each other."

"Gaoming's temper is strange," Rulan said, "but he looks pitiful too. He said he lived near the mountains in Guizhou, even planted potatoes in the fields. When he first came back, he was so thin. We asked if he had used drugs out there. He said he didn't."

"Even if his temper hasn't changed a bit," the aunt added, "now that your mother has this new apartment, you can give the old one in Luoqi to him. That would solve his housing problem."

…

Outside the park, Hanwei stood waiting. *Thirteen years… will I even recognize him?*

A taxi pulled up. A man stepped out—dressed in white, from shirt to pants. It was Gaoming. Hanwei recognized him instantly. While he was about to greet him, a second figure emerged from the cab.

He was young, in his twenties, delicate, with a carefully styled, flamboyant haircut.

A sharp wave of unease rose in Hanwei's chest.

"Let's find a place to sit," Gaoming said briskly, barely glancing at Hanwei as he led the young man into the park. No greeting, no warmth—just a stiff procession forward.

"Hi," Hanwei said to the young man. "I haven't seen my father in years. We have some family matters to discuss. If you live nearby, could you give us a moment?"

"It's fine," his father answered for him, giving the boy a quick look.

The young man nodded and left.

Hanwei and Gaoming sat at a stone table, angled ninety degrees apart.

"You," Gaoming said without meeting his eyes, "should wear brighter colors. At your age, dark shirts don't look sunny."

"Dad," Hanwei said, ignoring the remark, "how did you live all these years?"

"Oh, your father had many students outside. They respected me, brought gifts at New Year. And I never chased women—those rumors were nonsense. Your father isn't one of those who fool around. I lived alone all these years. When I came back to Chongqing, I stayed briefly in a retirement home—almost drove me crazy. A female administrator harassed me, wouldn't let go, even tried to force me to marry her. So I left. Living alone has its advantages.

"Sometimes I visit your mother," he continued rapidly. "She's a good woman. I learned a lot from her. But her relatives? They go around saying I'm gay, saying I'm mentally ill, saying I'm acting!"

He suddenly turned to Hanwei, eyes gleaming sharply behind his glasses. "Well, life is a stage. Maybe everyone is acting a part. And if we're talking about acting—your father can act too. Maybe better than most."

The lift in his father's voice, the sudden manic glint in his eyes—Hanwei felt a thin chill move through him.

"Mom said that during New Year, the family invited you for dinner, but you said you'd bring a young man."

"Yes. A migrant worker I helped when his wages were withheld. A young boy alone in the city on New Year's Eve—it's pitiful. I said I'd bring him. Your mom objected. Fine. She overthinks sometimes. What's wrong with bringing a young man for dinner?"

"There's nothing wrong with your spending the evening with him. But—" A middle-aged stranger approached. "Hope I'm not interrupting."

"Ah. You're here. Sit. You're not interrupting."

Gaoming's tone was casual, familiar. "This is a reporter from Chongqing Evening News. He wrote about me helping those migrant workers."

What is happening? How did a stranger suddenly join our reunion? Hanwei felt his composure slipping. This had to be arranged.

"Your father did a great thing for those migrant workers," the reporter said, taking a seat.

You arranged this, Hanwei thought, anger rising.

"See? Dad didn't lie," Gaoming said, now boasting. "My son just returned from America. Earned a PhD. Works in high tech."

"This must be your first meeting in over a decade," the reporter offered kindly. "Your father must be proud."

Hanwei said nothing.

"Once sons grow up, there will be distance from the father," Gaoming added casually. "All normal."

"Well, I'll leave you two to talk. After so many years, I'm sure there's much to catch up on."

Sensing the strain between them, the reporter slipped away. Silence closed in around the stone table.

Only then did Gaoming ask, "Do you want to come to my place for a bit?"

…

They passed several bright streets before turning into a narrow alley. The bricks underfoot were uneven and cracked, with puddles of murky water collecting in the gaps. Children pushed toy cars beneath windowsills, while elderly men in worn shirts sat on stools, smoking listlessly.

At the end of the alley stood an old residential building. Two rural-looking women knelt at the doorway washing clothes in plastic basins, while a dark, narrow staircase climbed upward behind them. A child played at its foot.

"Uncle Zhou," one woman greeted politely.

Dressed in spotless white, glasses gleaming, Gaoming looked almost surreal in the alley.

He nodded, then led Hanwei past the staircase and down a

small flight of steps. He opened a door.

Inside, another short stairway led down. It was an underground storage room.

Hanwei froze—four damp gray walls. No windows. No kitchen. No toilet. Nowhere to wash. A single bed sat in the middle. A few scattered belongings and books were stacked along the walls. Opposite the bed, a long table held an old computer.

"I live here," Gaoming said softly. "Small, yes. But cool in summer, quiet too."

He pointed at a rice cooker. "I cook everything with this. Rice, meat—convenient."

"Sit."

Hanwei obeyed. They sat shoulder to shoulder on the bed in the middle of the dim basement.

His heart broke.

Thirteen years ago, his father lived in a bright apartment with colleagues as neighbors, surrounded by furniture he had arranged, plants he tended on the balcony.

"You could buy Dad a TV," Gaoming said gently. "They're not expensive. It would make the days less boring. If you can... no rush."

"Okay," Hanwei whispered—and the tears finally came down his face.

He clenched his jaw, trying to hide the trembling in his breath. At that moment, all the walls he carried—anger, dignity, principle—collapsed under the weight of pity.

Sensing the tremor in his son, Gaoming said nothing. They sat shoulder to shoulder—no blame, no forgiveness—only silence.

Sometimes old wounds can't be reopened. Numbness

becomes the layer you need to survive, and silence is the only way to hold together the fragile pretense of strength.

On the way back to his mother's new apartment, Hanwei called her. He agreed to give his father the key.

Jay

The streets in Hillcrest, a prominent gay neighborhood in San Diego, were laid back and lively, exhaling youthful breath. On a Friday night, walking on the sidewalk of University Avenue, Hanwei could see young men stepping in and out of bars, drinking and chatting on patios, while occasionally brushing shoulders with residents who walked their dogs and folks on bicycles. He walked in leisure, paying attention to interesting men who occasionally came into sight.

While he was passing by a small bar, a fine-looking young black man standing by the side of the door caught his eye. The young man leaned his right shoulder on the entrance door frame, hands in his pockets, legs crossed. His soft gray t-shirt revealed his athletic physique. He had broad shoulders and long, strong arms. His rugged brown colored jeans were stylish and manly. The young man also noticed Hanwei. He returned the attention with a proud and flirtatious smile.

Hanwei walked up to the young man and spoke with a smile. "Hi, how is your night?"

"Not bad. How's yours?" the young man responded kindly in a masculine voice, looking into Hanwei's eyes with calmness. He knew he was hot.

Surprising, Hanwei didn't expect such a reciprocal response and had actually been ready for a humiliating snub. This close, Hanwei just realized how good looking this chocolate-colored young man was. Manly with a fine face, prominent jaw, strong nose and lips, his masculine look was complemented by his sensual eyes.

"You look cute," Hanwei complimented.

"Thanks. You too."

"I am Hanwei. What's your name?"

"Jay."

"Nice meeting you," Hanwei said warmly.

"Nice meeting you." Jay smiled with a cool yet arrogant expression. "So, wassup?"

"Nothing. Wanna hang out? Maybe go dance at Rich's? Did you come here by yourself?" A bit nervous, Hanwei gave it his best shot.

"Nah. Friends are inside." Jay pointed his thumb back inside the bar, and then stepped off the door frame towards Hanwei. "But they are okay by themselves. We can go."

Yes! Dang! Hanwei felt like he just hit the jackpot. His dating experience had been decent. But the rumor was that, when it came to hooking up, Asian men were ranked at the bottom and black men were ranked at the top; when it came to dating, the order was reversed. One thing was obvious, though: Asians and blacks were rarely seen dating each other.

The two walked into Rich's Dance Club next door. The dance room connected to the patio was playing hip hop. The crowd was energized by the beats, captivating those who were watching. Under the dazzling ballroom lights, the two stepped into the middle, surrounded by other young men and women. They moved together to the beat, face to face. Time to time, their bodies touched each other along with the rhythm, allowing them to feel each other's energy and warmth.

To Hanwei, Jay was everything he had wanted, sexy yet adorable, edgy yet fun. To Jay, Hanwei was mysterious, handsome and warm, especially as Asian men were virtually non-existent where Jay was from.

"Where do you live?" Hanwei asked under the loud music.

"Camp Pendleton," Jay said while using his hands to cover his mouth close to Hanwei's ears.

"Where is that?"

"Oceanside. Marine Corps," Jay explained. Camp Pendleton, situated in Greater San Diego, was one of the largest Marine Corps bases in the United States.

"Marine? Cool. Heard about the Marine Corps there."

"How about you?"

"I live in Rancho Bernardo."

"Cool," Jay responded, while he had no idea where that was. "How far is it?"

"Not far. We can go hang out at my place," Hanwei pursued.

"I didn't drive today. I came with my friends."

"I can drive and give you a ride home later," Hanwei offered.

"Thanks. I'd like to. But I've got training tomorrow morning."

Bummer. Maybe it's just an excuse.

The two guys continued their dance, bringing out their charms, facing each other within inches.

"We can go to my place," Jay said.

"Oceanside? Okay," Hanwei responded. *Oceanside is far. But why not?*

"Yeah. I just need to say bye to my friends." Jay then pulled out his cell phone and sent a text.

"Let's go!" Jay said.

The two squeezed their way out of the club into the street, breathing in the cool, fresh air.

"So, are you Chinese or Japanese?"

"Chinese."

"Cool."

"Have you ever dated a Chinese guy before?"

"Nope." Jay gave an amused smile, while walking in strides. "Asian is like a California thing. First time I met Asians was when I joined the Marine Corps."

While Hanwei drove the two toward the north, Jay tuned the radio to a pop music station. He shook his head along with the tune and moved his lips following the rap song's lyrics, "You can tell me where we are now. Cause my heart aches every time you doubt. Maybe, I'll move the world so one day our love will out…"

"So, where did you grow up?"

"Mississippi."

"Your family still live there?"

"Yeah. My mom. My aunt and cousins."

"How about your dad?"

"Not sure. Maybe somewhere in Tennessee," Jay answered.

Hanwei had yet to learn that it wasn't unusual for black kids to grow up without knowing their father. Some blamed the culture among African American men. But historians and sociologists had traced its cultural root to the slavery era, when black families' stability was under constant threat, where a child's father might have one owner and ended up being sold across different regions, while the child and mother were owned by someone else.

Hanwei took a look at Jay. His right hand touched Jay's left hand. Jay had long and strong fingers. A sense of warmth arose. "Are you comfortable?"

"Yeah. So, what do you do?"

"Engineer, wireless networks."

"Like computers?"

"Yes."

…

After about thirty minutes, a large sign came up on the freeway: "Camp Pendleton NEXT EXIT."

Off the freeway ramp, a gate encompassing all four lanes was revealed under the lights.

"This is the Marine Corps base?"

"Yeah. Follow the car right there."

As their car was approaching the gate, a soldier came up. Jay moved himself closer to the driver side window and showed his military ID. "He's my friend," he said.

Once in, Hanwei followed Jay's instruction, drove to the west side of Freeway 5 via an overpass, and soon reached a large flat area with barracks and open parking spaces.

The two parked in front of a barrack. Jay led Hanwei toward the first floor of the building. The barrack was three stories and looked like a motel with a corridor circling each floor facing the outside. Hanwei followed Jay's lead and entered his unit.

"This is where Marines live?" Hanwei asked.

"Yeah," Jay said, while reaching to the window and closing the blind. The light coming from the parking lot became much softer. The room was quite basic with two full beds, each with an end table, some storage cabinets by the side of a small desk and a TV.

"Where is your roommate?"

"I texted him. He went to his friend's unit."

Jay took off his shirt, revealing his amazingly athletic body under the dim light, every inch young and strong. Hanwei was breathless seeing Jay shirtless in front of him.

Jay slightly closed his eyes and reached his arms to Hanwei signaling him to come along. Hanwei pulled off his t-shirt, too, and revealed his body. Jay was very attracted. He leaned toward Hanwei, pulled his arms, and pressed his lips firmly over Hanwei's. Instantly fueled, Hanwei placed his hands on Jay's back and felt Jay's warm body and heartbeat.

Jay then pushed Hanwei onto his bed and moved his face close to him.

"You are so handsome," Hanwei said.

"Thanks." Jay smiled proudly and looked into Hanwei's eyes. He pulled off his pants and dropped them on the floor. With nothing on his body, his male beauty was now undeniable to Hanwei. While Hanwei was unzipping himself, Jay grabbed him and started passionately kissing him. With the touch of each other's flesh and scent, they became honest with their desires.

Having taken off his pants, Hanwei's arousal was exposed. Jay liked what he saw. He sat back against the headboard, pulled Hanwei to be on top of him and looked at Hanwei with passionate breaths.

"Do you have a condom?" Hanwei asked. "And lube?"

"Yeah." Jay pulled open the end table's drawer.

Hanwei put on the condom. The two immersed into each other's sweat and flesh. To Hanwei, it was like taming an alpha male of adversary. To Jay, it was like placing his trust in his fellow soldier and letting him get the closest to him in soul and flesh. It gave both men immense excitement and gratification.

The two came in an intense moment, watching each other's face in ecstasy..

"Do you like me?" Jay looked at Hanwei, asking with a smile like a big boy, while they sat together at the edge of the bed. That surprised Hanwei.

"Uh… I do." Hanwei hesitated then acknowledged. He held his tone carefully so as not to give away his feelings.

"How old are you?" Hanwei asked.

"Twenty-three."

"You are really young."

"How old are you?" Jay returned the question.

"I am older. Thirty."

"Ah. You look young."

"Thanks. What does the tattoo say?" Hanwei nudged the tattoo characters on Jay's arm.

"It's C.O.R.P., means Marine Corps. Many guys on the base have it."

"What made you want to become a Marine?"

"Nothing. They visited our town, told us it would give us good benefits, salary, and college scholarship. So, I signed up."

"It must be hard for your mom to give you up to the battlefield, right?"

"Nah. Not really. It was my stepmom and my aunt's side relatives in Mississippi I was living with. My real mom is in Rochester, New York State."

"Wow. Your parents left you when you were young?"

"Mom left around thirteen. Dad married my stepmom. They got divorced and then he left when I was fifteen."

Hanwei thought his childhood had been hard. Now he knew it had been tough for Jay too. "Did you guys go serve overseas?

I mean you and your Marine friends," Hanwei asked, while putting his pants and shirt on.

"Dispatched to Iraq twice, on the supply line."

"You cannot be gay in the military, right? Don't ask, don't tell."

"They say so. But no one really cares. I have two friends on the base, Dale and Jordan. They are like boyfriends. When Dale was dispatched in Iraq, Jordan received a letter from him saying he missed him."

"That's sweet."

"My roommate may come back soon. But you can stay if you like," Jay said while he stood up with his enviable naked body reaching for his clothes.

"I'll go home."

"Would you be my boyfriend?" Jay asked.

Hanwei was taken aback. "We can. We can get to know each other more."

"Alright. Text me." Jay smiled.

Hanwei drove off the Marine Corps base that night with his heart full of life.

#

"The Dow dropped 6.19 percent right now... The S&P 500 now down 7.88 percent in one day. Seven percent a day! If you got away with earning seven percent in your portfolio this entire year, I'd say you did pretty well," the financial news reporter talked to the anchor on CNN's Situation Room.

Hanwei and his coworkers stood in front of the big TV screen in their floor's break room, watching anxiously.

"Ali, the Dow drop just went up to 720,... 732 right now!"

Wolf Blitzer, the CNN anchor interrupted Ali Velshi, the financial news reporter.

"1.858 billion shares were sold at a loss today. This is unbelievable. We have not seen numbers like this before. Now it's 738," Ali commented.

Then he continued: "And this is not the story. The story here is that the credit market has seized up. The businesses that employ you may not be able to borrow money. And it could mean that you are going to be put out of work. It is very, very serious. The decision makers in congress are learning the economics lesson at the expense of your jobs and homes."

Lehman Brothers had filed for bankruptcy, Merrill Lynch had been sold barely days before, and A.I.G. had sought a $40 billion lifeline from the Federal Reserve. Now this.

"Oh my God," one of the colleagues gasped. Others were as nervous.

"You know? These people, who own Wall Street, they just want us, the regular people in this country, to work as slaves. They are creating a world that only allows us to have food, water, shelter, and maybe produce some babies as their laborers, without any chance to find joy in life," another colleague said in a solid and bleak tone.

"This is going to be so bad," another commented. "You'd think we escaped one bad fate just recently."

Standing by his colleagues, Hanwei knew he was referring to the brutal company-wide layoff that had taken place two months ago. He was among the few employees spared that day, when hundreds of employees were let go. He recalled seeing his friends streaming out of the stairway humiliated and shocked, seeing his Indian coworkers hugging one another outside the building to say goodbye, knowing they were facing a life-altering situation under U.S. immigration rules. Now, with one of the biggest financial meltdowns in U.S. history happening before their eyes, everyone, including Hanwei, would need to run for cover.

Hanwei walked back, sat at his desk, and tried to clear his mind. He was yet to become a permanent resident in the United States. If this company went down, he would have to find another high-tech job or leave the country within sixty days.

"Hanwei, do you have a minute?" a coworker came and asked.

"Yes?"

"Come here," the coworker gestured, suggesting they find a conference room.

"What's up?" Hanwei asked behind the closed door.

"I heard you're with a black guy. Someone saw that on Halloween night."

It was indeed on Halloween night. Jay and Hanwei joined the costume-filled street party in downtown San Diego. While Hanwei dressed in his fashionable slim cut Armani Exchange t-shirt, Jay was boldly only in his tank top. They bumped into two coworkers of Hanwei's, and Hanwei introduced Jay to them as his date. It was a real shocker.

"Whoa, news spread fast."

"You know, the company may not care too much if your date is the same gender. But dating the same gender *and* a black guy would not be what the corporate wants." The coworker slightly shook his head while talking, expressing his worry for Hanwei.

Hanwei interpreted this situation as his coworker caring about his standing at the high-tech firm. "I will be careful. My date doesn't have to be part of my work life."

#

Friday afternoon, Hanwei left his desk early. After the last layoff, the fancy office behind the glass wall was a lot emptier and demoralizing. Everyone suspected that others were either secretly interviewing for other jobs or were just desperately holding onto the once beloved start-up in the midst of a recession, where restaurants were empty, shops were closed and many home values were under water. Hanwei checked his appearance in the restroom before he got into his car and drove toward Oceanside.

After experiencing the insane traffic on Freeway No. 5, Hanwei arrived at the gate of Marine Corps base.

"What do you come here for?" asked the young black soldier at the gate.

"Visiting Jay Gilmore."

"Who?"

"Jay Gilmore. He lives in the barracks over the bridge."

"You have a driver's license?"

Hanwei showed his driver's license.

"Do you have guns?"

"No."

"You aren't gonna do anything bad, are you?"

"No."

"Okay. Go."

The Marine Corps base was active around dinner time. Jay was standing outside his unit in his tank top and uniform trousers as Hanwei walked up to the barracks.

Inside the unit, Hanwei saw three marines hanging out in

the room. They were young and good looking. A fair skinned Latino guy sitting on a bed looked at Hanwei as he entered the room. A square-jawed nerdy-looking young white guy with glasses was sitting on a stool with a book in his hands. He watched Hanwei curiously. Another tough-looking black guy, skinny and tall, was standing casually by the side of the storage cabinet, watching TV. The news anchor was reporting that Obama was five points ahead of John McCain and commented on the huge crowd he had drawn with his oratory skills on his campaign trail, and how transformational this moment could be while the nation was marred by the devastating 9/11 attacks and the ongoing financial crisis.

"Hi," Hanwei greeted these young soldiers.

The Latino guy nodded his head with a hand gesture. The nerdy white guy just watched Hanwei as if he were seeing an alien. The black guy greeted Hanwei before returning to the TV.

"This is my roommate, Jamie," Jay introduced the Latino guy. "Cedric, my friend," Jay said referring to the skinny black guy, and then about the nerdy guy on the stool, Jay said, "He is new. He is smart. Like you, he got a bachelor's degree." The freshman looked at Jay and Hanwei meekly, with his eyes wide open and hands holding his book.

"Dinner time, are you guys going?" Cedric asked.

"I will come," the freshman answered.

"I'll pass," Jamie said.

"We are going out," Jay told his fellow soldiers.

Cedric and the freshman then left.

"Can I use the bathroom?" Hanwei asked.

Jay pointed to the door at the end of the room. "Through that door."

Behind the door, there was a corridor connecting all units in the back. There were several toilet stalls. Hanwei went into one.

"He is your boy?"

"Yeah."

Hanwei could hear the exchange between Jay and Jamie. Then a very hip song arose from the room.

Hanwei stepped back into the room. Jay had put on a nice soft shirt and blue denim. Jay's outfit made him look rather sensual and macho.

"Nice song. Who is this?"

"Jennifer Hudson. 'Spotlight.'"

"Hey, Jay." Hanwei heard some female soldiers knocking on the window.

"Wassup?" Jay replied.

"Let's have sex together," another female soldier giggled outside while looking into the room.

"Jay is not gay. He is my boyfriend," the girl continued, while another female laughed and picked up from there. "Jay, when can we start making babies?" The two girls then laughed loudly.

"Geez. Go away," Jay said to the girls. "It's Nia and Sarah. Crazy girls," Jay explained, while the two girls walked away giggling.

"You are ready?" Jay asked.

"Yes."

"Have fun," Jamie said in his cool manner.

#

"How are you guys doing this evening?" a beautiful young lady asked Jay and Hanwei, who were seated at a contemporary-style dinner table on the patio facing downtown Oceanside.

"Doing well," Hanwei replied.

"Good," Jay responded with a smile.

"Good! I'm Jane. I'll take care of your table. Would you guys like to get some drinks while checking the menu?"

"I'll have strawberry lemonade," Hanwei said.

"You?" Jane turned to Jay.

"Same." Jay almost hesitated after seeing the price on the menu.

"Sure! I will be back soon. Take your time." Jane left the two by themselves.

While Hanwei decided to go for his favorite dragon roll, edamame, and miso soup, Jay couldn't decide.

"You can order for me," Jay told Hanwei politely.

"Are you sure? Have you had sushi before?"

"Ah. No," Jay laughed.

"Oh. But you chose the sushi place."

"You said it's good. And I've never had it before so I'd like to try."

Growing up, Jay ate burgers, fries, and buffalo wings. While Japanese cuisine was taking over in the United States everywhere, for a black young man raised in a poor neighborhood in Mississippi, sushi was an expensive foreign delicacy.

The two soon got their food. Summer breeze soothed the two under the edge of the patio roof. Fashionable music cheered up Friday night patrons in the restaurant. People in the street were happy for another weekend.

Jay tried using chopsticks with his trembling fingers to pick up a sushi roll. It was difficult. Obviously, what Hanwei had assumed that Americans were familiar with using chopsticks was largely a California phenomenon.

"You can use the fork," Hanwei suggested.

"Ah. Okay." Jay smiled. In this moment, Hanwei saw the tender side of Jay. A marine who was tough on the military base and thuggish in the street could feel a bit out of place in a socially pretentious situation, wanting to blend in to please his friend and be acknowledged well.

The roll instantly fell into pieces when Jay stabbed it with his fork. The two laughed out loud.

"What are your favorite movies?" Hanwei asked.

"*Batman. Fast & Furious.*"

"Yeah. They are nice."

"How about you?" Jay asked.

"*Monster*," Hanwei said.

"The animation movie?"

"I think the animation one is *Monster Inc*. The one I meant has Charlize Theron in it. It's the story of a real-life female serial killer in Florida in the eighties. The movie showed how she grew up from a broken family, and her life went down a misery. She committed multiple horrible crimes while desperately trying to hold onto the love she had with a girl, which she felt was her last chance of a meaningful life."

"Lesbians?"

"Sort of. It was a nice one. I always remember what she narrated in the end, when she was escorted to the jail for her death sentence."

"What did she say?"

"She said, 'Love conquers all. Every cloud has a silver lining. Faith can move mountains. Love will always find a way. Everything happens for a reason. Where there is life, there is hope.' The verdict and the sentence were almost a relief for her and the families of people she murdered."

"We've got to watch it together then." Jay touched Hanwei's knee under the table. Hanwei looked at Jay and saw warmth and sweetness in his eyes.

"Let me show you a place after this," Jay suggested.

#

The road along the coastline at night was dark and quiet, while the two guys drove south on Carlsbad Boulevard. The passing traffic lights and house lights shed orange colors into the car, illuminating the men's faces.

"Slow down. There will be a road forked to the right. Follow that road." Jay looked to the road ahead. "It's right there. Follow the road to the right. And go slowly."

Hanwei followed Jay's instructions. The view on his right-hand side opened up. The road was above a cliff over the beach. He could vaguely see the ocean and the beach hidden in the darkness, embellished with a few orange dots of bonfire.

"Pull to the right. You can park there. It's a lookout spot."

Hanwei drove his car carefully into a graveled area and parked.

"This is your spot?" Hanwei asked.

"Yeah. Some soldiers liked to come here."

Jay touched a button. The car's sunroof slowly opened up. Fresh, cool ocean air came in, humid and mixed with the scent of seaweed. He then turned up the car's stereo volume. Hanwei was playing a Chinese song from Andy Lau and Kelly Chen, "I Didn't Love You the Way I Should".

"You like slow songs," Jay commented.

"Yes. Do you?"

"Yeah."

"Was it dangerous for you to serve in Iraq?" Hanwei asked.

"It was. An IED bomb once exploded when our fleet was transporting supplies. One truck got hit and flipped on its side. The soldiers in that truck were injured. But they survived. We were lucky. Our truck only bumped into the truck in front of us. My nose was cut when my face hit the dashboard. I got some stitches."

"I noticed. Is the scar on your right nostril from that incident?"

"Yes."

"You're looking badass with that scar," Hanwei complimented with a smile.

Jay laughed.

"Thank God you made it home okay."

"What was the song about?" Jay asked.

"The lyrics say, in the night of darkness, they couldn't choose to close their eyes, 'cause they are afraid of each other appearing in their hearts and the sky. In the vast city, they couldn't choose to disappear into the crowd, 'cause regardless if they are alone or with others, they know they have lost each other as they didn't love the way they've vowed."

"That's sweet." Jay reached out and held Hanwei's hand.

Hanwei turned to Jay and looked at his face and into his steady, beautiful eyes. Jay lowered his gaze, leaned gently onto Hanwei's shoulder, and the two of them fell quiet. They looked at the ocean below the cliff, feeling comfort with each other. While the young men and women at the beach enjoyed their Friday night around the bonfire, the stars in the dark sky shone above them.

Hanwei now believed in Jay. It had been many years

since Hanwei saw himself in a relationship. In this foreign country, one of the most surreal feelings Hanwei had was that two people of different races, growing up in two vastly distant locations, raised in completely different cultures and languages, could communicate and see each other as humans, become friends, be attracted to each other, and fall in love.

That night, Hanwei and Jay crashed in the same bed in the barracks. Jamie, the roommate, was cool with it. Jay and Hanwei didn't know where their young love would lead them. Hanwei didn't know if he could secure his job and stay in this country so he could hold onto the love he had discovered with Jay. It didn't matter to him. You live only once. While life was hard and merciless, love was all he hoped for.

#

Jay and Hanwei differed in many ways.

Jay looked like a basketball player. Hanwei looked like a ninja. Jay barely went through high school and served his country as a Marine soldier in tough conditions. Hanwei worked with high-tech engineers behind glass walls. Jay could drink a lot; Hanwei on the other hand could drink one beer and then he was done. Jay had a poor sense of time. Hanwei was organized. Jay liked to hold Hanwei's hand in the mall. But Hanwei was reluctant, feeling embarrassed for his reduced manhood by the side of a taller and tougher-looking black guy.

Yet, they also had a lot in common. They both enjoyed nightclubs, music, and crowds. They both were bold, open minded, and boundary breaking, to some degree rebellious. They both longed for affection yet felt romantically insecure, rooted from a difficult childhood where love was often absent.

Jay eventually met Hanwei's LA Asian gay friends for the first time during their Memorial Day San Diego trip. Hanwei's friends were thrilled that he was seriously dating and was in love with a black man.

That evening, Jay and Hanwei walked along Mission Beach with Hanwei's friends by their hotel. While their friends were enjoying the beautiful view on the sandy beach, taking selfies and watching young lads playing sports, Jay caressed Hanwei's hair with his hand under the sunset.

He asked Hanwei, "Would you like to settle down some day?"

Hanwei answered in a sober voice, "Yes. I would."

The next day, Hanwei's friend blogged on the Internet with a photo. In it, Jay and Hanwei were facing each other on Mission Beach, their silhouettes accompanied by the golden sunset behind them above the ocean. Below the photo, it said, "The boy finally found his true love."

#

"Hey, what's up?" Jay said over the phone.

"I am trying to finish installing the home theater I bought today. It has taken me hours. What about you?"

"In Hillcrest. I was hanging out at my friend's house earlier. Can you come over?"

"Yeah? Sure. Give me half an hour."

...

"Where are you?" Hanwei asked after he parked the car.

"Across the street."

Hanwei saw Jay in his slim dark green t-shirt and brown

multi-pocket khaki pants, who then picked up his pace and walked over to Hanwei's car with a joyful smile.

"Where are we going?" Hanwei rolled down the window.

"Just get out of the car and come with me."

"Thanks, babe." Jay lowered his head and kissed Hanwei on his cheek, after Hanwei stepped out of his car. "Give me a kiss."

Although shy and scared to do this on a busy public street, Hanwei knew he had to match Jay's bolder personality. He raised his head and kissed Jay on his cheek. Jay then pulled Hanwei's hand into his and led them toward the University Avenue around the corner.

As the sun had just set and the streets became dimmer, the University Avenue was illuminated by the golden clouds, orange street-lights, and the lights coming from the nearby restaurants. Hanwei then noticed a crowd of people lined up along the curb. Many were holding protest signs and candle vigils. Among them were men and women, young couples, senior citizens, and families with kids. Many of the signs read, "Vote No on Prop. 8," "Love is Love," "We All Deserve the Freedom to Marry," and "Equality for All." Some signs held by LGBT couples were more personal: "In Love for 34 Years," "You have two wives. I just need one husband," and "Next time, can I vote on your marriage?" A sign held by a man who wore a thick pair of glasses carrying a backpack said, "We Will Eventually Win the Fight." While demonstrators waved their signs, many cars honked in return to give their support.

"Oh, people are protesting in the streets against Prop. 8…" Hanwei gasped.

"Yeah. While you are staying in your pretty little home, people are taking to the streets to fight for our rights," Jay responded with subtle sarcasm and a grin. *Yeah, it is a shame,* Hanwei thought. *Sometimes we may think we are doing good things, but apparently many other everyday people have done a lot more.*

"We can join now. But we'd better get a protest sign."

"Come here, babe," Jay pulled Hanwei toward the thrift shop around the corner. They could see "Vote No on Prop. 8" signs for sale through the window. Jay pulled the store's door handle.

"Ah." Disappointment, the shop was already closed. While the two were thinking where to check for another store, a young straight couple walked by with their bikes, holding a "Vote No on Prop. 8" sign.

"Can we borrow your sign?" Jay asked.

"Sure. You can have it." The man and the woman nodded with a smile.

"Thanks." Jay took the sign from the man. "You two have a nice day." He then turned to Hanwei. "Here. For you."

"You are good," Hanwei commented.

"Welcome. People are nice, you know."

The two walked back to the curb. Hanwei held up the sign and made sure cars driving by and people on the other side could see him.

"What is Proposition 4?" Hanwei asked a woman who was standing next to him holding a sign that read, "No on 4 & 8."

"Just another fascist law they want to pass," the woman responded, "If passed, doctors are required to inform a guardian and wait 48 hours before performing abortions on girls under 18. It sounds all good, and in most cases, it is better for parents to know and protect their daughter from making poor decisions. But in actuality, if a pregnant teenage girl can't go to her parents, she probably has a good reason. And when the girls know doctors will report on them, they might be desperate and force themselves into dangerous back alleys."

"True. I'd think doctors should only be required to take responsibility for those girls' medical treatment."

"This is really just the extreme right wanting to take away women's freedom of their own bodies."

"Yeah. We need to stop that together," Hanwei said, while he looked to the men and women who had taken to the streets. He continued holding up the sign, while Jay stood behind him and hugged him. He could feel Jay's warm arms wrapped around him and supporting him and Jay's kiss on the back of his head.

Mom's Blessing

Jay often stayed at Hanwei's place on weekends. They jogged together and visited the lake nearby. They started thinking about how they would like to settle down and build a good life in this wonderful southern California city.

"If this living room is fifteen feet by fifteen feet, how many square feet is it?" Hanwei asked, passing Jay a plate of fruit over the kitchen island.

"I don't know." Jay, in a thin white long-sleeve sweater, took the plate and shrugged. "Thanks." He took a bite. "Thirty?"

Hanwei laughed. Jay's innocent, slightly defensive look amused him—but it also unsettled him. A question this simple shouldn't have been a mystery for a high school graduate.

"Maybe that's not a great example," Hanwei tried again. "What about this: three times n equals twelve. What's n?"

"I don't know. I didn't learn." Jay was a bit annoyed.

"In high school, they teach you guys how to solve an equation, right?" Hanwei was curious.

"I said I don't know. What? Why are you laughing? You're looking at me like I am dumb."

"No. I am just surprised the school didn't teach you guys those basic concepts." Hanwei tried to make an excuse for Jay while still feeling shocked and sad for how uneven education was in different parts of America.

"They ain't teaching nothing. Maybe you can teach me."

The two finished the fruit.

"It's time for bed," Hanwei suggested. "We still need to get up early tomorrow for hiking around Poway Lake."

"Okay." Just then, Jay's cell phone rang.

"What are you doing?" "Just a second." Jay turned to Hanwei. "Babe, I need to talk to my family in Mississippi. You go to bed first. I'll come soon."

Jay went outside so he didn't disturb Hanwei and took this opportunity to walk around the neighborhood.

"Alright. What's up?" Jay asked.

"Aunt needs to talk to you. About your dad." It was Jay's cousin.

"Then let her talk," Jay said.

"Coco, how are you doing there?" Jay heard his aunt using his childhood nickname.

"I'm doing good. What's up?"

"Bad news. Your mom called me earlier today from Rochester and said your papa passed away. He had a heart attack."

"Papa... died of a heart attack?"

"Yeah."

"God. How did he have a heart attack?!"

"We don't know much. Haven't heard from him for a long time. Not sure if you are in contact with him. Your mom may know more, but she doesn't have your number. You might want to call her tomorrow. I'll give you her number."

After Jay's father went through two divorces and left for Tennessee, Jay mostly lived with his aunt, stepmother and stepfather in their old community. He was rarely in contact with his mother or father.

"What are they gonna do now? Where was he? In Tennessee?"

"I heard so. He had his own people in Tennessee. Your mom said they may hold a funeral for him or something. Call her." Jay's aunt gave him the number.

"Alright. I'll call her now." While Jay hung up with his aunt and started dialing his mom, he could see, in the darkness, two police cars driving into the parking lot with their lights on. He wasn't sure what was going on.

"Police. Drop the gun in your hand!" Jay heard a police officer shouting in his direction. He turned toward the police car and saw two police officers by the side of the first car pointing guns at him. Jay realized what was happening.

"Drop the gun now!"

"No, no—it's just my phone!" Panic and anger surged through him. "I'm just calling my family."

"Do what I said. Turn around. Drop what's in your hand," the officer insisted.

"Okay, sir. I'm putting my phone down. Please… don't shoot." Jay crouched and set the phone on the ground, hands shaking.

"Hands behind your back. Turn around. Walk backwards to me. Slow."

Jay obeyed. When he was close enough, one officer grabbed him and snapped the cuffs on; the other patted him down.

"Sir. I ain't doing nothing. It's just my phone. I am calling my family."

"What are you doing here? Do you live here?"

"I'm staying with my friend. He lives here. I'm in the Marine Corps."

The first officer picked up the object on the ground and turned it in his hand. "It's a phone," he said to his partner.

The second officer pulled an ID from Jay's wallet—a U.S. Marine Corps card with his name on it: JAY R. GILMORE.

"What's going on, sir?" Jay said, trying to stay calm.

"A neighbor reported seeing someone holding a gun in front of the building."

"Geez. Who does that? That's crazy."

"We're good now. We were responding to a 911 call. You can go. The neighbor must've misunderstood."

"So some neighbor's messing with me—and you guys are messing me up," Jay said, still shaking.

"We are just responding to the 911 call. We will talk to the neighbor about it. Sorry for misunderstanding," the police officer reiterated, then pulled out his walkie talkie and spoke to other responders. "Things are good here. We can leave." He then got back into the car and left the scene.

Jay walked into Hanwei's home, still physically shaking. He washed his face to calm himself down. The community was predominantly white with no blacks. *That must be the reason,* he thought. He remembered the first time he'd come over and joked, *God, you brought a Black person to a white neighborhood.*

Jay went upstairs and found Hanwei sleeping soundly in his bed. He pulled back the comforter and snuggled himself under it next to Hanwei. He hugged Hanwei's body from behind, laying his head by the side of this Asian man who was excited to be with him from day one.

#

"What happened? You are not in the Marine Corps anymore?"

Hanwei was very surprised when he found out Jay was now living at his friend's place in Oceanside instead of in the Marine Corps.

"Yes. I quit the military."

"But the Marine Corps takes care of you guys well, right?"

"Yeah. But it's boring. I don't like the strict rules in the military anyway."

"What are you going to do now? The job market's brutal since the financial crisis. Did you think this through?"

Jay shrugged. "You're telling me too late. I already quit."

"Why didn't you tell me earlier?"

"How was I supposed to tell you? I just don't want to be in the military anymore."

"Where are you looking for jobs?"

"My friend is helping me."

"I can check with my friends too. It's just that my friends in San Diego are all engineers. They may not know service sector jobs that you can do."

"I'll find something. Don't worry."

"Come to stay with me," Hanwei said while he knew that was a bold move as there is a big difference between two people dating and two people living together.

"Are you sure?" Jay replied.

"Yes. It will be easier. You can stay here until my mom comes in May. She will stay for a few months. I will introduce you to her. But we need to give her some time to process this and accept us."

"I know. We all need to get Mom's blessing."

"In the meanwhile, you can find a job. You should ask the Marine Corps for help. They should have programs for veterans."

What Jay didn't tell Hanwei, though, was that he hadn't simply "quit." He'd been forced out after someone reported that he was gay and dating men. Don't Ask, Don't Tell — the law that let gay soldiers serve only in silence — had taken the one institution that had given Jay structure, income, and a path forward, and thrown him out for being who he was.

…

Jay frowned at the job application form.

"'Have you ever used illegal drugs?' What kind of question is that?!" He tossed the pen onto the table in irritation. "Not every Black person does drugs!"

"It's just a routine question," Hanwei said gently. "Don't take it too personally."

Jay scanned the next line. "'Do you own a car? License plate number? Driver's license?'" His jaw tightened… "If I already had everything they're asking for, why would I need this job?"

"It is annoying," Hanwei admitted. "Maybe they just want to know if you can reliably get to work."

Jay flipped to another section. "'Last day at the previous job.' This is ridiculous. It's just a clothing-store job. Why does it have to be this hard?!"

Hanwei watched him quietly. He knew the market was tight for everyone—especially for a young Black veteran without a degree, separated from the structure of the military and trying to make it on his own.

"Just fill out what you can," Hanwei encouraged him softly. "Be patient. By the way—did that café ever get back to you about the interview?"

"No. Nothing. They're not gonna call." Jay shook his head with a bitter laugh. "That manager asked what coffee I liked. I don't even drink coffee. I'm there to work. What do they care what I drink? I told her straight up, 'I don't like coffee. I like beer.'"

#

"Mom!" Hanwei spotted Rulan walking into the LAX International Terminal reception hall. Rulan was wearing a beautiful lightweight, rose-colored down coat and pulled a small carry-on with her. Hanwei was excited to receive Rulan for the second time in LAX.

"You've got yourself such a big car?!" Rulan expressed the happiness she had for Hanwei, while Hanwei put her luggage into his car's trunk. Although his car was just an ordinary sedan, Rulan's simple praise and acknowledgment made Hanwei feel dependable and worthy.

When Rulan arrived at the beautiful home her son had bought in San Diego, she was happy for him, as she knew she couldn't help her son with any of this. All she could give him was love, care, and half of her income when he was young and vulnerable without a father.

Hanwei took Rulan on a five-day trip to Hawaii, then to Las Vegas and the Grand Canyon. Watching her laugh over buffets, snap photos beneath neon lights, and clutch the railing at the canyon's edge, he felt fiercely determined to make her life feel worth all she had endured.

On a Friday evening, at the dinner table, Hanwei told Rulan he was dating a guy. It had been a long time in the making.

Since young, Hanwei had heard from his mom that a man and a woman falling in love with each other was the most magical experience in life. While that was what he felt being with Jay, he knew the same blessing wouldn't come easy.

Rulan would prefer life to be simple, as simple as doing what everyone else did, and happiness to be rather easy to reach, as easy as earning an honest living and listening to wisdom from family and friends. This idea her son presented to her was too disruptive and dangerous.

"You call him your boyfriend. Then what does he call you, his girlfriend?"

"He also calls me boyfriend," Hanwei responded cautiously.

"It's hard for me to understand. It should be good enough for you guys to call each other friends or brothers," Rulan spoke to Hanwei. "I don't think you are gay."

Having seen her husband destroy every hope of a happy life for their family, Rulan thought her son was doing what her husband had done, likely from his influence, or perhaps it was only a phase.

"You can meet him, if it is okay for me to bring him over for lunch," Hanwei said.

Having survived a marriage from hell, and now having had a glimpse of a good life her son could bring after all the sacrifices she had made, Rulan felt it wasn't worth blowing things out of proportion, and it wouldn't be horrible to meet the guy his son spent time with and see how they were together.

"Okay," she agreed.

#

It was lunch time on a bright Saturday. The branches of the trees outside the large window of Hanwei's home moved along with the fresh breeze, reflecting the sunshine. They provided comfortable shade to families who were hanging around the community pool and people walking their dogs.

When the door opened, Jay walked in with Hanwei.

"Hi," Jay respectfully greeted the woman in her fifties busy in the kitchen.

"Mom. This is Jay," Hanwei introduced him in Chinese.

"Hi," Rulan greeted back with a soothing smile. Luckily, "hi" had become a universal phrase for people in different languages to greet one another. Rulan had a clear look at this black American, seeing his sturdy athletic frame, dark skin, and prominent facial features.

Soon, lunch was ready. She planned to treat the guest with comfort and compliments. She made Chinese food Hanwei liked and went out of her way preparing some bread and fried eggs she thought an American might like.

The three sat down at the lunch table and quietly started their meal. The moment felt surreal to all three. None of them knew if they would be received well by the others or how they should feel about themselves. Rulan tried to be a loving mother, carrying her facial expressions and body language with gentleness. Jay tried to behave as a respectful young man, curbing his free spirit and street vibe. Hanwei tried to be the man of the house, sensing the thoughts of his mom and his lover, adding fluidity to their conversation.

"Try this." Rulan presented one of the dishes to Jay. "Hanwei, ask him to try."

Hanwei hurriedly translated. Jay then tried it. After that, there was some exchange between Jay and Hanwei that Rulan couldn't understand.

"It tastes very good, Jay said." Hanwei told Rulan. Rulan could see Jay's smile.

"Your mom looks young," Jay said.

"Mom. Jay thinks you look young at your age," Hanwei

translated.

Rulan smiled, then laughed with Hanwei so she would be sure Jay could tell her delight from his compliment.

Even though they sat right by each other, every conversation seemed to have a long delay. It was like two people living on opposite sides of the Pacific Ocean trying to understand each other when talking over a choppy cell phone call in the early 2000s. Hanwei's translation helped, but he looked labored and was sometimes ineffective.

After they finished lunch, Rulan insisted she would clean up and let Jay and her son watch TV. While Hanwei and Jay sat down on the couch to watch TV, reality started to sink in for Rulan. *Is this the life for me from now on? Will my family in China find out? Will Hanwei be okay down the road? Is this a mistake of my son that only I can see and help? Is my life becoming once again what it was when living with Gaoming?*

"I am going to go have a nap upstairs," Jay said, while Rulan appeared to be reading a book in her chair.

"I will have a rest too." Hanwei followed Jay to the upstairs bedroom.

The two young men laid down in the bed. Consciousness soon blurred away as the food coma induced them into sleep.

"Hanwei! Hey!! Hanwei!!!" Hanwei heard someone calling in his dream. He always had vivid dreams, sometimes interesting, sometimes very strange, sometimes intense, even horrifying. *Was that Mom talking?* He tried to figure out what was happening in his dream.

"Hanwei! You really will cause your mom to die in despair!" Hanwei woke up. He just realized what he thought he heard in the dream was real. His mom was yelling downstairs in agony. He was not sure whether it was self-talk or directed toward him. He tried to get up.

"Damn!" He heard his mom curse hysterically in distress. He jumped out of bed and rushed downstairs. He didn't want anything bad to happen to his mom.

Then… *Bang!* The door was slammed. When Hanwei reached the downstairs living room, Mom was gone.

"What happened? Where is your mom?" Jay asked, following Hanwei downstairs.

"She was yelling at me and then left. She must be mad because of us."

"But we didn't do anything." Jay was shocked.

"Quick! We gotta go. I will send you to your place first, then come back and check."

"Wow!" Jay couldn't believe this was happening.

"Gosh. I didn't expect this to happen," Hanwei said while leading Jay out to the parking lot hastily.

Jay followed Hanwei and jumped into the car. Hanwei quickly backed his car out of his parking spot.

"It's over then! Your mom doesn't love you!" Jay commented anxiously knowing this was a big problem.

"No. She loves me," Hanwei steered the car toward the road.

"No. If she loves you, she wouldn't yell at you like that."

"There are many things that people in her generation aren't aware of and do not understand. But they do love their children. And it is hard for them."

"So, what are you gonna do? What about us?" Jay raised his voice while they got on the freeway.

"Maybe I couldn't do it in this life. If I have to, I will do it for her, by marrying a woman and having children. I can only give freedom and happiness to the next generation."

"So, you are gonna give up? How about your LA friends?

They are your family too." Jay questioned fiercely.

Hanwei didn't answer. While cars on the road passed by his car, Mom's image and anguished voice flashed in his mind.

They eventually reached Jay's place, an apartment in a ghetto area, where Jay rented with other guys.

"Hanwei, you gotta live a life that makes you happy," Jay said before he stepped out of the car. "We only live once."

...

Back at home, Rulan had returned heartbroken. Her tears had run dry. She told herself that a mother was supposed to love her children. If one day she had to die, she had to let her son live.

As Hanwei drove home, he watched the community for signs of his mom. After parking, he approached his house, opened the door, and saw his mom was home, safe and quiet, watching TV. She was calm, or at least pretending to be. She was warming water in the microwave for a drink. It was a huge relief.

"Mom. Are you okay? I am sorry. I assure you we weren't doing anything in the bedroom. I am really worried about you. You can talk to me," Hanwei pleaded in a soft tone.

Rulan got up from the sofa, grabbed the glass of water from the microwave, returned to the center of the living room, and faced the window outside. "I am okay." She took a sip of the water, and then held the glass with both hands.

"Hanwei, you are wandering at the edge of a cliff, seeking suicide. Mom does not know how to protect you from the abyss. And Mom won't be able to die in peace, knowing that your life is hanging in the balance at the edge of society," Rulan said seriously and calmly.

"Mom, I will protect myself and I will protect you. I have

friends here. I will be a strong man," Hanwei assured Rulan.

Love Can't Be Our Only Reason

While Rulan was living with Hanwei, Jay struggled with the unforgiving civilian life outside the military.

He worked briefly for GAP stocking clothes, but was fired after missing a couple of shifts from hangovers with his buddies. He later got pulled into a couple of "easy money" scams—exactly the sort of schemes Hanwei had warned him about.

His savings were nearly gone. His relatives had stopped sending money.

Hanwei would sometimes visit him with toiletries or groceries, and eventually broke his own principles by giving Jay money outright. He blamed himself for it; since childhood, he'd been taught you never hand out cash to friends who should be able to stand on their own.

This slow erosion devoured Jay's confidence.

A man who had once carried himself with the pride of a United States Marine now found himself relying on the help of a boyfriend from a developing country just to keep a roof over his head and food on the table.

Their meetings grew fewer. Their days apart grew longer.

It was a weekday evening. Hanwei's message to Jay was met

with no reply. He called Jay, but no one answered or returned the call for hours. It was never like that.

Soon, it was midnight. Hanwei texted Jay before he went to bed, "Text me when you get a chance. Let me know if you are okay."

…

In the middle of the night, Hanwei's cell phone buzzed. He woke up in a daze. The number was not in his phone's contacts and he missed it twice. Suddenly, he realized it could be Jay. He dialed back.

"Hello." It was Jay's voice. Hanwei could feel his tiredness.

"Jay? Is this your other number?"

"Yeah. I called using Google on my laptop."

"What happened? Are you okay? I texted you and called you earlier, but you didn't reply."

Hanwei heard Jay stifle a cry on the other end.

"I did something bad." Jay's voice was trembling.

"Tell me."

"I prostituted myself," Jay said. "I need money. I went to the street, El Cajon Boulevard. A client picked me up."

Upon hearing this, Hanwei could see how bad things had gotten for Jay.

"I am sorry," Jay sobbed.

"It's okay. I'm here. At least you're safe."

"I lost my cell phone at the client's place. I only realized that after the client dropped me off. I couldn't call you. I walked two hours to get back home."

"Oh my gosh. Don't worry too much. We can get another phone for you."

"I don't know who else to talk to. I only have you," Jay cried.

"Jay, I love you. I will always love you," Hanwei said. "I will come see you this weekend, okay?"

#

As Hanwei drove toward Jay's place, advice from his friends filtered through his mind.

You are going to feed him for the rest of his life. Are you crazy? Can he at least try working in McDonald's?

You can only give something to someone who would do the same if the situation was reversed. Do you know if he is that type of person?

Once you grow old, you think he will be able to take care of you? You cannot eat love for lunch.

Others were kinder.

If you love him, buy him a used car. Without a car, it's hard for him to get a job. It doesn't cost that much. You can afford a three-thousand-dollar used car for him. It will help him and help your relationship too.

Some were harsher.

What more do you want? It's not easy being gay. Many don't even have boyfriends, let alone a boyfriend as handsome as Jay. You want someone hot, and at the same time smart and competent? You are not that hot yourself.

Then there were Jay's words over the phone when their relationship was faltering. "Hanwei, I love you and you love me so we can be together forever."

…

The guys living in this poor neighborhood rarely bothered to lock the door, so Hanwei walked right in.

"Hey, Jay." Hanwei said, seeing Jay on a stool at his computer, immersing himself in a sad R&B song.

"Hey." Jay didn't turn around.

"I got groceries for you."

"Thanks," Jay responded. "I know, I am so broke, right?"

"Are you doing okay?"

"I'm alright. I know you don't want me anymore."

Hanwei went to Jay's side and sat on the mattress on the floor.

"It's not like that. I love you."

Jay stood up, ushered himself in front of Hanwei, grabbed Hanwei's arms, held him down onto the bed, looked at Hanwei with his whole life in his eyes, and said, "Then, what is it?" He started pulling off Hanwei's pants. "Is the sex not good enough?! You wanted me to be rougher, huh?!" He tried pulling off Hanwei's shirt and pants, forcing himself onto Hanwei.

"No. It's not that!" Hanwei looked into Jay's eyes.

"It's because I am dirt poor," Jay gave his own answer. Hanwei could see Jay's pride was drained. "Hanwei, but I don't love you for your money."

"No. I want you to make responsible choices for yourself." Pushed, Hanwei said what he had always felt.

"It's okay, Hanwei. You don't have to come. When push comes to shove, I gotta do what I gotta do."

"You can look for a waiter's job or even a janitor's job, right? At least I would see, when I need you, you'd try to give it all."

"Giving me a fucking million dollars, I am not gonna do a janitor's job," Jay shot back. "My friend, Cory, introduced me to a porn studio. Maybe I will be a good porn actor."

"Porn? There is nothing wrong with sex work. But it's not great for the long run. Think about the unlimited supply of young guys who can replace you and the stigma you'd face later when you need a different job. Are you sure you want to do that?"

"Well, you also said there is an unlimited supply of nerds who can replace you. And the only way to make a lot of money is to have your own business. Remember?"

"Okay, you are right. But what about us? Our lives will be so different. You think we can manage?"

"Hanwei, I am an American. You tell me something once, that's okay. You tell me twice and I still don't listen, you stop!"

Hearing that, Hanwei knew it might be time to leave.

He left Jay's place, not sure if he was a good enough person himself or if he had tried hard enough. He recalled the day he drove Jay all the way to Los Angeles for a job interview so life could give Jay another chance. He recalled the night he bailed Jay out of jail when he got arrested with his friends for reckless driving. He recalled those days he took a tutoring job to earn some extra money to help support Jay better, and then those days of endless arguments that turned a once sweet and warm relationship into a gut-wrenching pain.

#

"Hi guys, merry Christmas." Hanwei found his friends at their dining table. It was close to Christmas Day. Hanwei and his Chinese friends came to this all-you-can-eat hot pot restaurant to celebrate the holiday.

"Merry Christmas," his friends greeted back.

"What's up?" Hanwei asked, while he read the faces of everyone, "Is everything alright?"

"Jay isn't coming?" Ming asked.

"No," Hanwei exhaled. "We may be breaking up."

"I know! Jay called me at least ten times today. Every time I picked up, he hung up on me. I couldn't even make any of my own phone calls." Ming stared at Hanwei. "You guys fight and somehow I get involved." Their other friends all looked at Hanwei.

"Gosh. He called me at least twenty times earlier. He either hung up on me immediately or gave me complete silence." Hanwei shook his head. "I'm sorry. I will ask him to stop."

"Don't call him now. At least he stopped already," Ming said.

"Right. You should enjoy dinner with us and let us cheer you up," another friend added.

At the dinner table, Hanwei focused on his friends. In front of the delicious food and familiar faces, the get-together celebrating an important holiday made them feel as if they had a home and family in their adoptive country.

Zzz..., Hanwei's phone buzzed. He checked the screen. It was Jay, again.

"Hi, Jay." Hanwei picked up.

"What's up?" Jay spoke in a provocative tone.

"What were you doing earlier?"

"What do you mean?"

"Don't do this, Jay. Ming wasn't bothering you." Hanwei got up from his chair and went for outside.

"Sorry. I bothered your real boyfriend—Ming."

"Come on, Jay. You know this is ridiculous. If you want to talk, we can. It's a holiday. I want you to have a good time too."

"Good time? I had a good time. I went with Cory to do a private porn show for some rich old man in Rancho Bernardo. We got paid for fucking each other in front of him and letting him touch us all over in the middle of it."

"I'm not sure about this, Jay. I don't want you to get into trouble."

"But I made my own money, right? So, you don't have to worry about me."

"I love you. That's why I am worried."

"No, no, no. I loved you. I watched Chinese movies with you. I ate Chinese noodle with you. I hung out with your Chinese friends. I cleaned your house before your mom came. Maybe you don't really love me, Hanwei. Maybe you just want sex!"

"No! I love you. What if those people use drugs around you? What if you guys slip and forget to use a condom? What if you get arrested?!"

"Stop! Stop telling me what to do! A little yellow man trying to tell me what to do."

"What?! Don't do that, Jay."

"I did it! I did it! I just did it!!" Jay yelled.

Jay hung up. Hanwei stood there shaking, holding his fragile emotions together. How he wished he could amend the love they had had. But he also knew, unless he was free from all the other visions, convictions, and commitments he had for his life, he might not have the strength to live the dream Jay and he once had for each other.

Then the phone rang again. Hanwei picked up again.

"I am gonna ruin your life! I am gonna call your job!"

"Why are you doing this to me? I loved you too. I drove you all the way to Los Angeles for your job interview. I took you to the VA hospital for your surgery. I bought you a new phone and food so that you could get back on your own feet."

"Then why can't you accept me?!"

"Maybe love can't be the only reason for people to live

together," Hanwei answered in disappointment, a disappointment in Jay, himself, and life in general.

"Just stop calling me, Hanwei. You have a nice life." Jay hung up.

Hanwei returned to the dining table. Seeing his friends, he cried.

"It's probably just the holiday. Every lover's emotions run high on holidays," a friend commented. "Don't think too much. Maybe life has a plan for both of you. Maybe one day, you two will meet again, and that's when you two will never separate."

#

On Christmas night, Hanwei drove to Jay's place. In his passenger seat, there was an envelope.

As he was about to knock on the door, he heard another man talking behind the door, then came the familiar voice of Jay. Their conversations were calm and close.

I guess things have changed, Hanwei now knew. He stopped at Jay's bedroom's door. *At least Jay is okay, or at least he has someone with him.*

Hanwei went downstairs, took out a pen, and wrote on the envelope from his car. "Jay, Merry Christmas. Hanwei." Then he slipped the envelope into the apartment's mailbox. In it was six hundred dollars.

The next day, Hanwei received a text from Jay, "Hanwei, thank you. Sorry for everything. I still love you."

The remaining days before Rulan headed back to China were peaceful. Hanwei often walked with her and talked to her as an ally. As always, she reminded Hanwei that living was mostly about security and moments of comfort, not necessarily romance or excitement. "Even if you have a wife and a child, your life might not be as fulfilling in this foreign country. Your relatives all think, with your PhD degree in the U.S. and your friends and classmates in China, you would have a richer and more successful life back home."

#

Hanwei was on a bus on a freeway. He and his black friends occupied several seats on the empty bus. Some of them stood and some sat as they chatted with one another. Some held onto the handrail as they enjoyed the vast city scene outside the window. Hanwei was in the middle of them, listening to their conversation, happy that he was around his friends on the road trip to the big city he loved.

Suddenly, he realized Jay was nowhere to be seen on the bus. He also couldn't recall when he had seen Jay last. *Where is Jay? If I don't know where he is, I may never be able to find him again.*

"Have you guys seen Jay?! Do you know where Jay is?" Hanwei anxiously asked. His friends seemed to be oblivious to anyone missing; they smiled and continued with their cheerful chat.

Panic arose in Hanwei. He thought to himself that this was not real. He had always been with Jay, but now he was alone. Yet, strangely, he recalled Jay was in love with him and they were happy together.

"Where is Jay?!" he yelled.

All of a sudden, he realized it was all a dream.

With a pounding heart and racing pulse, he woke to find himself in his own bed. He felt feverish and shaken. *It was just a horrible dream. The sadness, and that Jay is gone are all a bad dream.*

He looked toward the end of his bed. Gray sky showed through the balcony outside—it was almost dawn. Looking around his bed, he could see his high school roommates still sleeping in their own bunks in the dorm. He felt a bit confused. *Is Jay somewhere in the building? Is he in another dorm room? Is Jay actually my classmate? Could someone know something and tell me whether Jay's around?*

"Hey, Feng." He tried to wake up his roommate on the other side of the room. Feng did not budge. Looking around, he realized all of his roommates seemed not to notice him. Panic rose; if this was high school again, then Jay couldn't exist.

Hanwei groaned loudly in agony. He must go back to the world he had come from, to reality.

All of a sudden, he woke up in shock. He found himself in his bed in his San Diego home in the middle of the night. He felt dizzy and his ears were humming. He was sweating all over. He just realized he had a horrible double-level nightmare. Jay and he had broken up half a year ago. He had not been able to get in touch with Jay the last three months, not by phone, email, or Facebook. This was now his reality. Hanwei wept loudly in his bed, wishing it was all just a dream.

That day, Hanwei had accepted an offer for a new job. He would leave San Diego for Silicon Valley, where more high-tech career opportunities existed.

Grown Up

In an era dominated by information technology and multinational capitalism, Silicon Valley had become the epicenter of the brave new world. It attracted scientists, engineers, and entrepreneurs from all over the world.

Before his relocation, Silicon Valley had been just another California town to Hanwei, with the extra benefit of offering many more high-tech job opportunities. But after he moved in, he soon noticed the difference.

Driving along Freeway 101, the ubiquitous presence of high-tech was visible on billboard signs. An advertisement for cloud data service promoted itself by taking a jab at two of the most popular cloud storage companies: "Your file should be neither dropped nor boxed." An advertisement for high-tech hiring had a simple line: "{first 10-digit prime in e}.com." Only if one could figure out the answer to that math problem, which would lead to another brain-frying puzzle on the website, would he arrive at a Google webpage that solicited resumes from the lucky few. To Hanwei, it was a complete cultural departure from Los Angeles, where movie posters and injury-lawyer ads ruled every corner.

The weekend scenes were also different. While Los Angeles' restaurants and bars were filled with street smarts, Silicon

Valley's restaurants were filled with book smarts. Once while dining in a restaurant, Hanwei noticed the diners at the table to his left were talking about genomics, and the diners at the table to his right were talking about SpaceX rockets; the rest seemed to be focused on comparing company stocks and experiences they'd had with their corporate rank and file. That was not a relaxed weekend to Hanwei, who was used to Southern California weekends at the beach with friends, ice cream and coffee in hand, drifting among vibrant crowds and pop-culture gossip.

Then there was the situation in Bay Area communities that concerned Hanwei the most: a scene of gentrification and self-segregation.

Technology had made life easier everywhere and capitalism had connected supply and demand across continents—but together they'd also accelerated the concentration of wealth into fewer companies and people, much of it pooling in Silicon Valley. Many locals were outbid in home prices, food cost, and educational resources. While many high-tech workers gladly referred to Silicon Valley as the "Center of the Universe," the locals called it the "Center of the Craziness." As a result, many of them chose to leave, contributing to a great exodus.

Making the matter more complicated, high-tech jobs were mostly done by recently arrived immigrants from India, China, and the Mid-East. They had little time to assimilate into American culture. Locals couldn't help them either. Black communities in Oakland mostly still operated within their own local economy and Latinos occupied the service sector, so different groups didn't get much chance to mingle. They tended to live and speak among their own, creating a de facto segregation in a digital age. That was not what

Hanwei was used to experiencing in Los Angeles where people of different backgrounds worked together in much more accessible professions, hung out, and blended among one another.

Although Hanwei had benefited from the tech boom, the inequality and segregation didn't inspire him. If he'd only wanted money and power, as his mother often said, he might have been better off going back to China.

#

When people are young, they feel invincible. Friends are easier to find and doors open easier. Once they get older, they tend to find themselves much less welcome, especially for gay men in the dating pool. While gay men often fixate on physical appearance and fitness, as they said in WeHo, it wouldn't work for a number ten looking for an eleven—especially when the eleven virtually didn't exist.

Now in his mid-thirties, although some still found him having a desirable look, Hanwei found picking up guys in nightclubs increasingly difficult. Since he last heard from Jay more than a year ago, hardly anyone or anything could bring back the joy Jay and Xiong had brought him.

...

One Friday evening, as Hanwei was driving towards Cupertino to meet friends for dinner, looking for a nice time during some lonely days, his phone rang.

"Mom. What are you up to?"

"Hanwei, I didn't want to bother you, but some trouble finds us at home." Rulan sounded troubled and tense.

"What is it?"

"Your father had a stroke. It happened yesterday. The factory called me, as I was the only family member they could find."

"What?! Was it really bad? Where is he?" Hanwei wasn't emotionally connected to his father, but he knew he had to make sure his father's situation was properly managed, especially when his mother was being burdened.

"He's been in the hospital since yesterday. I just finished my breakfast. I am about to go to the hospital again to check on him."

"How did it happen? What did the doctor say?"

"Neighbors first heard him calling for help. When they found him, he was shaky, had difficulty speaking properly, and had peed on the floor. Poor him." Rulan sighed.

"Is his mind still sound? Can he communicate?"

"He talks as erratically as usual. But he can talk, just a bit mumbled. And he seems to be still strong. They did an MRI on him and said he had a minor stroke. The doctor is giving him some kind of IV injection to see if his condition will improve. I need to go now."

"Okay. But don't rush. I am worried about you handling these things by yourself. Ask relatives to help you. Mom, I don't want you to get into any accident. Call me later when you get a chance."

"I know. But what else can I do?" Rulan paused for a second. "He is the father of my son. The factory representative even apologized to me when asking me to step up, as they know your father and I were divorced a long time ago."

#

The dinner table conversations carried out by Hanwei's friends ranged from the big sign-on bonus to the condo they just bought and put on Airbnb, and so on. The topics didn't excite Hanwei, but he enjoyed the brief comfort of their company.

Just as Hanwei was about to get back into his car and drive home, he noticed he had a missed call.

"Hanwei, this is Jay. If you can, please give me a call back."

He didn't wait for one second to dial back the unknown number.

"Hello?" Jay's voice came through.

"Hey, Jay."

"Ah, Hanwei."

"Where have you been? It's been more than a year. Your old number doesn't work." Hanwei's heart was pounding.

"I was just released from jail. I don't have my old phone number anymore."

"You just got out of jail?!"

"Yeah. Was in and out of jail for several months."

"What happened? Are you okay?"

"I'm okay. I was arrested for possession of marijuana, then got out on probation. But after a couple of months, I was put back in jail for threatening the probation officer during an argument. But I am okay now."

"Geez. Were you harmed in jail?"

"No. I kept a low profile. Some guys got jumped inside. I'm okay. The police injured my wrist during my arrest, but it feels a lot better now. It was scary, though, when the police pointed a gun to my head during the raid."

"Whoa. I'm sorry. Where are you now?"

"I am in San Diego. But I plan to leave for New York,

Rochester. My mom lives there."

"Can you stay in California?"

"Nah. It won't work out. Better stay with my family. My mom needs me too."

Hanwei used to tell himself, once he had better financial security, he would live with Jay, ignore their differences, and support each other. Now he felt that he had overestimated his audacity, as he wasn't sure if he had the capacity to live with Jay, now an ex-con and a felon who had grown into his own man.

"Where are you?" Jay asked.

"I am in the Bay Area now."

"Ah. I heard it's nice up there. Not sure if you can, but can I see you before I leave?"

"Of course. I will find a weekend to fly over." Hanwei didn't hesitate.

#

Getting back home, Hanwei dropped his backpack on the floor and turned on the TV. The news channel was still showing the video of the celebrations that broke out in every major city in America the day after the Supreme Court ruled to recognize marriage of same-sex couples on the same terms and conditions as marriage of opposite-sex couples in all fifty states.

Jubilant crowds were expressing their overwhelming happiness, waving rainbow flags and signs, honking horns, pumping their fists in front of news cameras in joyful excitement, and hugging one another in tears. The helicopter video feed showed the White House joining the triumph of the landmark civil rights case as it covered the entire building in rainbow-colored lights. There were people everywhere outside the White House, the United States capitol, the Lincoln Memorial, and the Supreme Court. Signs waved by people read, "Marry Who You Love," "Liberty and Justice for All," and then a very special one held by an exultant boy, "I Love My Gay Dads."

That's real human progress, Hanwei thought to himself. *What an exoneration for so many ordinary people. What a triumphant moment for those who have been fighting for human rights. What a proud day for the human race.*

Hanwei lowered the TV volume and called Rulan.

"Mom, how are things in the hospital?"

"Hey, Hanwei. Your father's short-term condition has improved. The doctor said the stroke caused some brain injury, but he should be able to recover and continue with his everyday routines. He will stay in hospital for a few more days. If no serious condition comes up, they can let him go home."

"Thank God. How are you doing? I hope you aren't too troubled there."

"I am doing okay. Let me tell you something," Rulan said as she changed her tone.

"There is a young man who came to help him. His name is Shiquan. When the factory representative found your dad, Shiquan also arrived. You know your dad's 'hobby' is not exactly a secret in the factory. The factory official couldn't trust Shiquan. What if he had stolen your father's money and property? So they gave me your father's bank card and ID card and issued an official letter that grants me temporary guardianship."

"Does the young man seem trustworthy?"

"He seems to be a nice and quiet guy. When we took the taxi to the hospital, I noticed your dad and Shiquan holding each other's hand tightly. The way they looked at each other seemed to be quite affectionate. Your dad is almost seventy. Shiquan said he is thirty-seven. I don't know how they found each other and get along like that."

"It's good for him though."

"And your dad was so erratic in the hospital. Yesterday, when he woke up intermittently from the hospital bed after Shiquan left, he howled in agony and insisted on leaving. The nurses tried hard to convince him to stay. Last night, the IV injection of medication seems to have made him feel a lot better. At one point, he took out the injection needle and monitor sensors by himself and tried to escape. It was so startling. You know he is strong. I wasn't able to stop him. Several nurses rushed over to calm him down," Rulan sighed. "Maybe your father always felt he was trapped in his life. When we were together, he wanted to escape the town. Now sick in bed, he wants to escape the hospital."

"Geez. It must be so hard for you to deal with the situation." Hanwei could feel the chaos and tension in his mother's words.

"Your father did bad things to you and me, and others. He was detestable. But in a way, he was also pitiful." Rulan exhaled with a deep breath.

"I know."

"Your father repeatedly asked, 'Where is Shiquan?' last night. We told him, 'Shiquan will come back tomorrow.' It helped him calm down. And you know Shiquan indeed came back this morning. He brought a pot of chicken soup with chicken meat in it, and he fed your father one sip at a time. You could see how warm your father was to him from his eyes.

The nurses were very moved and rooted for them, praising Shiquan for treating your father like a son does while his real son is in America and not by his side, admiring their loving friendship. Of course, they probably couldn't tell what was really going on between your father and Shiquan. If they knew, they may think completely differently."

"I am glad for him. It's very nice of Shiquan."

"Your father said he would leave all his money and legacy to Shiquan after he passes away. I am not sure what you think of that though."

"I think that's a sensible thing. He and I don't have much of a relationship. After he got back, I gave him some money. But that's it."

"I agree. Actually, I found your father's account doesn't have much money left. It is also now all being used to pay the hospital bill. I transferred some money from my account to his to make sure he won't run out of money."

"Mom, I will transfer money to you. You shouldn't put this burden on yourself. If the medical treatment costs more, I'll send you more."

"I don't need your money, Hanwei. You take care of yourself first. Your father said he would go with Shiquan to his village after this. Well, that's if Shiquan's parents would allow it. But I really doubt that. Though Shiquan did acknowledge that he would be okay to take your father to his place; there are nurses asking him to not be silly and to think about how he would be able to take care of an old man like this later on. So after this, your dad either needs to go to his place or go to a senior home."

"Yeah. It's up to them. I can call Shiquan later to see if they need something in case Dad goes to his place. If they do, I can send some money to Dad. How much he wants to share with Shiquan would be just between them."

"You can? I can give you Shiquan's number. But don't commit yet. You also need to make sure Shiquan doesn't look at you like a cash cow and try to use your father for it," Rulan said. "Okay. It's late for you. Try go to sleep. Don't worry too much."

#

In an older block of Chongqing's city center, a small neighborhood service office stood on a narrow street. Inside, a middle-aged clerk chatted with the young woman at the next desk.

"Those rich kids who grew up in villas—they never set foot in places like this," the clerk said, sipping his tea. "Ask them to come here and buy groceries? They wouldn't even know where the nearest supermarket is. Either their housekeepers keep everything stocked, or they only shop at those fancy markets in the wealthy districts."

"That's true," the young woman replied while sorting through several forms. "The rich are richer than ever, and the poor are struggling." As she lifted her head toward the open doorway, she noticed an elderly man slowly approaching—unsteady, bewildered, as if he had lost his way.

"Hello, sir. Can I help you?" She stepped outside to meet him.

The old man's hair was short and gray, his face exhausted and slack around the mouth, the wrinkles hanging downward. Behind his glasses, his eyes looked anxious, hollow, and lost. His short-sleeved shirt and shorts were clean and presentable, yet he looked worn down—fragile, despite the remnants of a once-sturdy frame.

"Excuse me… is this the reception for the shelter?" he asked in clear, formal Mandarin.

…

The young woman exchanged a quick glance with her colleague, then lowered her voice. "He says he's from the factory in Luoqi. Can you see if we can reach anyone there? If they confirm who he is, maybe someone from the factory can come pick him up."

Turning back to the man, she asked gently, "Sir, where is your family? Do you have any relatives we can call?"

"I have no family…" The old man suddenly burst into tears, crying like a child.

"How did you end up outside like this? What is your work unit?" she asked softly.

"I have no relatives here," the old man replied. "I came from Suzhou. A kind young man from the countryside took me in for a while. But his parents were harsh to him. I was only making life harder for him. I couldn't bear to burden him, so… I left."

"Why didn't he take you home before he left?" the young woman pressed gently.

"He went out of town for work these past few days. While he was gone, his parents forced me out. They said their son had been in a car accident years ago and wasn't right in the head anymore… and that I must have tricked him into keeping me." His voice trembled.

Another staff member approached and whispered to the young woman, "The Luoqi factory confirmed he's one of theirs. They said he used to live alone, and he recently had a medical episode—nearly didn't survive it. Ask him whether he wants their people to take him back to town, or if he prefers going to a senior care facility. At least there, someone will keep an eye on him."

#

One weekend, as promised, Hanwei flew to San Diego to meet Jay in Oceanside. He saw Jay again as he had seen him in the past—walking across the street toward him with a kid-like smile and burst of energy and playing basketball at the beach park.

Before parting ways, they sat in the car. Hanwei put five hundred dollars he had prepared earlier into Jay's hand, and then added all the dollar bills he could find in his wallet. "Please take good care of yourself," he said.

"Yeah, I will," Jay nodded. After pausing for a second, he took out a ring from his pocket and put it into Hanwei's hand. Hanwei looked at Jay with eyes wide open, speechless.

"Keep it for me," Jay lowered his eyes and said. "I'll see you later, 'cause you'll always be my babe."

They held each other one last time. Then Jay stepped out of the car. Hanwei watched him walk away until he disappeared. He sat there, the ring still warm in his palm, unable to move, weighted by regret, and yet knowing, somewhere deep down, that some things, no matter how much you love someone, are simply beyond you.

...

Before flying back to Silicon Valley, Hanwei drove to Los Angeles to see his Chinese gay friends, the only "family" he had in America. At the dinner table, those familiar faces made him feel secure, their jokes made him laugh, and the stories they told breathed life into his aging soul.

That night, Hanwei revisited his familiar gay bar. He saw, under flickering lights, a young, handsome Mid-Eastern man with a lightly-haired, ripped body, wearing only his underwear as he moved his body along with the music on the go-go boy bar. His content and calm demeanor touched Hanwei.

Hanwei walked up to him and pushed a dollar bill through the slit of the man's underwear. The young man squatted down and lowered his head to reach Hanwei.

"Thank you. What is your name?"

"You're welcome. I am Hanwei. You are remarkably handsome."

"Thank you." The young man looked into Hanwei's eyes.

"Are you from the Middle East?"

"Israel. A Palestinian from Israel."

"Cool. You made everyone happier in this place tonight."

"Thank you. I am Iman." The young man kissed Hanwei on his cheek.

"Thanks. For real. You did. It is not only about your sexual appeal. It is your spirit. People like you make the world better for many and show us what a better place it should be."

The young man moved back to his position and looked across the bar with a bright smile. He was the gladiator of the night, giving his audience something to admire.

There is something for everyone in this place, Hanwei thought to himself, *be it a Palestinian or a Chinese, be it a go-go boy or an engineer, be it a straight man or a transgender, be it an introvert or a socialite, and that is how things should have always been.*

#

Returning to his small apartment in Silicon Valley, Hanwei found life growing unbearably heavy. He felt like an addict deprived of his fix—unable to recover even a shadow of the happiness he once knew. Television no longer entertained him; weekends offered no motivation for learning or renewal. His dates had increasingly devolved into one-night stands, leaving him feeling less like a human being and more like a piece of flesh passing through strangers' hands.

Night after night, he woke from tangled, suffocating nightmares, then lay awake for hours unable to pull himself back together.

Work was the one place that still held him together. In the rhythm of code and problem-solving, among colleagues who needed his input, he could still pass for someone with worth.

In the weekly calls with Rulan, he kept his voice steady and cheerful, hiding the guilt that gnawed at him—the guilt of not being the son she deserved. Only by pretending could he let her keep the fragile peace she now lived with.

To reassure himself he still had people in his life, he kept a private list of cherished friends on his computer. One day, while sifting through old folders, he stumbled upon a forgotten audio file. He faintly recalled it was from one of Gaoming's emails. Gaoming had said the file was a recording from the time he left home. Back then, his father had sent rambling messages from Guizhou—often so incoherent that Hanwei barely paid attention.

Hanwei clicked play.

"Who said that? Was it Director Liao?"

It was Rulan's voice—familiar, younger, edged with worry.

"Yes!"

The instant his father's voice entered the room, Hanwei's heartbeat lurched. His breath caught.

"He threatened you? Said he would do something to our family?" Rulan's tone was cautious.

"Yes. Said he'd 'deal with me.' Said others in the unit were whispering that I had filthy conduct. Said if I kept talking, *the organization* could act at any moment!"

"Secretary Qi from the hospital also came to talk to me. He said you were spreading things about the leadership. Why did you have to say those things? I heard others say Director Liao even said you were… nothing."

"Why can't I speak? When leaders in the factory are corrupt, shouldn't someone expose them?"

"They say—because your promotion never came through, you're bitter, so you're stirring trouble."

"One thing has nothing to do with the other! Someone *should* speak up about what's happening in leadership. And you—you're my wife. You can't even stand on my side?!"

"You still have to think about what you can handle… think about yourself for once," Rulan said, her voice starting to shake.

"I, Gaoming, am not someone like you—only thinking about yourself! Do you know? At the office—someone called me a dog… and you aren't defending me!"

"If he calls you a dog, you can call him a pig."

"They want to push me out—dump me in the retirement service office! How am I supposed to stay in that unit? All of this is because of you!"

The audio cut off abruptly.

Hanwei turned to his bedroom, lowered himself onto the

bed, and broke down in tears—trembling uncontrollably, as if all the years of humiliation, anger, and buried sorrow had found their way out.

Fate or Fight

"Hey, Mom. Is everything okay?"

"Your dad fell from the staircase in the senior home. He cracked his head. He is now in a coma in the ICU. The doctor said he might not live through the night, or if he survives, he could become vegetative. Let me hand over the phone to the doctor."

"Okay," Hanwei answered.

"Hello. You are Gaoming's son?"

"Yes."

"The situation is that your father now has massive bleeding inside his skull, accompanied with infection in many areas. He is on a ventilator, as he is unable to breathe on his own and relies completely on the machine to suck mucus and fluid out of his respiratory system. The pressure built up inside his skull from bleeding has damaged his brain. We have two options: one is to transfer him to the best hospital in the city for surgery, potentially saving him from becoming permanently vegetative. However, the transfer will be very risky, as his condition is unstable; moving him can be fatal. Even one gulp of phlegm in his windpipe would lead to death. Another option is to treat him in our hospital for now. Once his condition is stable, you can consider transferring him out for brain surgery. But the risk of him becoming permanently vegetative is higher. Either option needs your verbal agreement over the phone witnessed by hospital staff and your mom. From what I heard, you are the only relative who can make the call now for him."

Hanwei paused for a second, then responded. "Thank you, doctor. Understood. Can you please hand the phone back to my mom for a second?"

"Yes. You heard what the doctor said, right? What do you think?"

#

As he pulled up his luggage handle, Hanwei stepped onto the stone platform before the gate of Rulan's residential community. Small kids were running next to their parents around the mobile food stands. Seniors stood around chatting with one another. Young guys and gals occasionally walked in and out of the community gate. Their pretty faces, fresh clothes, and chill attitudes projected the comfort and confidence of the good time in today's China.

The security guard at the gate's sentry box asked the traveler, "Who are you visiting?"

"My mom. She lives here."

After strolling his luggage around people coming in and out of the apartment building and rising up in an elevator squeezed with unfamiliar faces, Hanwei arrived at his mom's home.

Rulan opened the door and saw her son standing in front of her, smiling and looking tired.

The mother and son were now again sitting side by side, in

the small but clean apartment they had bought together. Rulan had prepared dinner so Hanwei could enjoy home cooked food again. She briefed him about Gaoming's latest condition. The doctor stopped Gaoming's internal bleeding, saving him from an immediate death. But his brain had been severely damaged and his infection had become pervasive. He could die any time.

"Your father has done terrible things. But he also went through misery. No one goes to visit him. It's just me and your aunt who accompanied me once. Nurses used to gossip among themselves when I was there, saying things like, 'The old man is miserable, the son is not here, yet the wife and relatives don't even want to come.' I had to respond to them, 'He tormented us for years and ruined part of our lives. We have been divorced for many years. I have already gone out of my way to come here.' Since then, they have stopped gossiping."

The doorbell rang—*ding-ling*.

Hanwei stood up to answer it. At the doorway stood the elder he respected most: his grandmother, Wanqing, now frail with age but still dignified.

"Grandma!" Hanwei's eyes brightened, and he hurried forward to greet her.

"I heard Hanwei came back," she said gently. "So I came to take a look."

Wanqing sat down with Rulan and Hanwei, the three generations gathered once more in the small living room.

"Grandma, I'm really happy to see you." Hanwei placed a steadying hand behind her back as she settled into the sofa.

"Ah, Hanwei's grown sturdier," Wanqing said with a smile, squeezing his arm with her thin hand. "Your arms are so firm now."

"Ai… you're a good boy," she nodded while continuing, eyes warm with approval. "You came home to see your father. That means you still have a filial heart." She turned to Rulan. "How is Gaoming now?"

"Not well," Rulan sighed.

Wanqing lowered her eyes. "He's had a hard life too. Back then, he never wanted to stay here—always dreaming of getting out. In the end, he stayed… and the son went everywhere he once wished he could go."

She paused, then turned to Hanwei. "I don't know if your mother ever told you this. When you were five, your father took with you to Suzhou on a business trip. When he came back, he came back alone—without you. When we asked where the child was, he said he left you at a friend's home because 'the education conditions were better' there. Your mother was heartbroken—she cried and cried telling us. Your grandfather was furious. In the end, he stormed into the factory leadership office, made a scene, and only then did they order your father to go back to Suzhou and bring you home."

"Oh my god…" Hanwei whispered. He suddenly realized how close he had come to being taken away from his mother forever.

"Ai… talking about it now is pointless," Rulan murmured, her eyes turning faintly red.

"Your father's temper was strange, but we never blamed him much," Wanqing continued, her voice soft but steady. "All we ever wanted was for him to live a steady life with your mother, take care of each other. But he wouldn't. Your mother's life has been hard… and I'm old now. My hearing is fading. When

I'm gone, who will she have? You've done well out there—treat your mother kindly. If you can, take her to live with you someday. That way, I can rest peacefully."

"I understand, Grandma." Hanwei nodded, his voice steady.

"Your father… no matter what he's done, he's still your father," Wanqing said gently. "And now he has no one but you."

Rulan hesitated, then asked quietly, "After dinner… do you want to go see him? He's on the sixth floor, in the cardiac ICU."

#

After the nurse and the doctor led Hanwei to the ICU bed of his father, he came into the room to see Gaoming lying there with tubes plugged into his body. His head was covered with bandages and his nose and mouth were connected to the ventilator machine. His eyes and other parts of his face were very swollen. His high heart rate and low oxygen level were displayed on the medical equipment by the side of the bed.

"Mr. Zhou, your son is here. He has just come from America to see you," the nurse talked to Gaoming loudly, trying to solicit a reaction. "You are a very lucky father."

There was no sign of movement.

The doctor pushed back Gaoming's eyelids.

"Can he hear us? Do you see him giving any sign of response?" Hanwei asked.

"He is not processing sensory stimulation yet, at least not in a conscious sense," the doctor said, while looking at Gaoming and then at the equipment. "His body is fighting severe and massive infections. We are still unable to stop them with blood serum and our best medication. He is quite strong as an old man going through such severe injury and surviving this long. But he is weakening by the day and could pass away any day. We are trying our best."

"Thank you. Let me know what he needs. I can get it for him," Hanwei said.

"She is the nanny helping the ICU patients with cleaning. Since your family hasn't come here much, she has brought her own tools." The nurse pointed to a middle-aged woman in plain clothes in the ICU room.

"I will get the things she needs here," Hanwei acknowledged.

#

Although born and raised in Chongqing, having not lived in the city for more than twenty years, Hanwei was no longer familiar with the way locals conducted their business. He didn't want to bother his mother's relatives for the errands, as he knew, although they would support him, in their heart, they were not supportive of his father.

Hanwei tried to find an effective way to communicate with the doctor and nurses. He tried to figure out how health insurance worked. He visited the senior home to learn about his father's earlier life. He visited local shops to buy buckets, soaps, brushes and towels for the nanny who took care of his father. He looked into how to organize a funeral in case his father passed away and looked into care centers for those who are terminally ill in case his father would live a long-term vegetative state.

The news of Gaoming's ordeal spread to his siblings who lived in other cities in China. But their sour relationship in the past didn't help. They lent their sympathy to Hanwei and encouraged him to stay strong and focus on his mom who truly loved and sacrificed for him.

Other than two factory officials who paid a visit to the hospital, Gaoming's old friends in the factory town did not show up. They had moved on with their lives.

Hanwei visited his father in the hospital everyday. He didn't love this man on the ICU bed. He hated him. He could not feel sympathy or pain. He came here to care for this man in his last few days.

"I don't think your father had a sad and pathetic life," a female high school classmate of Hanwei's who accompanied him during his hospital visit one day, said calmly, looking at the ICU room.

Startled, Hanwei turned his head to her and looked at her with his fatigued eyes.

"I think he had a worthy one," she continued. "He lived the life he wanted. Many people want something in their life, but never have the courage to go for it. They stay living under the dogma of our society, much of which often represses the humanity among us. Not to say what he did was fair to you or your mother, but society had not been fair to him from day one."

#

A week passed. Any hope of Gaoming's recovery had faded; his life lingered only through machines. The doctor told Hanwei the time had come—he needed to decide whether to withdraw life support or wait a little longer and eventually transfer his father to a hospice facility for the terminally ill.

"Sigh… When you were little, your father made you suffer. Now you're grown, he still leaves you with a difficult burden." At the dinner table, Rulan spoke carefully, almost tenderly. "Keeping him alive like this… it doesn't mean much. Even if he survives this way, no one will visit him. That's not a life he would want. If it were me, I wouldn't want to live like this either. Your dad has lived through everything he was meant to live. His days are over. When it's time to let him go, you should—and then take care of yourself. Live your own life well."

…

"This way. Up here."

The administrator led Hanwei into a narrow concrete corridor. Elderly residents shuffled in and out, some stooped, some confused, all moving slowly through the dim space.

Hanwei followed him up a long, narrow stairwell.

"This is where he fell."

They stopped on the landing between the second and third floors. The administrator pointed toward the stairs above. At the top was a locked metal gate.

"For safety, we keep the third floor closed most of the day. We only open it during meals and group activities." He unlocked the gate as he spoke.

Inside, Hanwei saw them—one elderly figure after another, drifting through the corridor, staring blankly out a window, sitting in silence. Lives worn down to a slow, quiet erosion.

"Your father used to sneak out on his own. He would take taxis by himself. We couldn't keep track of him. We kept calling the police station to ask if they'd spotted him."

He brought Hanwei into a narrow room by a small window.

"This was his bed." It was a low, simple cot—just a thin sheet over a wooden frame. Two other old men sat silently on the beds nearby, their expressions unreadable.

"The things in this nightstand are his. The blankets he brought are in the shared cabinet. We had sorted everything and kept it here for you. His phone and documents—here, I put them all in this bag."

"Alright," Hanwei said quietly. "Please go ahead. I'll come find you in the office."

When the administrator left, Hanwei opened the nightstand.

Inside lay a stack of old photographs.

The first showed Gaoming as a young man—handsome, lean, caught mid-strike in a martial arts pose, his expression sharp with vigor.

The next was taken by the Yangtze River: shirtless, arms around two friends, sunlight on their laughing faces.

Hanwei flipped further.

More young faces appeared—boys his father had known decades ago.

One photo caught Hanwei's eyes: It's Gang, the "big brother" who used to visit their home, who took him on outings, who once gave him that Legends of Gods picture book.

In the picture, Gang was naked in a bathtub, smiling straight at the camera—bright, carefree.

At the bottom, in his father's neat handwriting: "Gang, age eighteen."

Another photo showed Gaoming with three young men flashing victory signs, all grinning wildly. His father stood behind them, smiling so broadly it seemed almost too big for his face.

Page after page, the years moved on.

Gaoming aged—lines carving into his cheeks, hair

thinning—yet the young men around him remained full of life, their eyes bright with the electricity of youth.

Holding the photos, Hanwei felt a heavy breath rise from deep inside him. *Who, in all of this, could grant them the dignity and happiness of being whole?*

Then he found it — a photograph from his own PhD graduation. There he was in his gown and hood on campus, surrounded by friends. But among their faces stood his father, smiling.

Hanwei stared. His father had not been there that day. Looking closer, he could see it — the edges slightly off, the lighting wrong. Gaoming had photoshopped his own head onto one of his friends. Hanwei didn't know whether to feel anger or sorrow. He could only imagine his father showing this to people — presenting himself as a father who had been there, who had proudly witnessed his son receive his doctorate. And yet underneath the lie, Hanwei sensed something true: a wish his father had carried that could never be fulfilled, for a moment that had already passed, for a bond that both of them had let slip away, each in their own way.

#

"I consent to unplug his ventilator but keep his life support for now," Hanwei said to the doctor the next day.

"Okay. I will get the paperwork ready for you," the doctor responded.

Hanwei went to the corridor outside Gaoming's ICU room and he sat on the bench, alone. He knew this old man had been alone for a much longer time. In all his life, this old gay man wanted to be loved by someone he loved. He struggled against his fate, damaging one thing after another on his journey. If anything, Hanwei wished the journey this old man had chosen had given him a taste of sweetness in all the bitterness. Looking around, Hanwei realized that for what life could not offer to this older gay man, it had at least offered something to his younger gay son. Yet, this younger gay man was also fighting his own fate, one that could easily be dismissed by his friends, his family, or other fellow gay men, one in which he could also be alone.

Hanwei cried on the bench, covering his face with hands and resting his elbows on his legs. *Do we choose our fate, or does fate choose us? Would life be more merciful if one accepts his fate or stays defiant?*

Outside the hospital, Hanwei saw trees and sunlight and people going about the hustle and bustle of a familiar life. Inside Hanwei's heart, his journey of life was never certain. Instead, it was downright scary and painful.

Then Hanwei thought to himself, hadn't life already given him and his father another chance?

Two days later, Gaoming passed away. To honor his father's long-stated wish, Hanwei donated his remains to a medical school.

The America Between Us

"Hanwei, can you help me print a few documents?" Rick asked, eyes still on his laptop as the two sat in a small café.

"Sure. Send them to me. I'll print them at the office tomorrow. What are they?"

"Some oceanographic data and charts for my climate-change lesson."

"You teach this stuff in high school?"

"I go over basic scientific concepts—climate, data literacy, that sort of thing."

"No wonder the far-right Republicans are always trying to start culture wars at schools," Hanwei laughed.

"You have no idea how hard it is teaching in the Bay Area's Chinese community," Rick sighed. "The moment we cover reproductive biology, sexual orientation, or gender identity, Chinese parents storm the office."

"Of course," Hanwei said, well aware of how Chinese parents think. "Doesn't your school give you printing?"

"My school gives printing, but with a quota. Sometimes we have to fundraise from parents just to buy teaching supplies. Teacher salaries are a joke. And you tech guys make more than the U.S. president." His humor only half-concealed resentment. "I've got a PhD, was an assistant professor back in Louisiana, and I still struggle to rent a one-bedroom here—forget buying."

"I know."

"People think guys like me have white privilege. But here in the Bay Area, after my day job, I still pick up shifts waiting tables to make ends meet—and the people I serve are almost all immigrants: Indians, Asians, Middle Easterners. What privilege?"

Hanwei smiled faintly. They had met at a trans rights rally in San Francisco. Rick, handsome and broad-shouldered, had grown up poor in a white working-class mountain town in Louisiana—living in a trailer on a slope with parents and three sisters who'd never finished school. When the local mill closed, most of the men lost their jobs. Only his second sister's husband earned steady money as a long-haul trucker. Rick had been the only one to excel academically.

He was charming and talkative. He often invited Hanwei along—to discuss politics, economics, and social issues. They became close friends. Hanwei liked him, but Rick had not shown much romantic interest, and his confident, forceful personality convinced Hanwei early on that they would not make a good couple.

"Next weekend there's a charity event supporting people with depression," Rick said. "Want to come?"

...

They crossed the lawn toward a cluster of tents. Each belonged to a different organization: support groups for people with depression, reproductive-health nonprofits, trans rights associations, and a network for parents who had lost children to suicide. Volunteers handed out pamphlets, collected donations, and recruited helpers.

At the tent for suicide-prevention parents, Rick picked up a strand of purple beads labeled *Survivor* and hung it around his neck.

"Rick… you haven't ever tried to kill yourself, right?" Hanwei asked.

"I have. Once."

Hanwei froze. "Was it because you tested positive for HIV?"

"Partly. But it's complicated. When I tested positive, I had just turned thirty. I thought my life was over. I panicked."

"You must have been under a lot of pressure. But HIV medication is easily accessible now—you can live normally."

"I was young, stupid, ashamed. I started using drugs to numb myself. Things spiraled. In my third year as assistant professor… I attempted suicide. Woke up in the hospital."

"My god. What drug did you use?"

"Meth."

"What's that? Like ecstasy?" Hanwei asked, unfamiliar.

"Worse."

"I have friends who party sometimes—they take stuff occasionally. As long as it's not hard drugs or overused, they seem okay."

"Anything that gives you pleasure can become addictive," Rick explained. "Because once that comfort disappears, your brain keeps chasing it."

"Like sex… or coffee, or boba tea?" Hanwei mused.

"You got it." Rick nodded. "My past was a disaster. But I am all good now."

#

One bright morning, Rick stepped into Hanwei's newly finished home.

"Wow. Congrats! New house—finally done," Rick said, wandering through the rooms.

"Thanks. You're the one who pushed me to buy the lot last year," Hanwei replied, leading him through the fresh-paint smell of the place. "I'm going through the inspection list—have two weeks to send issues to the builder."

"I'm good at this." Rick immediately crouched near the corner of the living room. "This outlet isn't sealed with caulk. It needs fixing."

He pointed at the stairs. "That plank isn't aligned. And these small mistakes? Someone could trip."

He flipped light switches, examined pipes under the sink. "These Mexican workers… No wonder Trump is winning people over with all that 'MAGA' nonsense. Their work sometimes looks third-world quality. People nowadays don't take pride in their craft any more."

"It's not a race issue," Hanwei replied. "Third-world societies face upheavals and instability. When dignity is fragile, people think short-term. I am worried the U.S. is becoming oligarchic—heading in that same direction."

Upstairs, Rick tugged on a loose signal wire protruding from a sealed wall.

"What's this?"

Hanwei burst out laughing—it was the unused conduit for the bedroom alarm system he had declined during signing.

"Come on. Let's get Chipotle to celebrate." Rick ushered Hanwei into his red coupe.

As they drove down the hill, Rick pointed at a Chinese woman dragging two large cardboard boxes toward a dumpster.

"She's totally going to toss them in whole."

The hillside community had been filling with Asian buyers—wealthy international students helping parents secure U.S. property.

Clang! The woman shoved the two intact boxes inside, instantly filling the bin.

"See?" Rick shook his head. "What are you Chinese thinking? She should flatten the boxes first. Now no one else can use the dumpster. Who does she expect to fix that?"

"Many countries have become rich faster than their civic norms can keep up," Hanwei said.

"You know," Rick sighed, "I used to be a left-wing liberal. After a few years in Silicon Valley, I'm drifting right. Feels like immigrants are turning the country upside down. Sometimes this place doesn't feel like my country anymore. Half the people in the mall speak languages I don't understand. It makes me want to move back home."

#

On Hanwei's TV, a clip replayed: Mitt Romney denouncing Donald Trump.

"He creates scapegoats of Muslims and Mexican immigrants, he calls for the use of torture and for killing the innocent children and family members of terrorists. He cheers assaults on protesters. He applauds the prospect of twisting the constitution to limit first amendment freedom of the press... His promises are as worthless as a degree from Trump University... His imagination must not be married to real power..."

"Wow… that was brutal," Hanwei said. "But Republican voters don't care."

The screen cut to interviews at a Trump rally.

"What makes you think Hillary has AIDS?" A reporter asked a man in a red MAGA hat.

"Probably got it from her husband."

"How did Bill Clinton get it?"

"Probably from his friend, Magic Johnson?"

"My God," Rick groaned from the couch.

"Crazy," Hanwei agreed.

Another interview asked a woman about Obama's birthplace.

"What would convince you Obama was born in the US?"

"A birth-witness," she said.

"His mother was there. Does that count?"

"No. She'd lie. She has a reason to."

"So even if Trump produced the birth certificate, you wouldn't believe it?"

"Oh, I'd believe Trump. He's been here the whole time."

"And how do you know that?"

"His parents were here."

"But you said we can't trust his parents."

Rick and Hanwei burst out laughing.

"White rural folks support him," Rick said. "My entire family does. I'm the only one against him."

"Obama being president probably shattered the pride of many insular, under-educated white communities," Hanwei said. "Combine that with globalization hurting them—they just want to tear everything down and return to a past that never truly existed. China has plenty of people like that too, stuck in nostalgia and slogans."

"Exactly," Rick nodded, chewing his nail.

"But Trump *is* smart at manipulating people," Hanwei added.

"Please don't call Trump smart in this house," Rick groaned. "He's destroying my country."

He glanced at the clock. "Anyway, it's late. You're flying to Europe tomorrow, right?"

"Yeah."

Rick stood, gave Hanwei a firm hug. "Safe travels."

Someone to Listen to

Once again, it was the face-to-face meeting of one of the world's largest wireless industry organizations. Hundreds of delegates from different companies, including Hanwei, came together to discuss the latest developments of the wireless industry and spend time socializing with one another, as some of them had become good friends over the years. This time, it was in Barcelona, a fascinating city of Spain along the coast of the Mediterranean Sea.

While the conference was filled with interesting presentations, debates, straw polls and motions, and the hallway conversations were busy with greetings and skirmishes, Barcelona beckoned the visitors. No one wanted to miss the chance of appreciating the magnificence of the world famous La Sagrada Familia, the invigorating beauty of La Barceloneta Beach, the romance of La Rambla, the delicious tapas in warm and delicate Spanish restaurants, and the beautifully dressed pedestrians who brought corners of the city alive from sunny mornings to the lively nights.

While Barcelona was exciting and therapeutic, Hanwei's depression had taken a toll on him. He used work to distract himself from negative thoughts. He dressed sharp and groomed himself to cover his sinking feeling. But he could not shake off the anxiety and occasional panic, as he saw his chance at having a stable and loving life dissipating and his promise of security and peace to his mom elusive.

In the conference hotel's lobby, Hanwei sat down with one of his most trusted industrial colleagues and friends, Yanqiang, a woman in her early fifties. Their professional discussion took a turn.

"Yanqiang, how have you been?"

"Doing good. How are you doing? It's been a while. I sometimes go to San Jose for business trips. But I always rush back on the same day. I haven't had a chance to see you until now."

"I am doing alright," Hanwei responded.

"Just alright? How's work? How's your mom? How is everything?"

Hanwei had worked with her in the startup before it fell apart. During those days, she was Hanwei's boss's boss. Hanwei trusted her. "I am having a hard time in San Jose and increasingly feel so," Hanwei spoke in a humbled personal tone.

"What happened?" Yanqiang asked in an urgent and caring manner.

"You know I lived in Southern California when I first came to America. I loved the culture and life there. My adulthood grew with it. And I got used to it. After I moved to Silicon Valley, I've had a hard time adjusting to the life there."

"Do you have any friends there?"

"I have some," Hanwei responded. His eyes gave away his lost feeling. "My close friends are mostly in Southern California. It's only after I moved to Silicon Valley that I realized it's a lot harder to make friends in a new location as a gay man in his late thirties. I feel very lonely. I have never felt like that before. I often feel tired after dinner, wake up three to four times at night, and sometimes have panic attacks."

"I am sorry to hear. Have you thought about coming back to San Diego?"

"I thought about it. But I still want to give myself a chance in the Bay Area. After all, I love the work there. And my work is the only thing that I can still count on."

Yanqiang nodded her head. "Well, the good thing is you love your work. And you are doing well with that. Work is an important part of life. But when we grow older, our health and our mental health are also important. Friends are a part of that. We all need someone we can come home to. After a whole day of busy work, with all the troubles and successes we had outside, when we go home, we need someone who would ask, 'How are you? Are you okay? Tell me,' someone who listens to us, someone who cares. And we want to do the same in return. It doesn't matter whether that someone is a man or a woman, a family member or a friend."

Someone who would ask, 'How are you? Are you OK? Tell me.' Hanwei thought that was exactly what he had now come to realize.

"When we are young, the world is very forgiving to us. Once we grow up, the world isn't as much. Sooner or later, we become as vulnerable as those who we saw falter before us, and we all need a little help, we all need to give and share." Yanqiang tried to help Hanwei embrace himself.

#

Barcelona's nights were enchanting. The streets were adorned with delicate restaurants. Lovers carefully picked their dining places, longing for the romance they anticipated. Night clubs were filled with charming young men and women looking for their love at first sight. Alone, Hanwei walked into a large and beautiful gay bathhouse in this live and let live city.

"Hi," Hanwei greeted the staff at the reception desk, who came to meet him from behind a glass window.

"Hi. Twenty euro," the staff spoke in a Spanish accent.

Hanwei then placed his credit card and ID into the tray below the glass.

"Do you know what this place is for?" the staff asked, staring at the innocent-looking Asian man.

"Yes," Hanwei replied in a confident manner.

The staff processed the credit card. The door was automatically unlocked and Hanwei walked in.

The staff greeted him inside. "Here is a towel and slippers. This is your locker room key. You have the blue color band. It's for guests." The staff pointed to the band attached to the key.

Hanwei undressed himself in the locker, wrapped his lower body at his hip with the white towel. After all these years, Hanwei still looked athletic and fresh. He put on the blue color band with the key, and then walked toward the inside.

The tunnels were dim and the walls were covered with large, polished stones, reflecting orange light from the embellished fixtures mounted in the corners. Soft R&B music played throughout the maze-like structure. The temperature inside was perfect for walking around without clothes. Along the tunnels were private rooms for patrons and cozy lounges with mounted TVs on which handsome men were in action.

Some corners had open showers and sauna rooms. Some were dark dead ends where guests went to unleash their devious desires using chains and straps. Men came to this place filled with tension and hormones, leaving their trouble outside to have a taste of what they wanted from another man just for a moment.

Turning a corner, a square-jawed young Brazilian man smiled at Hanwei. *A very handsome guy*, Hanwei thought to himself. Before he could give him any more thought, the man moved close to Hanwei's face and gave him a passionate kiss. His masculine scent, naughty smile, and strong maneuver were irresistible. Before Hanwei could react, he grabbed Hanwei's hand and put it between his legs to feel his large member.

"I just got here," Hanwei said, startled, as he smiled at the Brazilian. "Let me check out this place a bit first."

"Find me later," the young man said.

He left the young man and rounded the corner, surprised that he had gotten the attention from such a sexy fellow.

Hanwei gradually descended to lower levels, walking into different pockets inside the bathhouse, like a hunter inspecting the bushes and trees.

Around another corner, a rough muscular man with darker skin greeted and smiled at Hanwei. On the stairs, a timid-looking, slim white man took a seductive look at Hanwei. *Guys here are attractive,* Hanwei thought to himself, and *somehow they are paying a lot of attention to me.*

The central enclave at the bottom of the bathhouse was spacious, built with a large pool, a Jacuzzi, and a stylish lounge with a bar. Several men were sitting around. A good-looking bartender was catering toward them amid tempting hip-hop music. Hanwei walked to the bar and seated himself on a bar stool.

They noticed the arrival of this Asian man. One of them was senior in age, quiet and comfortable in his skin. Another man was in his middle age, hairy, in decent shape, with wrinkles on his face giving away his experience. Among them was one athletic black young man, who was vividly expressing himself. He caught Hanwei's eyes.

"I like that town. Nice beach and fun night-clubs. I'd visit there again if I get a chance," the black guy said.

"Which town were you guys talking about?" Hanwei asked.

"Cagliari," the black guy replied.

"The one in Sardinia. Yeah. That's a nice place," Hanwei followed.

"Oh, you've been there too? How are you?"

"Doing good. This place is nice," Hanwei responded and checked out the black guy.

"Where do you come from?" he asked.

"California."

"That's a nice place." The black guy smiled.

"So, you are a bloody American." The middle-aged man joined the conversation with a grin on his face, while raising his beer bottle.

"I grew up in China but have been living in the U.S. for a while." When asked that question on his overseas trips, Hanwei usually said he was from California so as not to trigger the distaste people around the world had for the recent U.S. politics and devilish scams on Wall Street. Plus, he knew most people would assume he was ethnically Chinese despite his American tone, and everyone knew California was filled with Chinese.

The bartender came over to Hanwei. "Do you want a drink?"

"Can I have a Coke?"

"Sure."

"Election night is tomorrow. Who do you think is going to win?" the middle-aged man asked Hanwei.

"Hard to tell. Hillary seems to be still ahead in the polls," Hanwei replied.

"I like Hillary," the black guy said.

Hanwei smiled. "I support her. But I rooted for Bernie Sanders in the primary. He wasn't well understood in America, especially with his democratic socialist label, which everybody here in Europe seems to be okay with."

"Do you support this man?" The middle-aged man pointed to the news program being played on the TV. Euronews Channel was replaying Donald Trump's speeches to his massive audience, giving ideas on how to treat protesters against his campaign: "In the good old days, this doesn't happen, because they used to treat them very, very rough. I'd like to punch him in the face, I'll tell ya. Try not to hurt him. If you do, I'll defend you in court. Don't worry about it."

"No. What he is doing and preaching is not good for our civilization."

The middle-aged man gave a thumbs up to Hanwei.

Hanwei continued, "It's sad that the Republican Party in recent years offered increasingly defective candidates. Their platform worsened; just look at their stand on gun violence, anti-intellectualism, misogyny, and racism."

"So much gun violence and deaths are happening there. When asked what the solution is, their answer is more guns! The Republicans. It's crazy!" the senior man seconded.

"It's deliberate," Hanwei followed. "A stance disguised under the name of self determination to guard the old privilege and dogma, however obviously unfair, irrational, and uncivil it is."

"Do you like America?" the middle-aged man asked.

"I do. I love those American strangers who kindly wave to me while driving, reminding me of my open gas cap, just like I love those Chinese classmates who rushed back to pull others out of the crowd during an earthquake stampede. It's people like this man on TV who manipulate others to pick a side without letting them be close to the truth who are damaging lives and civilization."

The middle-aged man nodded. "Exactly."

Hanwei raised his glass of Coke. "At least I don't have to worry about those things tonight."

"So, what type of guys do you like?" The black guy made a move.

"I am into many different types." Hanwei was no longer interested in the black guy. He was a bit too campy for Hanwei's taste. "Nice chatting with you guys. I'm gonna use the pool."

Hanwei pulled off his towel, put it aside on the chair, and stepped into the water. The water was warm and clear. He flexed his muscles and floated around a bit. Some older men in the pool peeked at him from time to time.

After relaxing in the water for a few minutes, Hanwei jumped out of the pool, dried himself, and was ready to try his luck in the maze tunnel.

A manly voice came from behind. "Hey, how are you?"

Hanwei turned around. A tall and handsome man stood in front of him. He was Arab looking, with dark hair, large sensual eyes, and a charming and friendly smile. His shirtless body was on full display, showing off a wide chest and broad shoulders, strong arms and legs, and athletic waistline with a white towel covering down below. Hanwei was in awe of his beauty.

"Doing well. You?"

"Doing well. I am Ramses, by the way." The man reached out with his hand.

"Marco." Hanwei brought up an English name he uses in Starbucks to avoid the difficult pronunciation and spelling of his real name. He shook hands with Ramses. It was a warm, strong grip.

"Are you visiting Barcelona?"

"Yes. For a conference."

"Cool. Are you Chinese?"

"Yes. I am."

Ramses nodded his head, friendly and calm. "We can sit down and chat. Hope I didn't bother you."

"No. Not at all."

The two sat down on the chairs by the side of the pool.

"Your English is really good."

"I have been living in the United States for many years."

"I see. You are a handsome man."

"Thanks." It felt flattering to Hanwei. The man in front of him would be a dream man to many. If being approached by several handsome men earlier was puzzling, this made no sense to him at all. Hanwei started to suspect this place was actually a male brothel.

"You are remarkably handsome."

"Thank you," Ramses smiled.

"Are you from the Middle East?"

"Yes. I am from Egypt. Been in Barcelona for a couple years."

"What do you do?" Hanwei asked.

"In the daytime, some small jobs. At night, I come here. Are you looking for a companion tonight?"

"Are you…ah…" Hanwei searched for the right word, "…looking for clients?"

"Are you looking for boys? You saw my red color band? Red color band is for boys."

"Blue color band is for guests," Hanwei recalled what the staff said at the entrance. Looking across the pool, he noticed the black guy also wearing a red color band. Now it all made sense.

"Whoa. I actually didn't know; I didn't plan on hiring an escort tonight. I came here to try my luck. If not, at least I'd enjoy the ambiance."

"You seem to be a nice guy. You can still give it a try. We can have a good time." Ramses looked into Hanwei's eyes and approached him calmly and romantically.

"You are really attractive. But I didn't plan for this. I am not sure I'm carrying enough cash for this." Hanwei was nevertheless tempted.

"No worries. We can find an ATM outside. My rate is two hundred euros. We can go to your hotel. We can chat, relax, have sex, or whatever you feel comfortable with. I'll take care of you. But really, no pressure." Ramses reached out with his hand and held Hanwei's.

Hanwei looked at the Egyptian man.

"Okay. We can go to my hotel."

#

The temperature outside was pleasant. Wearing a jacket with a steel zipper and blue jeans and carrying a gray leather handbag over his shoulder, Ramses walked confidently with Hanwei by his side.

"How do you like living in Barcelona?" Hanwei asked.

"It's nice and many things are happening. But it's expensive, hard to live only doing restaurant work. I am trying to get into modeling. But in the meantime, I do escort work to save some money."

"Do you get family support from home?"

"My family is poor. The economy in Egypt is bad now. Hard to find jobs there. I decided to stay in Spain and give it a shot when I visited here with a tourist visa."

Soon, Ramses and Hanwei reached the hotel.

As the two walked into Hanwei's room, Ramses crossed the room and sat on the couch.

"You look as good as any model, you know," Hanwei complimented.

"Thanks." Ramses gave a gorgeous smile. "Come over here. Don't be shy." He pulled Hanwei in front of his lap.

Hanwei was turned on by Ramses' masculine scent, although still holding himself back with an instinctive hesitation from the fear of being emasculated by such an attractive macho man by his side.

"Hope you make it in the modeling industry one day. Escort work may only last for so long."

"Yeah. But that's the same for many other professions. And many don't pay that much. Working as an escort helps me save money. I plan to buy myself an apartment and look for other opportunities later. Hopefully start a business with friends too."

"That sounds like a good plan."

"It's also not as bad of a profession as people think," Ramses continued. "Some people say, 'Oh, sex and affection should be earned and not bought.' To me, clients who appreciate me also earn my affection. Many clients are decent people. Some are successful in their own career. But they have relationship difficulties. They feel lonely. They often adore the ideal men they want themselves to be, or they think they cannot be, or they desire to be with."

"Right."

"At least I can help them a bit emotionally, especially during a crisis in their life. Sometimes, the job is to listen to them, like being a therapist."

"I can see that," Hanwei said. *Indeed, everyone has something to offer and something to admire.*

"So, what's your story? You don't come across as a typical client. You look young and lovely," Ramses asked.

"I am not that young. I am almost forty. That's probably part of my crisis."

"Do you have a family, wife, or boyfriend?"

"No. My ex-boyfriend and I broke up years ago. He is black. Life is tough for him. Was in and out of jail. Almost homeless after that. I tried hard to help, but our differences grew too large. It was so hard to be together. He went back to where he came from."

"You seem to be a good man. You'll find someone. How about your parents? Do you have relatives living around?"

"No. They are in China. Actually, my dad was gay. He passed away a year ago. But even when he was alive, he wasn't really around. It's just my mom and me for each other."

"Your dad was also gay?! Shoot. That must have been hard for your mother."

"Yeah. He brought guys home all the time. Those days were hell for us."

"And your mom was okay with that?"

"She was either in denial or just numbing herself. She lived her life all for me. She used to think she was married to a devil, and then the old devil gave her a younger devil. And she sometimes felt her life was ruined because of my father and me."

"Whoa. That must be hard for her and for you."

"She is remarkable. She eventually turned around, rose above the dogma, and now hopes I'll meet someone who loves me and who I can live happily with. While sometimes I feel depressed because I think my dream is slipping away, what worries me most is still her."

Hanwei paused while looking into the void. "She did so much for me. I am so afraid that I will fail her, that she will think my life at the end doesn't amount to anything, or being gay is destined to failure, sadness and pain, like my dad's life."

Hanwei took a deep breath. "I feel I am obligated to live through a gay life to exonerate my father and feel obligated to have a good ending so that she can see she made the right choice to trust her son and that there is a good life for every decent honest human being."

"I am sorry to hear your story." Ramses hugged Hanwei, and then turned him front and center.

Hanwei stopped talking to make sure he could hold back his emotion.

"You have not done anything wrong in your life. You are a responsible person, caring about your mother and your loved ones. You've done well at work. You have many good friends." Ramses touched Hanwei's shoulder. "You will do well."

Ramses looked into Hanwei's eyes passionately. "I want you to have a happy time today."

Ramses removed his polo shirt, revealing his remarkable physique, and then pulled Hanwei's t-shirt over his head and shoulders.

"You are very cute. I already have a hard on." Ramses smiled, and put Hanwei's hand onto his private part.

At that moment, Hanwei flashed back to his childhood encounter with his father's young man when he was startled by the vitality of a grown man and had admired them when he was little.

"Thanks. It's late already. You must be tired. We don't have to do anything. I can pay for your escort time. I am happy that I get to talk to a likable guy like you."

"No, no. It's not late in Spain time. And I want to have fun with you. You have a nice slim body. I saw it when you were naked in the pool. I want to give you a good time."

Ramses took Hanwei by his hand and led him to the bed.

…

"You can stay here tonight. It's already two o'clock," Hanwei told Ramses.

"I'll go home. You still need to fly out tomorrow. I'll leave you to have a good sleep."

Ramses turned around and gave Hanwei a long hug before he walked out of the door. "If you need someone to talk to, text me. Take care of your mom. She is a remarkable woman. She needs you. At the end of the day, we all need to give to those who love and support us."

When the door clicked shut behind Ramses, the room fell quiet. Hanwei exhaled, letting the stillness settle over him. He reached for his phone to set an alarm—and only then noticed several messages he had missed.

They were all from Rick.

Hanwei, your front door was unlocked. I went in—someone's been through your place. It looks like the police were there. Get back as soon as you can.

Ally

Rick, what happened at my place?" Hanwei typed, his fingers tense. "I'm still in Spain—I'm not home yet. Where are you right now?"

Minutes crawled by. No reply.

Growing uneasy, he called. Each attempt rang out and slid into voicemail.

He decided to call his neighbor.

…

"I just checked," the neighbor reported. "Your door's closed tight, nothing unusual inside. I also reviewed my camera footage—no one stopped at your door except people passing by."

"Thank you," Hanwei said, though the confusion only deepened.

…

Finally, Rick's message came: "Oh—I forgot you were in Spain."

Hanwei frowned. Rick had hugged him goodbye only days ago. How could he forget?

A second message appeared: "Hanwei, can you come get me? Meet me on the street by the café we always go to. I'm on the freeway—there are thirty police cars chasing my car right now."

"What? What happened? Why would the police be after you?" he typed back.

"I'm in Spain," Hanwei wrote quickly. "Whatever is happening, please try to stay calm and stop whatever you're doing. Call me when you can."

He waited. The clock ticked past 2:00 a.m.

Finally, a message came: "I'm okay now. I hid in my friend Sarah's house. I'm safe."

Hanwei stared at the screen. *No one escapes thirty police cars. That's not possible.*

Then a memory hit him—Rick had once said he had used meth in the past, and the "police chase" likely existed only in hallucination.

A long, helpless sigh escaped him. At least now he might manage a little sleep.

#

Early the next morning, Hanwei started packing for the flight back to the US. He turned on the TV. The US presidential election was all over the news.

A few minutes past nine o'clock in the evening in California, CNN News Channel announced that Donald J. Trump had taken Ohio, Florida, and North Carolina. With his wins in these battleground states, Trump's path to the White House had suddenly become a lot clearer.

The polls are off, Hanwei thought. He quickly pulled up his cell phone and checked the election statistics on Fivethirtyeight's website. Nate Silver's estimate of Hillary Clinton's chance of winning had dropped from above seventy percent to below twenty percent.

Clinton's campaign had to pin their hope on Pennsylvania, Michigan, and Wisconsin. Hanwei then checked the numbers in those three almost must-win states and glanced over CNN's live coverage. Trump was already ahead in both Wisconsin and Pennsylvania.

Shit. Polls have never been this wrong in modern times this close to the election, Hanwei was shocked. To him, Trump's win would be disastrous to this country and its people. *This is a person who narrowly focuses on his personal gain over everything, has little regard for laws, profits from pitting one group of people against another, and slandered honest work of scientists and hard-working people,* Hanwei thought to himself.

Standing in the long line at the security gate of Barcelona's international airport, Hanwei checked his cell phone again. Trump had won Pennsylvania. And that just made his White House win unassailable.

My God. Hanwei's heart sank.

…

Seated at his window seat, his bag finally stowed overhead, Hanwei refreshed the news one more time. The numbers hadn't changed. Trump's victory was now all but certain. A hollow disbelief pressed against his chest.

Then his phone lit up: "Hi Hanwei. I just want to say I'm sorry." It was Rick.

Hanwei sat up straighter. "It's okay. Are you alright? Whatever happened, you can tell me."

A pause—then another message appeared: "I think I had some kind of psychotic break. I might have ruined my life today. I'm so sorry for everything."

A familiar ache settled over Hanwei. "Don't think that way.

Whatever happened, don't panic. Just stay safe. My plane's about to take off. Once I land in San Francisco, I'll come see you. We'll get through this."

"Thank you. I hope your business trip went well in Spain. I'm really happy for you—for your work, for your life."

The aircraft rumbled as it pushed back from the gate. Hanwei set his phone into airplane mode, the cabin lights dimming around him. Hanwei haplessly laid down in his business class cabin, seeking any comfort he could find, and plunged himself into unconsciousness for his long flight across the Atlantic.

...

Ten hours later, the flight landed at San Francisco International Airport. Hanwei pushed himself up, dragged his luggage out of the plane, and lined up for the customs. He could hear many in the customs lines talking about the unsettling news that Trump had now won the US presidency; he would be forty-fifth president.

Waiting in those long lines were Asians, blacks, Spanish, and many white Europeans.

Looking at the crowd, knowing this would be a world changing event, his mind started racing.

Ever since homo sapiens had walked out of Africa one hundred thousand years ago, they gradually migrated and lived in different pockets of the Earth, evolving into who we are today, different skin color and shapes, different skills and cultures. Those tribes looked after their own kinds. But now is the first time in human history that children of humankind are meeting one another again. Different tribes won't be able to avoid one another anymore, but will live and grow together, morph into one another, become something bigger. While many have to do it for their common needs and for settling differences, some would do that for a better meaning of human life, dignity, and justice. But, not without growing pains, I guess. And how easy it is for people to walk back to what is every man for himself.

Walking out of SFO, Hanwei breathed the fresh air. He was back in Silicon Valley where he had seen people from all over the world working hard side by side, setting aside their differences, suspending their prejudices, and learning to understand beyond their own little tribes.

#

Hearing the doorbell, Hanwei rushed to open it.

The moment the door swung wide, he froze.

Rick stood there looking like a different person entirely—ashen, gaunt, hollow-eyed. His clothes hung off him as if he had shed ten, maybe fifteen pounds in a matter of days.

"I'm sorry," Rick murmured, head bowed, his expression that of a man awaiting judgment.

"I had no idea meth could do this to you," Hanwei said, his brow tightening as he watched Rick shuffle weakly toward the sofa.

"I barely ate those days," Rick replied.

"Oh my God..."

Rick nodded faintly. "Four, maybe five days. I was with... them."

"Who is 'them'?" Hanwei asked.

"A group I know—people who can get meth. Others just drift in and out. We do... things we'd never do sober. Time passes fast. Everything feels amazing—until you come down."

"I don't really know much about it. But you know—you

have to stop. For yourself."

"I'm sorry." Rick lowered his head again, crushed under shame. "My landlord gave me three days to move out."

"What? How did it get that bad?"

"I went to school. I was high while teaching."

"Oh my God."

"The students noticed. They told the school. The administration confronted me and sent me home. After that, my landlord figured something was wrong. Then my roommate said the police came to check the house for drugs. I don't know who called them—maybe the school, since they emailed me demanding a drug test. Maybe the landlord. I wasn't home when the police came, but once the report was made… he told me to get out in three days."

"What will you do now?"

"I don't know. I can't go back to school. I didn't save anything living in Silicon Valley. I need to find another job, then a place to rent. But time is running out."

"Will the police come after you?"

"No. Police don't bother with simple possession. But if things fall apart, I'll have to go back home. And then my born-again sister will say this is just God's punishment for gay people going to hell."

Hell. What crime earns such a sentence? Hanwei thought. *In the dark months of his own loneliness and despair, Rick had stood by him more than once.*

"You can stay with me temporarily," Hanwei said after a moment. "I can help you for a couple of months. Hopefully, you'll find work and then a place soon."

"No," Rick said, shaking his head weakly. "I don't want to drag you into this. You have your own life. Let me see what

I can do first." He looked around the room, exhausted. "I'm just… really tired. Can I lay down here for a bit?"

#

"When you use meth," the YouTube animation explained, "you feel euphoric, invincible—like Superman. Everything is thrilling, everyone is fascinating. But when the drug wears off, the only thing on your mind is getting that feeling back…"

The narrator shifted into a carnival metaphor:

Imagine it's the weekend, and you've gone to an amusement park. At the entrance, a strange circus clown waves you in with a big, welcoming smile.

You climb onto the roller coaster. Sunlight, laughter, families crowding the walkways—every ride feels like pure bliss. For a moment, life seems effortless, almost tender. You think: So this is happiness.

But after a while you grow tired. You glance at your phone—it's past midnight. You remember you have work tomorrow, errands overdue. You tell yourself it's time to leave.

Just then, the clown reappears, smiling warmly at you. He waves you back inside: You still have time. One more ride won't hurt.

You hesitate, then follow him back in. You climb onto the roller coaster again. The joy returns. You wander to your other favorite attractions. The fun is still there, but something feels… off. Less intense. Less magical.

You check the time again. It's already 2 a.m. You have to handle your errands, get some sleep, and go to work tomorrow.

But the clown glides toward you once more. Same smile, same gentle wave: Just one last time.

You tell yourself you can push those tasks to tomorrow. Just one more ride—then sleep. You'll manage somehow. You return to the park.

You play through all your favorite attractions again. You smile... but it feels thinner now. Something in your chest tightens— Tomorrow is coming, and you're not ready.

You look at your watch—and freeze. It's already morning. You've missed your meeting. You didn't prepare the documents. The parking ticket still hasn't been paid. Your utility bills are overdue. Panic spreads through you.

And then the clown appears again—closer this time. His smile no longer looks warm. It stretches a little too wide, the corners curling unnaturally. His voice softens: Don't worry. Call in sick. You can play... one more time.

Behind him, you hear it—the rumble of your favorite roller coaster, speeding by in the distance. Passengers scream with joy, oblivious. On the ground below, crowds cheer, eyes bright with hope and excitement...

It was terrifying. Hanwei stared at the YouTube video. The narrator's voice chilled him to the bone.

Hanwei clicked on another site:

"Meth triggers dopamine levels three to four times higher than cocaine, about five times higher than sex. While using, many users engage in sexual marathons lasting dozens of hours. Without treatment, fewer than five percent remain abstinent after three years."

My God, Hanwei thought.

Scrolling further, he stumbled onto a documentary about rural white communities in the American South, ravaged by meth:

"Our towns used to have factories," a man in the documentary said. *"Then they all closed. No jobs. People sat around with*

nothing to do. Then meth came... and it destroyed one village after another. These were ordinary people. At first, you hear someone in the next town get hooked. You think it's not your problem. Then a while later, you hear a friend—someone you actually know—has gotten hooked. And before long, you find out... your own mother is using it too."

How unbearably tragic, Hanwei thought while he watched, heart sinking.

A middle-aged woman appeared on screen, speaking with a haunted heaviness:

"When I use meth, I always go to a friend's place. I would never use at home. If I used at home... I'd probably end up having sex with my own son."

The camera then cut to an elderly woman sitting beside a daughter with vacant eyes.

"She got addicted," the old woman said softly. *"Lost her job. Lost her house. So she came to live with me—because I'm her mother, after all."*

She paused, her voice steady but unbearably sad. *"I'm old. I'll be gone first. I don't know what will happen to her after I die. But I am not worried about that. Because by then... I won't be here anymore."*

#

"I'm Tony. I'm a meth addict."

"I'm Holland. I'm a meth addict."

"I'm Rick. I'm a meth addict."

About twenty people sat in a wide circle in a community room—mostly young, white, with a few older faces in between. It was a Narcotics Anonymous meeting.

Hanwei introduced himself when his turn came.

"I'm Hanwei. I am an ally."

"I've been off meth for seven years now," a middle-aged man said from the podium, drawing a warm round of applause from the circle. "Even though I rarely feel the urge anymore, I can't say I'm cured. Recovery is something I have to choose—every day, for the rest of my life."

He gave a small, self-conscious smile. "I still remember the things I did back then… the kinds of things most of you here know all too well—those marathon sex binges that lasted ten, twelve hours." The room chuckled knowingly.

"Sometimes I miss the highs. But I choose the life I have now." He paused, steadying himself. "I always remember the morning I was supposed to make breakfast for my daughter and take her to school. Then I got a text from a friend—inviting me to a party at someone's house to use meth. At that moment, the only thing running through my mind was meth, and how good it would feel to use with them together."

He swallowed, voice tightening. "When their van pulled up outside my house, my daughter stood at the door crying, yelling, 'Daddy, Daddy, don't go.' But I walked away and got in that van. I left my little girl behind for meth."

The man's eyes reddened. "I ended up on the streets not long after. But by the grace of God, I'm still alive. I found a job. My daughter has her own family now, and I—well, I still get to be her father. I can still help her when she needs me."

He lifted his gaze at the circle around him. "This quiet life I have now… it's worth fighting for. And the love of my family is what gives me the strength, and the reason, to stay clean."

The room erupted again in gentle, encouraging applause.

…

"Rick," the host called. "You're next."

"Thanks. It's been six or seven years since I first used. Three weeks since my last relapse. I carry a lot of guilt. I've hurt people who trusted me. My lies, my irresponsibility… they pushed people away, one after another."

He paused, but his voice stayed level.

"I still remember that night in the parking lot with my ex — the night he tried to stop me from going off to use. When he said he'd seen my messages, the ones where I was arranging to meet other users, I threw my phone in the air twice in anger until it shattered into pieces. Then I got in my car and drove off. The look on his face… I'll never forget it. After that, I stopped believing I deserved anyone's love."

"I'm grateful for my ally sitting over there—Hanwei. He's from China. He helped me through a lot, even gave me a temporary place to stay. I just hope he meets someone better than me in this country."

...

"Come on, the movie's about to start," Hanwei said after the meeting wrapped up, sticking to the plan they'd made for the evening.

They got in the car. As Hanwei turned right onto the main road, they passed a white woman in tattered clothes rummaging through a garbage bin.

"That'll be me someday," Rick said with a dry, self-mocking laugh.

"Don't say that," Hanwei replied. "You'll do better."

#

Days passed. Then weeks. Hanwei made a quiet decision:

he would give a few months of his life to help Rick get back on his feet. During that time, Rick worked days at a small restaurant, spent his evenings applying for jobs, and on weekends sometimes hiked with Hanwei to clear his head. Whenever he had downtime, he went to NA meetings, letting the community there help keep him accountable.

Four months went by.

Then one day, Rick finally received an offer for a high-school teaching position, and he rented a small side unit behind a Vietnamese family's house.

"When you need someone to talk to, you can always tell me," Hanwei said when he dropped Rick off at his new place. "And if you ever want to go out, call me. In the hardest stretches of life, only honesty and a quiet mind can become our own salvation."

#

"Hey, I decided to move back to China. I found a company to work for there. Will leave the US soon." A Wechat message came to Hanwei's cell phone screen.

Ming was Hanwei's close friend in San Diego, a fierce intellectual. He had difficulty living as a single Chinese gay man in a predominantly white neighborhood, feeling his potential unfulfilled.

Hanwei quickly called back. "Hey. You are really leaving for China?"

"Yes."

"Is that because you were fed up with US politics?"

"I am fed up with the stupid uprise of racism, xenophobia, sexism, and anti-intellectualism. But, I am sure other places can be worse with those things. The US still has its charm. I am leaving because my life has stagnated for many years. I want to experience more. Life is about experiences, right? That's how we get wiser."

"I hope one day you'll be back. We can retire together."

"Maybe. By the way, I will send you the key to my condo in case I need your help with the property."

As Hanwei hung up the phone, he realized his life as an immigrant and a gay man had become even lonelier. While life had been full of hope thirteen years ago, his life now felt wasted and underachieved, with many friends lost along the way.

To The Heartland

One Saturday morning, Hanwei was reading the list of beliefs he had written down following his therapist's advice.

"I believe a person can change over time."

"I believe I should take care of my mom for her remaining years."

"I believe it is entirely possible that everything and every congregation of things are conscious, but to different degrees in different ways."

It is indeed therapeutic, Hanwei thought.

The therapist had given him a new assignment this week: to write down his understanding of the meaning of life and his feelings for the world and its people. Hanwei thought for a few minutes, and then started writing.

History of mankind is like a fractal.

When progress is made, darkness follows.

When hope fades, a better world arises.

...

Zzz... His cell phone vibrated, before he could finish his writing. It was a "Hi" message from the OKCupid app. A picture of a smiling, good-looking South Indian man appeared on the screen. His name was Rahul. A match score of ninety-six percent was displayed below Rahul's profile.

Interesting… Hanwei had never dated an Indian guy. Although there was virtually no escape from Indian engineers in Silicon Valley, it was rare to see an Indian man come out as gay, let alone approach a Chinese man.

"Hi. How's your weekend?" Hanwei replied.

"Good so far. I liked your profile, your mentioning of your interests in science and arts, and especially that sometimes you do things in the hope of making the world a better place."

Hanwei responded with a smiley face emoji and said, "I like your picture on top of Mission Peak standing on the pole with open arms. You have long arms and a great smile."

Apparently, Rahul was a nature lover. Besides the picture on Mission Peak, in one of his pictures, he stood on a trail of green bush and yellow flowers over a cliff above the breathtaking Pacific Ocean in Big Sur. In another picture, he carried a large camping pack on his back, held a sun hat in his hand, and was standing on a rock slab at a ridge above a vast basin of trees and river branches.

With a short chat, they decided to go on a date.

#

It was early in the afternoon and many families were gathering on the small beach of Shoreline Lake, having picnics and enjoying the sunny view of colorful recreational boats on the clear blue water. Hanwei came to a coffee shop next to the lake. Through its large windows, he could see many customers lining up at the counter.

"I am here," Hanwei texted Rahul.

"I am here too, by the coffee shop," Rahul's reply came

promptly.

Walking around the corner, Hanwei came to the parking lot side. An athletic, casually but nicely dressed Indian man stood in the walkway among other passing visitors.

Very good looking and well mannered, with good taste in style! Hanwei's energy rose when he saw the man. *It's funny the way he moves himself back and forth, like an innocent boy.*

"Hi, Rahul?" Hanwei walked over. His fit shape, good looks, swift moves, deep and friendly voice instantly warmed Rahul.

"Yes. Hanwei?" Rahul smiled. His fuller face, large and beautiful eyes, and innocent and inquisitive expression were mesmerizing.

"Yes. Nice to meet you. Wanna grab a coffee inside?"

Hanwei ordered a cup of coffee and blended it with milk and honey. Rahul ordered a small box of coconut water and some cookies. The two sat down in the coffee shop's sunroom so they could enjoy the colorful scene outside the window.

"Do you need to drive far to get here?" Rahul asked gently, after taking a sip of the coconut water.

"Not far. Only thirty minutes. You live in Palo Alto?"

"Yes. My friend and I rent a condo there."

"That's a wonderful place, very lively and happening there."

...

One exchange at a time, the two slowly got to know each other. Hanwei learned that Rahul was a bioinformatics scientist and liked cooking and hiking. Rahul learned Hanwei had many friends in Los Angeles and San Diego, liked pop music, going to the beach, and dancing at nightclubs. Most intriguing, they found they both immigrated to America not long ago before 9/11, got their PhDs around the same time, survived the 2008 financial crisis in their early career, relocated to Silicon Valley in the same year, and now both desired a committed long-term relationship.

#

"How was your date?" David, Hanwei's visitor from San Diego, asked.

"Good. But this guy is in remarkable condition."

"Remarkable condition!? Ha-ha. Same as with women, men are not objects, okay?"

"Yeah. I doubt it will work out. He is handsome, fit, intelligent and very much a soft spoken gentleman. He seems to be out of my league." Hanwei shook his head.

"Come on. You aren't bad at all. Give it a try!"

...

"Would you like to go hiking together on Mount Umunhum this Saturday? It is not far from where you live," Rahul suggested to Hanwei over the phone.

Mount Umunhum, a towering mountain located in the 18,000-acre Sierra Azul Open Space Preserve, stood on the ridge of the south rim of Silicon Valley, separating the Valley from the Santa Cruz beach town. At its summit, visitors had a spectacular 360-degree unobstructed view, ranging from the Pacific Ocean to the Sierra Nevada. A cubic-shape concrete building at the summit, a retired military facility, was so prominent that it could be seen far away from Hanwei's home community. Rahul apparently had done his homework.

#

That Saturday morning, when Hanwei stepped out of his car

in the parking lot of Sierra Azul Open Space Preserve, Rahul was there waving at him.

Hanwei looked street and fashionable, wearing his black t-shirt with a strip of silver beads lining his chest. Rahul looked fresh and energetic, wearing a gray t-shirt and brown hiking pants.

Hanwei smiled when he walked up to Rahul. He mustered the strength he had when picking up guys in nightclubs. Rahul was shy, but the light and warmth in his eyes had given him away.

"You are ready?" Hanwei said.

The trail ascended gradually with its twists and turns on the back of the hill. Large trees offered hikers cool shade and fresh air. Silicon Valley occasionally revealed itself through the gaps of hills, giving the two men a delightful view.

"Watch out for the leaves of those bushes," Rahul said, pointing to a group of plants by the side of the trail. "They are poison oak. Be careful not to touch them with your bare skin."

"Good to know. You seem to be into plants and nature. How were your PhD years in Florida?"

"It was actually not an easy time for me," Rahul answered.

"PhD life in this country can be hard. Was your professor difficult?"

"He was nice. But he was old and had lost interest or energy in research. I couldn't get much guidance from him. I struggled to find the right direction myself. And because I had little money, I couldn't go out and do fun things. I was sending my savings to my mom in India."

"That's tough. But it's nice you were sending money home. I was once in a similar situation. My professor had funding issues. I ended up writing teaching materials for him and doing under-the-table jobs, like babysitting and tutoring."

"Whoa. That's hard too."

"Does your family know you are gay?" Hanwei curiously asked, "It is usually very hard for Indians to come out. You actually had the courage."

"They don't know about it. My father already passed away. My mother and I no longer talk. I also haven't told this to my aunt and uncle, who adopted me when I was little."

"You were not raised by your biological parents?"

"No. My birth father was a womanizer. He barely paid any attention to the family. My birth mother was somehow dragged into his drama and gave me away to his sister when I was two years old."

"Whoa. That must have been hard for you, especially when you realized you were abandoned."

"Yeah. My aunt said I cried badly for days at the beginning. But I was also lucky they raised me. They are educated and financially comfortable. My aunt is a prolific novelist and a feminist. She wrote many books advocating rights for women and poor people; she inspired many people in India. And she inspired me, taught me how to read in my childhood. I was reading newspapers by the time I was four. How about you? Does your family know?" Rahul asked.

"My family situation is a bit unusual." Hanwei opened up and shared his family's story.

"I am sorry for what you've been through. It seems we both did not have much of a father figure at home," Rahul commented. "And I can't imagine the hardships your mother has been through."

"Yeah. Society has suppressed women's rights and wills so

much that many women, like my mom, have once accepted bearing babies and following what their husbands say as their fate, not thinking for themselves, fighting against injustice done to them, and pursuing their aspirations."

"That's what's happening in America too. Look at how supremacists and far-right politicians haven't stopped trying to overturn Roe v. Wade," Rahul pointed out.

"I know."

"I can also see that life was hard for your father too," Rahul commented.

"Yeah. I admire his defiant spirit against cruel dogma and social pressure. But ironically, while he was discriminated against as a gay man, he was misogynistic at the same time," Hanwei said with a bitter laugh.

"Misogynist while being gay? That sounds like some of those closeted gay republicans," Rahul pointed out sharply.

"Ha. Yes. It's like they are gay themselves, so they are able to grasp the concept. But since they aren't women and aren't into women, they then lose their empathy, respect, and understanding toward women," Hanwei said.

"And if they were not gay themselves, they would be anti-gay," Rahul followed.

"I know, right?" Hanwei commented. "Sadly, that is one of our weaknesses as humans. We often pick up prejudices from our own limited experience. That tendency also breeds racism and xenophobia."

"Yeah. Those prejudices are easily exploited by ill-willed politicians. They stoke people's fear of losing their privileged status to others whom they perceive as inferior," Rahul said alluding to the current political climate in the US.

"That seems to be what's going on now around the world,"

Hanwei followed. "Unless we are highly aware of our own thoughts and the grand scheme of things, we are all prone to only attending to our immediate interests rather than nurturing a win-win resolution."

"The extreme right wing in this country seized and capitalized on such tribalistic sentiment and blamed this nation's decline on minorities, while the real cause of this nation's decline is unregulated capitalism and foreign competition," Rahul shared his thoughts.

"I know. With so much power and resources being concentrated in the hands of few, the majority of people will suffer," Hanwei agreed.

"Besides unprecedented power and resource concentration, the sad thing is this once brilliant country seems to have all the ingredients now for the rise of authoritarianism. It will be hard for many people when that comes," Rahul expressed his deepest worry.

"Ha. Like Princess Padme said while she was witnessing the triumph of autocratic rule over democracy in *Star Wars*, 'This is how liberty dies... with thunderous applause.'" Hanwei said.

"That's a nice quote." Rahul's eyes brightened while he looked at an opening on the trail. "We reached the summit!"

In front of them, a well-maintained concrete staircase wound up toward the mountain-top, segmented by a couple concrete pads accompanied with beautifully polished wood benches. The two quickly ascended to the top of the mountain.

The space around them opened up. The sun was bright. The air felt fresh. The entire Silicon Valley was at their feet, hugged by heavily vegetated mountains.

"Look at the structure over there. That's the one I can

see from the hill I live on!" Hanwei pointed to the large cube-shaped concrete building standing next to the visitor's pavilion. "I like how mystic, alien, and stylish it looks."

The two walked up to the visitor's pavilion, climbed up the concrete wall on the lookout deck, and sat side by side.

"It's magnificent." Hanwei couldn't help but stand in awe of the view beneath their feet.

"Yeah, it's beautiful. This view never stops to amaze me."

Rahul handed over a water bottle. "Are you hungry? I brought some snacks," he asked, while he pulled some small bags out of his backpack. There were grapes, bananas, nuts, and cereal bars.

"Thanks." Hanwei chewed on the cereal bar and then looked at Rahul smiling. Up close were Rahul's big and warm eyes, gentle smile and fuller face. While Hanwei had been drawn toward clubbing and parties, in Rahul he saw a man with a good heart who enjoyed life with less and felt content being close to nature.

"So, when democracy dies, we'd need to run for cover together?" Hanwei smiled at Rahul.

"Okay, we can run together." Rahul smiled. "But there is still hope. Many Americans are already fighting back, especially the progressives in this country. It won't be easy. There will be setbacks, but we have to fight back. And we cannot stop fighting back," Rahul said while he looked toward the valley and the mountains around it.

"Yeah. And our liberty is owed to those who fought before us," Hanwei followed. "I am happy to be here with you."

"Me too." As the warm feeling arose, Rahul reached out with his hand and touched Hanwei's. "Although we both lost something precious in our original families at home, we can build our own home here and we would have each other," he moved himself closer to Hanwei, feeling their shoulders touch as they sat side by side.

Sitting on top of the mountain, the vast landscape in front of the two men felt clearer. At that very moment, they both felt they had found someone they could care for, resonate with, and love.

#

"Fifteen seconds left…"

Rahul encouraged both of them as he followed the fitness coach on the YouTube video playing on the TV. Breathless, he jumped and squatted on the living-room floor. Hanwei's forehead was already dripping with sweat as he pushed through the final seconds of the thirty-minute workout.

Buzz. Hanwei's phone vibrated. He picked it up, still breathing hard. "Hello?"

"Is this Hanwei?"

"Yes."

"This is Gary… I don't know if you still remember me."

Of course he remembered—Rick's friend, from the meth recovery meetings. A good man carrying too much sorrow for his age.

"I remember. How are you, Gary?"

"I'm alright. Thank you. Did you see the news?"

"No. What news?"

"It's Rick. He passed away. His body was found near the edge of the Guadalupe River, close to downtown San Jose. The police are investigating. It's already on the news…"

Hanwei froze, stared blankly ahead for a second, then

turned to Rahul. "It's about Rick," he said abruptly, fumbling for the remote.

He pulled up the news on YouTube.

Headline: "San Jose High School Teacher Found Dead in Guadalupe River."

And then—Rick's smiling portrait on the screen—full of sun and youth.

The anchor continued:

"Shock remains in the San Jose community as the body discovered last week in the Guadalupe River has now been confirmed to be Dr. Rick Rowland, a teacher at San Jose High School…"

The screen cut to a field reporter under the overpass.

"The body was found by a hiker walking the riverside trail. The stretch of the Guadalupe River near downtown San Jose has long had a visible homeless population; the city has been working to address encampments along the corridor, citing pollution concerns. Some residents describe parts of the area as unsafe. Others point to it as a known spot for drug use. At this time, we still do not have enough information to understand what exactly happened. In his school, Dr. Rowland was beloved by students and staff. Since the announcement of his death, more than two hundred condolence messages have been posted on the school's website. According to school officials, Dr. Rowland had recently decided to leave San Jose and return to his hometown to accept a university teaching position…"

Rahul didn't speak at first. He simply reached out, placing a warm, steady hand on Hanwei's shoulder. "I'm so sorry," he whispered.

Hanwei's eyes stayed locked on the television. Dinners with

Rick. Their long late-night talks about American politics. The hikes they took together. Those weary months when Rick slept under his roof, fighting through withdrawal one day and one night at a time.

He remembered Rick's anxious voice, confessing his fears about the direction of his beloved country—and his own reply to him during their walk:

"America will one day survive this and move beyond it. What the American people learn from these hardships and atrocities will help them build a better union. And that day will not be far."

Those words now echoed in his chest like a distant, unanswered prayer.

#

"All of our liberation is linked together. Think about the people you are fighting for and say it with me from your gut: 'It is our duty to fight for our freedom. It is our duty to win. We must love and support one another. We have nothing to lose but our chains!' That's what we're here for, to love and support one another. I come from the Black Lives Matter crew, right? And that's what we believe. That's what we are fighting for. We are fighting to liberate. So let's go out there. Let's bring this political revolution to the front door steps of the oppressors. Make sure that we defeat them in November. Let's do this!" The crowd roared inside the convention center, while Kendrick Sampson spoke to them with a quote from Assata Shakur. Bernie Sanders had just won another resounding victory on his road to becoming the Democratic Party's nominee for the 2020 United States presidential election.

This is exactly what those pioneers did decades ago when they fought for the rights of LGBT people. It's time for people to do the same for everyday people in this country who earn an honest living, Hanwei thought, while watching the TV with other volunteers at the Bernie Sanders campaign headquarter in Silicon Valley.

Rahul appeared at his side, already holding their precinct maps. He leaned in and pressed his lips firmly on Hanwei's temple — warm, still, the rest of the room falling away for just that moment.

"Let's go. We are knocking on doors in East San Jose today. Do you have the streets you will cover?" Rahul asked.

"Yes. I will call to meet you once I'm done."

...

Driving across downtown San Jose to East San Jose, Hanwei could see homeless people curled up outside closed stores, tents scattered around public parks, and coffee shops closed early due to a shortage of staff.

He parked his car on a street in East San Jose. A row of run-down houses jumped into his view.

One house after another, Hanwei knocked on doors, patiently talked to them about Bernie Sanders' political positions, listened to their opinions, encouraged them to go vote, and kept a log on the campaign app. For houses where no one responded other than some loud dog barks, Hanwei stuck a campaign flier beneath their front doors.

"Hi, ma'am," Hanwei stopped in front of a rather shabby house. An overweight Caucasian woman in her late fifties with messy hair and dirty clothes wobbled around her belongings in a front yard full of junks.

"What are you looking for?" She looked at Hanwei inquisitively.

"I am campaigning for Bernie Sanders."

"Who?"

"Bernie Sanders."

"No. No Bernie Sanders. Why? The economy is doing great."

"The economy is doing great, but only for the top one percent. The wealth gap right now has widened to that of the 1920s. You saw those ordinary people living in tents and families packing up leaving their homes in pain."

"The stock market is doing good," the woman said in a questioning tone.

"The stock market has much less to do with most Americans. Only half of them have a single stock."

"We voted for Trump. I don't want democrats. Everyone wants to come here. Now Chinese people want to come."

Hanwei laughed. "I agree with you. The immigration policy should be sensible. The border must mean something. However, human migration is driven by supply and demand of the labor market. America is benefiting from it. It's just that the rich, who benefit the most from it, aren't paying their fair share. It ends up that ordinary Americans pick up the slack while working two jobs to make their ends meet. This country needs to invest the wealth created by everyone in public education, health care, and infrastructure to help American families grow. That's what Bernie and his supporters are fighting for. We are fighting for you."

The elderly woman looked a bit confused.

"By the way, does Max live here? Can I talk to him?" Hanwei asked while checking his campaign app.

"Oh. The transgender. She is my daughter. She doesn't live

here anymore."

I see. That's why the app directed me to a Trump supporter's house.

...

"Where are you?" Hanwei called Rahul as soon as he was done.

Walking into the middle of an apartment complex, Hanwei saw a crowd of young men and women gathering around on second floor railings, on stairs, and in the courtyard, carefully listening to a familiar voice. It was Rahul. Joining them, Hanwei saw the man he loved standing out front, warm and inspiring, touching the ordinary souls he cared for.

"The Bay Area has the highest income level in the entire country, yet people here are going down everyday, not because they don't work hard. They are restaurant workers, handymen, and teachers. It's because, even when they work ten hours a day, they can't make their ends meet. When you are only one hospital bill away from being bankrupt, or one car breakdown away from being unable to pay your mechanic, you can't catch up as fast as you are being left behind. What is happening in this country is that the wealth concentration under unregulated capitalism has caused a level of power concentration that corrupts government institutions, rips off hard working Americans, deprives young Americans of opportunities, and wastes their potential and talent."

Hanwei walked up and joined Rahul. "Yeah, and the system is pitting one group of people against another. The confident young man who once happily helped us in a hotel lobby can no longer be happy. Instead, he is now resentful and despises those homeless people more than we do. Neighbors who used to support each other can no longer feel delight in each other's successes. Instead, they would be bitter because earning an honest living is no longer something they can believe in and honor. And the young man and young woman who used to capture each other's heart with their charm or wisdom might no longer believe in love, because love might have failed them when they were struggling to put food on the table."

"But doesn't socialism encourage laziness?" a young woman in the crowd asked.

"Good question. There are multiple interpretations of the S-word. Some are made up. And some aren't as nuanced. But we can't box our thinking in one English word," Hanwei followed. "I share many values advocated by conservatives, like being disciplined and prudent, upholding responsibility and having entrepreneurial spirit. So, yes, if what a man gets does not reflect on what he gives, it will encourage laziness. But at the same time, if the opportunities for a man to grow and subsequently contribute only depend on the resource he controls, society will lose its steam in innovation and productivity."

"There needs to be real changes. You know, if the system stays the course, people like Hanwei and I probably would do okay, but that wouldn't be the case for the majority of the people in this country. As young Americans, your future and this country's future depend on you to fight for democracy, to fight for your fair opportunities and treatments, to support and love one another, and to vote when you still have the power."

#

Two years later…

On the rooftop lounge of the Diamond View Tower near the San Diego Bay, family and friends quickly seated themselves and greeted one another on the patio facing an outlook deck. Among them were Hanwei's Los Angeles friends from his West Hollywood days, Rahul's friends who supported him in his difficult PhD years in Florida, Hanwei's friends from the startup company that went down in the 2008 financial crisis, Rahul's close friends from work and members of Silicon Valley's tech worker rights group.

The fifteenth floor penthouse and its rooftop patio boasted a breathtaking view of downtown San Diego, Coronado Island, and San Diego Bay, the quintessential beach city of America's Pacific Coast. The lookout deck was styled with steel rail, midair above the Petco Baseball Stadium, reflecting lights from different directions.

While the afternoon sun descended at five o'clock, shedding gold color across the bay water onto the patio, the music beats became stronger, and the seated guests got livelier. Just at that moment, Hanwei and Rahul walked onto the patio from the penthouse in blue suits. They walked down the aisle toward the lookout deck, filled with gratitude and joy as they passed their seated guests.

While the music started to fade and the view began to blur, what became crystal-clear to those who had supported Hanwei and Rahul was that they now stood by each other in front of the officiant, a role served by Hanwei's longtime friend.

During the previous two years, the world had become a much more dangerous place.

Autocratic rulers had risen around the globe. The United States suffered a constitutional crisis during its transition of power. Works of intellectuals were attacked by authoritarian leaders and their followers. Lies and conspiracy theories were spread rampantly over social media. The world had experienced a pandemic of vast proportion, only rescued by modern medicine. Human migration was abruptly halted by international travel bans instigated by the distrust and hostility between countries. Racism that had been largely shamed in public life in recent decades had crawled its way back following the dog whistles of powerful politicians. Women's reproductive rights in America were again under grave assault after the balance had been tilted in the Supreme Court. And wars of aggression had just put the planet at the brink of World War III.

"So now we are all here, in California, the land of fruits and nuts as they used to say, to celebrate the wedding of Rahul and Hanwei. What a wonderful story of the American melting pot." The officiant opened the wedding ceremony. "Hanwei, a man with his roots in Chongqing, China, worked his way up and out through sheer brainpower and determination. No help from anyone besides the love of his mother. His father probably would never have imagined it a possibility for his son to be in a lasting relationship with another man for all to see. Rahul, with his roots in rural Andhra Pradesh, India, adopted and edified by his Aunt, an accomplished author of feminist novels and text books, and his Uncle, a university professor, came out to himself at age thirty-one. To illustrate the struggles facing gay men and women worldwide, Rahul's family is not aware that he is getting married here today because his impression is that they would not approve. And, there, thanks to the powers of social media, they met. They fell in love and recognized in each other a shared sense of purpose and the opportunity for a balanced and intellectually stimulating lasting relationship. Now, I invite the couple to express their vows to each other. I understand that Rahul is going first."

Rahul took out a piece of paper while he looked into Hanwei's eyes with a sweet smile. "Hanwei, when we met three years ago, I did not know where this life would lead me or whether someone would love me and understand me. I have found the answer. I remember the day we went on this beautiful hike at Mount Umunhum and we both were totally infatuated with each other. I still remember the feeling—that feeling of elation when the rest of the world does not matter. We both did not have it easy in life, we both had to struggle and beat the odds and, to a certain extent, were lucky. I like how passionate you get when you start talking about the theory of relativity, I like how there is a lot I can learn from you. I see in you the fighting spirit that I once had, one that makes you feel that you can do anything, and occasionally accomplish seemingly impossible things. As I stand here before you today, I feel the same way I felt during the hike to the summit of Mount Umunhum. You are an amazing person to many and to me. You have a heart of gold. I will love you and support you always."

Watching Rahul read his vow, Hanwei knew it was with this man—abandoned by his mother and father, an advocate for the rights of ordinary people—that he shared a profound sense of human intellect, progress, and love.

With all eyes on him, Hanwei looked to the family and friends in front of him. Among them was Rulan, his dear mother, dressed in light yellow and sitting upright accompanied by Hanwei's friends. Her life's stories could be read on the wrinkles of her face. Her kindness and strength shined through in her calm smile and traces of dried tears.

She had come a long way. She struggled for many years living under the shadow of her gay husband. And only because of her own son was she able to give up her pride and dream and put herself on a journey of understanding homosexuality, along with the people, the culture, and the politics surrounding it.

Hanwei still remembered every word his mom said the day he broke his wedding news to her: "Hanwei, ever since you left Mom when you were fifteen, Mom rarely interfered with your decisions. Mom trusts your effort and judgment. You went far away. You made many decisions and moves in your life without really consulting Mom first, including applying for Beijing University and going to America. Your decisions sometimes also have a great impact on Mom. You did always tell me, but usually after things were done. Mom is not well educated, couldn't comment or ask for something different in those turns of your life. You probably know much more than Mom does. Mom can only hope you made the right decision for yourself. And Mom will be happy if you can live the good life that you always wanted."

"Thank you, Mom. And Rahul also thinks you are the best mom he knows." That was when Hanwei understood how much he owed to this woman.

What Hanwei didn't know, however, was that his mother cried profusely in front of her family while telling them she was leaving for the United States for Hanwei and his love amid the COVID-19 pandemic and travel ban. She said to them, "this will be my last fight."

"I want to thank everyone for coming. Mine is slightly

longer. Please bear with me." Hanwei cleared his voice, while he took out his notes and faced toward Rahul.

"Rahul, I remember the evening you anxiously rubbed my feet when trying to comfort me while I was sick with the flu. I remember the day in Hawaii when you saved us by flipping our capsized kayak with one strike of your arm, while your feet were under turbulent ocean water, punctured by sea urchin spines and in severe pain. I remember the days you went to the street waving signs supporting farmers rights in India, protesting police brutality against underprivileged people, and organizing meetings of Silicon Valley's tech worker rights group. To me, you deserve the deepest love and respect from other human beings. I am very lucky to have met you and earned your affection."

After a pause, Hanwei continued. "Life is short and can be very hard for many. There are still many people of color, immigrants, and women being discriminated against, disenfranchised, or enslaved around the world. There are still intellectuals and honest, hardworking people being oppressed, smeared, and persecuted inside and outside this country. There are still lesbians, gays, bisexuals, and transgender people being excommunicated, bullied, and killed in many parts of the world. Our little story is only one of the many that ordinary people, including many of my friends in the audience, have had. So I am aware of how lucky we are and how precarious life can be. We owe debts to those ordinary people who fought and sacrificed for human rights. I promise that I will never let you be alone. I will always learn to be a better person, always fight in the face of darkness, and always love you the best I can."

The crowd was silent. Some wept in joy.

"Now you may have each other," the officiant announced. While Rahul and Hanwei hugged each other with music turned up, the crowd cheered in thunderous applause.

Rulan witnessed her son's happiest day in her seat among the crowd. It was also her proudest and happiest day. It was her love and fight that had led to this wonderful day of human life.

#

The next morning, Hanwei stopped at the small desk by the study window. As he put things in order, he lingered over the wedding cards and their heartfelt messages. Then he uncovered a notebook he hadn't opened in years—the one he had filled during one of the lowest chapters of his life. He opened it gently and reread the beliefs he had once written to steady himself:

History of mankind is like a fractal.
When progress is made, darkness follows.
When hope fades, a better world arises.

We have only one life.
Our journey enlightens us in a limited time.
Everyone carries a talent.
No one survives alone.
While many do harm to benefit themselves, we don't
have to.
While others expect us to be different things, we can
become our better selves.

Everything is connected.
Love is the first act of our defiance.
Some come to this world with stars aligned.
Some come with little, left to struggle.
Then some are born to fight for justice, for us, and for the world.
May we respect everyone who lives in honesty.
May the fruits of our civilization be shared with every soul.
May our struggle be answered in our heartland.

— Hanwei